WHEN THINGS HAPPEN TOGETHER

JORDAN CLAYDEN-LEWIS

DDP
DEEP DESIRES PRESS

Winnipeg, Canada

Developmental editor: Margaret Larson
Proofreader: Francisco Feliciano

Published Oct. 2022 by Deep Desires Press, an imprint of Story Perfect Inc.

Deep Desires Press
PO Box 51053 Tyndall Park
Winnipeg, Manitoba R2X 3B0
Canada

Visit http://www.deepdesirespress.com for more scorching hot erotica and erotic romance.

Publisher's Note:
While this book has a British protagonist and is set in Australia, it uses standard American English. Australian spellings have been maintained where appropriate or no equivalent American translation is available.

Subscribe to our email newsletter to get notified of all our hot new releases, sales, and giveaways! Visit deepdesirespress.com/newsletter to sign up today!

When Things Happen Together
The Novel Playlist

Listen to the official novel playlist, curated by author Jordan Clayden-Lewis, featuring sounds that inspired the book.

https://sptfy.com/when-things-happen-together

For Amanda
That long bus trip was quite the unexpected one. You know the one.

WHEN THINGS HAPPEN TOGETHER

Newfound Home

"Synchronicity: a meaningful coincidence of two or more events where something other than the probability of chance is involved."
– Carl Jung

Powdery red dirt covered me from head to toe, my former olive skin now a tinge of sunburnt orange. The desert sun's rays scorched my already-burnt skin, and the bloody wound on my knee seeped. I couldn't have walked even if I wanted to.

Sprawled in the dirt, I sheltered under an immense tree with a thick trunk and very few leaves. Endless desert plains enclosed me. Spiky spinifex grasses at each glance, its long hairs sharp and coarse. I'd worn black shorts, my legs lacerated. As sinister as it might sound, the stings of the spinifex soothed the throbbing pain of my knee wound. I held a dusty, cream-colored piece of paper, trying to preserve its longevity with equally dusty hands. Small black handwriting was scribbled on the page.

Hands shaky, I tried to imagine that Bruce was reading me this letter again, just like he had when we sat by that fresh-flowing brook. When all that mattered was how lost I became in those alluring almond eyes. When I'd breathe a sigh of relief each time he touched me. When he'd smile, and I'd smile.

It was in those initial moments that I realized all the chaos, the explosions, the race to the finish line; stopped completely.

I hoped that wherever you were, whatever you were up to; that you were doing okay, and that you'd found peace.

"I fell for you like a waterfall," I recited from the page with a soft whisper of sadness.

I couldn't read any more of that page-long poem. It was too much. Instead, I folded the piece of paper back together in fours and burrowed it back into my pocket. And then, shifting my feeble gaze up to the sky, I studied a bald eagle soaring high above my brow. Its wings didn't even flap. It just hovered from side to side.

Only then did I make a wish, like it was eleven-eleven or something. I wished to be this eagle, able to fly away. To the highest of mountains. To the bluest of waters. To the greenest of forests. To *him*. Pretty much anywhere that I didn't have to catch sight of this tangerine sea of sand was fine with me at this point.

Six Months Prior:

Not a cloud lingered in the May sky as our flight touched down in Brisbane. For those of us used to the gray skies of London, it seemed as if the blue hues did not dull for days. The sun sprayed its shine—the kind I was ready to copy onto canvas. Australia was the ideal backdrop for a working holiday, there was no denying it. I had no idea it would lead to what it did, though. I expected a whole lot of nothing during my twenty-fourth lap around the sun, yet I got much more than what was bargained for.

But how could four numbers change the course of my entire life? The signs were clear as day in hindsight, most of the time screaming at me from the face of a clock. It was the clashing of two comets, unwilling to break apart. And a less-than-subtle message, that the timing was *now*. It intrinsically made me think of life like dominoes from then on. That when they tumbled, they sometimes only took a few with it. But then on other occasions, they would tip the whole lot.

I phoned Dad not long after our arrival at the hotel, the king bed's mattress soothing the ache in my back the moment I lay on it. Much better than curling over like a prawn in economy class plane seats, that was for sure.

"How was the flight?" Dad asked after a yawn.

I chuckled, glancing over at Courtney taking selfies outside, the sun kissing her cheeks. Her long blonde hair shimmered. "Well, we got a little drunker on the plane than we expected," I replied, rubbing my left eye. I clicked the loudspeaker button so I could rub my right eye and smooth over my short dark hair in the mirror. I desperately needed a haircut, but perhaps a proper sleep first.

Dad laughed. "I told you that altitude gets the better of you." Agreed. One drink felt like five. "Got much planned for your first night?"

Eavesdropping, Courtney scrunched her fist up into a ball and raised it back and forth to her wide-open mouth, her eyes rolling into the back of her head.

"Uh…we might go grab some food and, uh…see what the city has to offer," I said with a growing grin, controlling myself from bursting into laughter as Courtney moved her fist back and forth more rigorously.

"What about you? Much happening back at home in The Big Smoke?" I asked after turning away from Courtney.

"Not a whole lot. Just going out for lunch with Abigail."

"Nice. Things seem to be going well between you two."

Dad exhaled a sigh of relief into the phone. "It's been a long time, Thomas. It feels nice."

I paused for a moment, catching my own azure eyes in the mirror, my smile fading but my tone still as cheery. "I'm really happy for you, Dad."

"Thanks, son. Do you and Courtney have a plan of where you'd both like to base yourselves there?"

I chuckled. "Not entirely sure yet, but we'll find somewhere. I'm hoping I can get back into my art ASAP. Already getting lots of ideas and it hasn't even been a day here."

"That's what you want. Try to get a place where you can set up a little studio or something."

Dad sprinkling his two cents into my life was something I hadn't always appreciated. But, better late than never.

After another short ramble, he finished with, "All right, well, keep me updated, and enjoy your first night. I'll speak to you soon."

"Will do, Dad. Bye."

I hung up the phone, casting my gaze to a now star-fished Courtney on the bed.

"So, what *are* we going to do tonight?" she asked seductively. "I'm way too excited to sleep off this jetlag."

Two fresh white bathrobes were folded neatly on the end of our bed. "I don't know. As long as I get to wear this sexy getup wherever we go," I joshed. "What do you want to do?"

"You know what I want to do, Tommy boy." Courtney lifted her leg up in the air at a forty-five-degree angle. "I want to *dance*."

Brisbane, or "Brissy" as the locals called it, had great gay clubs. A bundle of the tanned beautiful men in this country instantly melted me with their curious stares. I must have looked extremely pale to them, though, as Courtney and I ambled through the club. They gave me sidelong glances, thinking that I didn't notice.

"The guys are loving you here," Courtney teased as we chugged down a beer in the smoker's area. Another group of young men strolled past, one of them lending me the lets-fuck look.

"Well, we *are* in a gay bar," I reminded her. "Hmm, I wonder if I'll get myself a sexy Australian boyfriend in the land down under."

Speaking to Courtney was a bit like having a conversation with my conscience sometimes. A conscience I'd known for nineteen years of my life, ever since I learned how to read and write. She had been my best friend for as long as we had both known the term.

"Thomas—you will *not* be getting yourself a boyfriend and leaving me alone over here!" she piped up.

"Settle down. I'm kidding," I answered. But was I? I had been dreaming of delicious Australian men for days now.

"Good," she said. "You literally just got out of a relationship late last year. You do *not* want to get in another one, especially when we're here in Australia to explore together."

I assured her, "Yeah I know. Don't worry." But deep down I craved that limitless love I had lost all of a sudden with Peter those months ago.

Was it even love, though, or just uncontrollable lust that, when faced with reality, faded like breath on a flame?

She chuckled. "I'm so jetlagged. Oh look, finally, some girls!"

Two young women around the same age as Courtney and I walked into the smoker's area. They cackled loudly, continuing to do so as they sat across from us.

"Five-dollar basics get me messy," I overheard the paler and skinnier of the two say. "Oh, fuck. I think I've lost my lighter. Hey, excuse me, guys!"

Our first encounter with the locals. *Please go swimmingly.* "Do you guys happen to have a lighter by any chance?" she slurred, stumbling over to us while the other sat in her seat and chortled at her phone.

Courtney pulled one out of her handbag. "Yeah, I do. Here you go, darling."

"Oh my god, I *love* the accent!" the girl gushed, sparking her cigarette and handing the lighter back to Courtney. "Where are you both from?"

"England! We just arrived in the country this morning actually," I said gleefully.

"No way!" the girl squealed. "I have family that lives in Manchester."

"Oh fab. We're from London," I announced.

"Brissy must seem like a walk in the park then?" she remarked. "Do you mind if we join you guys? We're really drunk and need friends tonight."

"Absolutely," Courtney agreed. "New friends are always good."

"Brie, c'mon, get your arse off Tinder and come over here. We're making friends!" the girl called out. She shook both our hands. "I'm Kat. And this is Brie."

Court and I reciprocated the introduction. We couldn't believe how friendly Australians were on those first few nights in the country. Kat and Brie lived on the southern Gold Coast, about an hour and a half drive south of Brisbane. They were so lovely, to the point where it almost seemed too good to be true. They even mentioned that the café they worked at in Coolangatta was hiring new staff if we wanted a job. That was something we thought we'd have to search aimlessly for. But nope, it came to us.

I couldn't have predicted that we would spend a few more days in Brisbane and then hop on a one-way bus down to the beachside town of Coolangatta. Nor did I think I'd end up in my first one-night stand that night, or that I would have that much choice between who I'd rustle under the sheets with. His name was Sam I believed: chiseled chest, big cock, and a shaved ass that I just so happened to slip into.

I had to pat myself on the back for how quiet I was slinking through his bedroom the next morning, stepping over islands of clothes to get to the door, lube on the bedside table with the lid off, sticky condom hanging off the side of the black metal bin, and no intention of seeing him again. It was good while it lasted, but who knew when I'd be back in Brisbane next.

Sandy Frogs

"It's official," I declared, waving our employee detail forms in the air. "We live in Australia now!"

Courtney and I sauntered along the Coolangatta esplanade, the cerulean sea sparkling on this ever-so fine day.

"We've only been in the country for a week, and everything has fallen into place pretty damn perfectly if I must say," she mentioned, talking so fast I could barely keep up. "We're renting our own unit. You bought a car. Now we're working at the cutest café-slash-bar in town."

Face now buried in my phone, I glanced over at her and shrugged. "When things happen together, they happen together I guess."

Courtney chuckled. "Um, and where the hell did that phrase come from?"

Shifting my eyes to the left, I couldn't have replied any more casually. "It's a way to explain the definition of synchronicity."

Courtney arched a brow. "*Riiiiiight*," she murmured.

And just like that, I was back to swiping left and right hastily on my screen.

Alongside Courtney, Tinder was my other best friend in town. Some local lads liked to meet up for drinks or food, others preferred one-night stands. But most didn't even want to meet up at all. They preferred to become friends on Snapchat and watch each other wank, swapping a folder full of photos and videos until someone came. I mean, it *was* an easy way to get one's rocks off right from the comfort of their own home. And much better than watching porn.

I'd spent almost every day with my feet dipped into the fine white sands, looking out onto the horizon. The town birthed some of the best sunsets I'd ever seen, illuminating the dramatic city skyline in the distance. It might've been the vibrant daily rays that felt so beautifully foreign, but I could feel myself changing already.

I'd subconsciously flown halfway across the world for this feeling. It was as if this life lived back in London didn't mean anything anymore, and I could recreate myself here in Australia if I wanted to. I could be anyone I wanted to be. Perhaps, I'd finally be myself.

I had certainly been myself at that little nook by the beach, two towels in the sand under the pandanus trees. Mackenzie, with his wavy light brown locks, wearing a red bandana to keep it all under control. He had the thickest, sexiest Australian accent I had come across thus far, as well as a peculiar twitch that lasted no longer than a second after we first met, which I presumed was just the cool breeze that suddenly blew in.

The smell of salt and sweat wafted from his hair, right under my nose as he sucked my nipples. And due to the hypersensitivity of said nipples, I came in about a minute, and he licked it up. Extra protein for him and those tanned, freckly muscles of his. My stomach copped a second load of jets from him while he ate his early afternoon snack. Then, he was a gentleman enough to wipe his spunk off me with a handful of tissues.

He laughed, laying on his side, facing me. "I don't think I've ever used these to blow my nose."

"You must have a decent immune system then." I winked, poking my finger into the tissue to stop it from dripping. Then, I licked it. "Tastes like...a healthy boy."

He was already busy drawing something in the sand with his finger. "Only the healthiest," he said smoothly. "Lots of pineapple."

Eyes narrowing, I peered down at his shrine. "What the fuck are you doing?"

"It's a frog squatting on a big dick." His reply was as blatant as my question. But honestly, why? This guy was peculiar, but in an amusing kind of way.

Most of what we discussed that day was all the sex he had been getting as of late, and the lads he was yet to fuck in the area. Zoning out at some point, I gazed at the waves tumbling onto the shore. The sun hovered its glow over the ocean. I had never seen water as blue as this.

Mackenzie then asked something that caught my attention, "Do you like outdoor music festivals?"

"Is the Pope a Catholic?" I quipped. "Boomtown Fair has been an honest favorite for years."

He gaped. "Get fucked! I've seen photos of that one. Looks *absolutely* unreal."

"Yeah, me and my best friend love it," I reminisced. "We've

been to four of them already. Hopefully many more in the future too."

"You'd probably dig Aussie bush doofs then," he suggested. "There's actually one happening this weekend. You should come."

Something similar to the magic of Boomtown? Enticing.

"Bush doofs?" I asked.

"Yeah! *Raves*," he piped up.

Now, there was a term I was familiar with.

"They're like hippy festivals out in the forest," he explained. "Everyone camps. It's an all-around good time."

I didn't have work that weekend. With no plans, it would've been rude not to go. I thought about Courtney. "Sounds fun. Can I bring my friend? She's a hoot."

"Uh, sure! My next question was going to be asking if we could take your car, cause it's a two-hour drive inland and my car still needs fixing."

For Australia, two hours inland from the coast meant the middle of fucking nowhere, but also the perfect spot to set up a festival. A place where no one would be bothered by the sound of ground-rumbling bass and shenanigans beyond comprehension. Courtney couldn't have squealed "yes" any louder when I invited her to the doof.

"Those shitty nightclubs again on a Friday and Saturday are getting old," she sighed.

I told her about Mackenzie and his frog drawings.

"He sounds fucked. Perfect."

She hadn't even scraped the surface on describing Mackenzie. We picked him up from his house in Murwillumbah, a small country town inland from the coast. He walked out of a small tattered unit across from the tennis court. Another young lad around our age was with him, his blonde hair slicked back.

Glitter was strategically patterned on their faces, and they both wore DIY crop tops made from old fishing shirts.

I complimented them as they hopped into the back seat. "You lads look fab!"

"We just got a little bored waiting for you guys," Mackenzie mentioned. "But we can totally share the glitter around."

Courtney smirked. "Yeah, honestly, we've gotta step up, Tommy. We can't have this."

Mackenzie—after twitching for a moment upon meeting Courtney, just like he had with me earlier—introduced us to the dazzling blonde next to him. "So, this is my boyfriend Stu."

Courtney and I instantly exchanged glances, eyebrows raised.

"We're in an open relationship," Mackenzie added, grabbing Stu's hand and smiling at him. "Sorry for not telling you earlier, Tommy. I just didn't know how you would take it."

How did I take this news? I mean, with a sinking of the stomach and a fake smile of course. But it didn't stop me from having a wicked time at my first bush doof. Everything, from the sunset drive in the countryside to the lush private property in the wilderness. It was intimate, maybe a thousand people at the most.

My eyes were fixated on fire twirlers most of the night. They moved in sync so perfectly to the sound of trance music.

A bonfire bellowed behind the dancefloor, warming everyone to an icy winter's night in the forest. People around the fire spoke about events like this, and how it was a place they felt truly free.

Indeed, having to watch Mackenzie and Stu make out on the dance floor every five minutes when we'd all taken caps was a little strange. It was also a little strange when the two invited me to sleep in their tent. And well, I didn't say no to the threesome because what did I have to lose? That's right, nothing except another Tinder match that wouldn't progress past a hookup.

Warm and weathered, I woke up between Mackenzie and Stu the next morning, all of us *very* naked. I caught Mackenzie's eyes. He stared up at the dew drops scattered across the roof of the tent, cocooning himself within the blankets. I could still hear music thumping across the field. Faint laughter echoed in all directions. Mackenzie looked over to Stu, then to me, rolling his eyes. Stu snored loudly, and I hadn't even noticed until Mackenzie took an eyeballing stab at him.

"I feel fucked," Mackenzie whispered, clearing his throat.

Come to think of it, so did I. I felt sad and sore, and I wasn't sure which one was more prevalent. Every cackle from outside the tent irritated me.

"I might go see where Courtney got to," I said, pushing the thick blankets off me.

"I think I vaguely remember hearing her getting back to the campsite laughing with some guy," Mackenzie explained. He glanced back over at Stu sleeping. "I'm gonna leave him here a little longer."

We both emerged from the tent. Our body warmth must've been something strong, because the cool air slapped us, sending goosebumps crawling. We turned to the morning rays spraying through the trees.

Mackenzie shivered. "We need to get to that sun, boyo," he declared with a sudden sense of urgency.

"One sec." I walked over to the tent Courtney was sleeping in. From the looks of it, she was cuddled up to some tanned lad with dreadlocks and tattoos. They looked too comfortable to disturb, and I was too cold to even try to wake her up.

Mackenzie now jogged on the spot to warm himself. "C'mon, Tommy. Let's get to that fucking sun."

"You're right," I giggled. "This is a life-or-death situation."

"Damn fuckin' right it is," he answered, linking his arm with mine as we strode through the sea of tents to the sunlight over in the trees. The grass was moist, painting patches on our shoes and pants.

In the distance were perhaps a few dozen people on the dance floor. By the looks of it, they were nowhere near as energetic as they were last night. They just swayed and twirled their arms around.

"Dance floor or sun?" Mackenzie asked.

I scoffed. "Are you crazy? I am *not* ready for that dance floor just yet."

"Sun it is, my friend."

Mackenzie must've appreciated my decision because as soon as he stepped foot in that glow, he absorbed it into his face with a relieved, "Ahhhh."

Our bodies thawed as we stood there with the rays on our faces, smiling into it.

"Much better," I noted.

After we sat up against a tree log, Mackenzie began rolling a cigarette. He then stared at it like a campfire. Smoking was the last thing I could think of doing. My throat was already fragile from the amount I puffed down the night before. Mackenzie sighed as he breathed smoke out. "You ever had to break someone's heart, Tommy?"

I was taken aback by the question, and it took me a moment to think. I thought back to last November, to the sleepy town of Hakuba in Japan. The "Peter" Chapter. "Yeah. I have. Why's that?"

Mackenzie sighed again. "If I tell you something, you promise not to tell anyone?" He gave me this stern look, one of which I couldn't take seriously.

"Honestly, who would I tell?" I asked.

He shrugged, moving his head from side to side. "That's a good point. Okay, so, I'm just not sure I'm in love with Stu anymore. It's been two years and, I dunno, I feel as if we're both just holding on because of the convenience. And lately, I've just been feeling that it doesn't feel right. We're only intimate when we're fucked up. At home, we just argue, or go and sleep with other guys." He shook his head. "I just don't know if I can do it anymore."

I knew how he felt. I had to break Peter's heart, and it was the first time I'd had to do that to someone I was in a relationship with. I tried my best to give advice to Mackenzie as I knew that's what he was seeking. "I've been there. And from experience, lad, the longer you leave it, the worse it gets. Sometimes, we think something's going to really work out with someone. But then life comes in and is like, nope, *plot twist*. I believe you're meant to be with people, but some only for a specific amount of time."

"A year ago, I honestly thought I'd go on to marry Stu," he explained. "We did everything together. We were joined at the hip."

Sometimes when people cried in front of me, I didn't know how to respond, or what to say. I would just sit there and pat them, kind of like a pet. *There, there. There, there.* It seemed to work. It worked with Dad when we both grieved over Mum's death, and with Courtney when she'd lost her father. And now with Mackenzie. I felt like he needed someone who could relate to him on that frosty morning. He didn't cry for very long. He just lay in the grass, staring up at the clouds.

"Tommy from London, I do hope we someday find our soul mates," he said with a sigh.

I messed up his hair playfully. "There's no rush, lad. It'll come at the right time for both of us. I trust that."

Probably when we least expect it.

In The Distance

The new week crept in, and so did a hefty comedown. Monday wasn't excruciating as such, but Tuesday was rotten. Fake smile plastered on my face, I had a rather large section of the café to look after on my own for a lunch rush. Kat dropped a full tray of drinks in the middle of service, including some cocktails for my tables. So, it looked like they weren't getting drinks for another ten minutes. A stout bald man then complained about his fish size being too small for the price he paid.

"Sir, you *did* purchase the Goldband Snapper, the most expensive and quality fish on the menu," I said restlessly, eyes narrowed, realizing table 10 had finished their entree and needed mains, table 14 needed more water, and table 17—well, I'd lost my mind, so I wasn't sure what table 17 needed. They just naturally looked like they weren't having a good time. Of all the days our fellow waiter, Sebastian could've called in sick, it just had to be today, didn't it?

The man with the fish problem huffed and groaned and told all the staff he was never coming back. I emphatically told him not to be so rude, that we didn't want his business if he was going to treat our staff like that.

Our bosses were out doing fuck knows what at this time, so we were all left to deal with the nasty prick. The customer was always right, my arse.

Courtney had been where I wanted to be that entire time: behind the bar. So, after the man left in a theatrical exit, I vented to her immediately.

"Literally, fuck people," I ranted, pouring myself a glass of cola filled with ice, and taking a seat on the blue milk crate next to the fridge. "Why do they have to be so insensitive? Like, can't they see I've had a big weekend? I'm fragile. Do your research on what you're ordering, you piece of shit!"

Courtney polished glasses, trying hard to hide a chuckle coming on. "Sounds like I missed quite the problematic customer," she smirked. "I didn't miss all those drinks smashin' on the ground, though. That was the icing on top of the cake for me."

I sighed. "I feel like I need a guided meditation or somethin', and maybe a live-in husband to nurse me back to health."

"I feel you, Tommy. But, look, the upside is that by tomorrow, our serotonin should be coming back to greet us with open arms, right?"

I rolled my eyes and crossed my arms. "You'd want to hope so."

It did. Wednesday wasn't too bad. I painted on my day off work and gave Tinder another whirl. I also partook in a guided meditation with Courtney. We lay in the backyard on a floral picnic blanket, a Bluetooth speaker in between us. The practitioner had this deep soothing voice I could have listened to all day.

"Settling down, wherever you are," he said. "Closing down the eyes. Just bring your awareness to your position, and how you are sitting."

We were laying down, but that was okay too.

"Feeling the connection to the ground," he added.

After taking a deep breath, I could feel the soft hairs of the grass beneath our blanket: soft like plush. "Notice what's going on around you."

The faint sound of a lawnmower in the neighbourhood. "Feel the weight of your hands resting in your lap."

They were a little cold from the light breeze.

"Start breathing in and out through your nostrils, clearing the passageways with the deepness of your breath." They were a little stuffy, but it was self-inflicted, and I knew it. "Focus on the breath, and with each exhalation, focus on letting go."

In and out.

"See if you can move that breath down the body, to the upper torso. Slowly filling up those areas of constriction."

I could definitely feel my sternum retract as I breathed in heavily. "And as you breathe out, let go of that constriction."

He then moved our point of focus to the nostrils, and the temperature of the air we inhaled: hot too hot, not too cold. Then, I exhaled, the air much warmer.

"Become aware of your ribcage," he told us. "In between the bones on the ribcage, there's this muscle called the intercostal muscle which connects each of the ribs. As you breathe, these muscles allow the rib cage to expand to create space for the lungs. And as you breathe out, they close in around the lungs, helping to expel the air. Can you feel a sense of the rib cage opening?"

Whoever this guy was, I would love to meet him someday, so he could guide me through these mind journeys every day.

I hadn't meditated in years. The last time would've been with Mum when I was around ten years old. Dad was working, and our dog had a fit that morning, so I took the day off school to help take Meg to the vet. I was feeling a little shaken, so Mum introduced me to meditation. The practitioner was nowhere near as mind-altering as the guy that day in Coolangatta, though.

Courtney and I spent the afternoon down at the beach with a few bottles of beer. The **New message received** notification appeared on my phone several times. We watched the usual string of surfers in the water, waiting for their golden wave.

"Maybe I should learn how to surf," I thought out loud.

Courtney laughed into her bottle of pale ale. "*Right.*"

"What? I was being half-serious," I replied, nudging her.

"That's what you said when you wanted to learn how to skateboard when we were, what, twelve. *Four stitches later.*"

Surely falling into the water from a board couldn't be as bad as falling from a half-pipe onto my head, because that's what had happened to me.

After a laugh and a silence, Courtney's smile faded. "Are you getting bored yet, Tommy?"

"What do you mean?"

"Of this place. There's not exactly as much going on as London, right?"

"A little. I mean, it's beautiful here, but we're probably so used to the fast life."

"Look, yeah, we probably should give it a good shot here. You never know what could happen. And if nothin' does, we fuck off to Sydney."

"Sounds like a plan," I agreed, unlocking my phone, my eyes instantly glued to it.

"You've had your face in that thing all afternoon!" Courtney piped up. She poked her head over to catch a glimpse. "Oh, you're on Tinder! Of course you are!"

Caught red-handed, I smirked and continued to sip on my beer. "I'm talking to this really cute guy," was my excuse, something Courtney had heard a thousand times before.

"I wonder if he'll be like any of those other meaningless one-night stands you've been on here," Courtney teased. "You want more, Tommy, I can tell. But none of these guys are worth your time."

When I started talking to Bruce, I thought he would be like the rest of the guys I'd met so far in Australia. Oh, how wrong I was. Those wavy brown locks and alluring almond eyes drew me in right from the beginning.

THOMAS
Hey man, how was your weekend?

BRUCE
You know what, it was maybe the strangest one I've ever had
I had no Saturday
It was definitely the shortest

THOMAS
Oh yeah? Care to elaborate on the strangeness?

BRUCE
Hahaha
Well I left Hawaii on a Friday and landed on a Sunday
So, there was basically a day where I didn't exist

THOMAS
Ahhhh I see

BRUCE
Still not sure what to make of it 😄

THOMAS
It's mad though, isn't it? That we can disappear in time like that

BRUCE
It's hard to get your head around 😄
Definitely flying home that way to get that day back

Disappointment set in. This cute boy wouldn't be sticking around for long, I presumed.

THOMAS
Are you from Hawaii?

BRUCE
No, Ireland 🌸

THOMAS
No way!

BRUCE
Was visiting a friend on my way to Aus
My best friend

THOMAS
Nice! I'm from London. We're pretty much neighbours
Hawaii looks so beautiful

BRUCE
We had a class time 🏄
Finally learnt to surf properly!
It's awesome that we're almost neighbors!

THOMAS
I've always wanted to learn how to surf but I've got
    terrible balance!
Are you just visiting the Gold Coast or Byron or what?

BRUCE
I'm here for at least a few more days
Staying in Burleigh
I just moved to Australia

THOMAS
Oh beautiful! You'll have an awesome time over here

BRUCE
Yeah, I think so
Definitely feels like a good move

I wanted to know more about this guy. He seemed so
interesting, but not in the way a good book or film would intrigue
its viewer. Bruce felt like the home I could be anywhere to feel,
even just by talking to him on a dating app.

THOMAS
Have you got Insta there lad?

BRUCE
I don't actually
Have been trying to spend less time on my phone

Tinder's a necessary evil 😆

THOMAS
Tinder's good for some things
Like talking to cute lads like you

BRUCE
Hahaha
Truth
Likewise
I better go
I'm getting all jetlagged

THOMAS
Yeah I'm about to pass out too
Goodnight mate and welcome to the land down under
👍

BRUCE
Cheers dude! 🕺
Sweet dreams 😴

THOMAS
Hope to catch you one day before you venture on 😊

BRUCE
Yeah that'd be nice. Hopefully we can arrange
something

The next day, I spent the morning doing what I did best—
the sketch and paint game— creating something from the depths
of my imagination and itching it onto paper, or canvas if we were

talking about preferences here. I used our carport as a studio for my art and parked my car on the road.

With a cup of coffee in arm's reach, hands and bare upper torso dirty with dry paint, I created a Cupid-like character. But not the Cupid you would see on an old oil painting. An angel bursting with color, shooting rainbow arrows aimlessly, planting love deeply within the hearts of two people who crossed paths.

Deep down, this winged companion almost seemed like a self-portrait; just wanting someone to love for himself, and for someone to love him the same way.

My phone buzzed.

BRUCE
Hello there handsome

THOMAS
Hey lad, up to much today?

BRUCE
Just been helping my friend move out of her place all morning
She goes back to Ireland today :'(
Now we're just chilling on the beach
She's got to get as much Vitamin D as possible before she goes home
This is not winter 😂
What about you?

THOMAS
I feel for her! She might not see sunshine for a long while! Hahaha
This is beautiful weather compared to back in our neck of the woods

Never going back lol
Not that much at the moment
Just doing a bit of painting

I peered over at my half-finished masterpiece and smiled in accomplishment. It felt like a rare thing, and a step up from my normal work.

BRUCE
Ooooh, painting?

THOMAS
Yeah, fine art is my thing. I love it

BRUCE
That's so cool!
I want to hear more about this
I've always had a soft spot for art and literature
They tell a story in a way like no other

THOMAS
Totally agree! Would you be down to hang out later on?

BRUCE
I'm meant to be going to Brisbane for the night
That said I'd like to meet ye
Where are you based? 😊

THOMAS
Coolangatta
So not far from you
Have you got a car?
Cause I do if you don't

BRUCE
No, the only wheels I have are on my suitcase 😆
What were you thinking for later?
If I'm staying around, I'll have to sort accommodation for tonight
So, we could choose somewhere closer to you
If there was anywhere that you thought would suit

THOMAS
Well I was thinking
We could get food or see a movie
I dunno, I guess we could always camp somewhere too

BRUCE
I'm open to camping
Or I can just grab a hostel somewhere in Coolangatta
I'll be finished at 5 with my friend
I'm cool with food or a movie too 😊

THOMAS
Want to meet me in Coolangatta? At the surf club?

BRUCE
Yeah, no prob

THOMAS
Six o'clock?

BRUCE
Six o'clock!
Looking forward to it

"You're looking a bit handsome there, Tommy," Courtney

complimented me as I walked into the kitchen for a glass of water.

I was wearing beige chinos, a black button-up T-shirt and black Vans. "Thanks, Court." I then laughed awkwardly.

"So, what are you and this Irish fella getting up to tonight?" Courtney winked. She watched television on the couch, biting down on a Toblerone.

"I honestly have no idea," I admitted, shrugging. "Could be dinner, or a movie, or we could go fuck in my car. I'm prepared for all three."

Courtney giggled. "You're fucked up, Tommy. Get out of here."

I loved getting Courtney's approval. She felt like my big sister sometimes; weighing up my actions and supporting me through my quests.

I stepped into the night, hoping my rugged comet edges were ready for this collision. They were, it turned out, but with a hefty price.

Collision

A cool breeze crept onto the beachside. The restaurant lights glistened. Coolangatta was a popular spot for dinner any night of the week, and I presumed I had dressed appropriately for the occasion, whatever that may be.

THOMAS
I just parked lad, where are you?

BRUCE
Sweet! I'm just beside the Tweed Heads Surf Club

THOMAS
Coolangatta Surf Club?

Pretty sure I'm on that street

BRUCE
Are there two surf clubs?
Outside the Ripcurl shop now

THOMAS
All right, on my way

BRUCE
Nice one 🕺

I thought I knew where the Ripcurl shop was. Though, I seldom roamed the streets here. Except when drunk on a Friday or Saturday night.

THOMAS
Hahah where the fuck is the Ripcurl shop?
Are you inside the shopping center?

BRUCE
Hahahaha
Well this is getting off to a seamless start

I walked into the shopping center and then back onto the street, hoping I would perhaps bump into him on the way, that he was just walking around aimlessly trying to find me too.

THOMAS
Stop running away from me hahahaha
I'm nice I promise lol

BRUCE
Gotta go 🏃,

I smiled.

THOMAS
Ahahaha
In all seriousness though, where the fk are ya?

BRUCE
Hahaha
Ok
The Ripcurl shop I'm at is beside Pan Asia
Are you next to Woolworths?

THOMAS
Yess ahahah

BRUCE
Ok
Imma find you

Please do, Bruce. Come find me.

BRUCE
Who's the local now? Ahahah

THOMAS
I'm outside Woolworths

BRUCE
Ok see you in 2 mins or maybe never

THOMAS
Hopefully never 😖

BRUCE
Hahahaha
You should be so lucky
I see ya
I think 😅

After glancing up, I spotted him, twenty meters from me, approaching at high speed. We locked eyes. He looked even better than his photos, and he was well-built with a muscular upper torso bursting out of his T-shirt. Those legs looked absolutely delicious in his black tight jeans. We smiled at each other. He neared, and I peered down at my phone.

THOMAS
Nah that's not me

I appreciated my own sense of humor, even when no one else did.

Bruce's hair was slicked back. He wore neatly polished black Doc Marten low-tops. *Dashing* was the first word that came to mind. And he spoke in this deep tone that I inhaled with the silent relief of instant attraction.

"Hey, Thomas," he greeted me, and we hugged for a moment. "Do you prefer Thomas or Tom?"

"I don't mind," I replied, getting all shy. "Tom. Thomas. Tommy. I get it all."

"Me too," he said. "Either Bruce, or Brucey! But don't call me Brucey."

I liked this guy already. And he was *so* handsome. I knew I wanted to spend the night with him, there was no doubt about it. We strolled down the street, the ocean air crisp and salty.

"How was your day?" I asked him, even though I'd been speaking to him all afternoon. He'd told me most of what he had done already, but I guess a part of me just wanted to hear it again from his voice. Either that or a part of me knew that some people talked absolute shite over dating apps. They could very well live completely different lives than what they project online.

"It was long, but it was good," he mentioned. "Said goodbye to my friend, Lila which was sad. But it's okay."

"You're here on a work visa, yeah?"

"Yeah, I am. I'm guessing you are too?"

"Yeah. Been here a few weeks now," I said.

Bruce giggled. "I bet it's been nice having sunshine all the time, right? You know as well as I do that we don't get that very often in our corner of the world."

I studied him as we walked along the footpath further into the heart of town. I saw him looking at me too. We both beamed.

"You're right," I agreed. "How long do you plan to stay in Australia for?"

"I'd like to stay for the full two years and do some farm work. Your man I was speaking to on the bus was from Ireland too and he said his partner found it easy to get residency here. She's a doctor, though."

I laughed. "Or you could just marry an Australian."

He followed suit. "Or that."

Our silences were awkward to begin with, but the more we got to know each other, the more normal they became. It didn't take long at all.

"What about you?" he asked me. "What's your plan?"

I exhaled heavily.

"I don't know yet," I said, truthfully. "I'm just going with the flow for now."

Bruce waggled his eyebrows. "And what better place to go with the flow, right?" He gestured his hand toward the sea.

"This is true," I agreed.

"Staying in Burleigh was so nice," he then said. "I don't know, I really want to go up north. It looks amazing up there. Less tourist-y too."

"Oh yeah? What would you do up there?"

"Err, well back in Ireland I had a background in writing for digital media publications, but there's not a lot of that work around here. All those jobs seem to be in Sydney and Melbourne," he went on. "Besides, I want to be where the waves are, and maybe try something different for work."

I knew this guy was unique, and I wanted to find out everything I could about him.

"That's very cool," I exclaimed. "I haven't checked out much up there. I'd love to, though. I just haven't had that much time with work and stuff."

"Maybe you'll have to come up and visit sometime," Bruce winked at me.

"Maybe I will."

"So, tell me about this art of yours," he said.

I told him all about it, which fascinated him. I showed him photos of my past prints, which fascinated him even more. I always got so passionate when I spoke about my art, and how through sketches and colors I could craft any scene I wanted and have that scene forever. He told me he had a portfolio full of poetry, upon which I wanted to see so badly. He also spoke about wanting to write a novel one day.

We strolled aimlessly along the windswept beachfront, until

we had to decide on what we'd do that evening. Neither of us could decide.

"What do you think of getting a takeaway pizza and taking my car somewhere and watching Netflix?" I finally suggested. "My car's an estate and turns into a real comfy bed."

He nodded his head. "I love this idea."

We stopped outside the bottle shop. "Beer?" I suggested.

The corners of his mouth quirked up. "You read my mind."

We purchased a six-pack of a new Pride beer that had a rainbow label on the bottles. The brewing company selling the beer was also donating some of the profits to an LGBTQIA+ community charity, so that was even more incentive for us to buy it.

"What kind of pizza do you want?" I asked as we arrived at Domino's.

"Well, I'm vegetarian so something without meat if that's okay?" Bruce replied shyly.

"Good answer," I winked.

I was looking to give being vegetarian a try and I couldn't have met Bruce at a more fitting time in my life. Cutting meat from my diet was one thing that rubbed off on me from him. We ordered a cheap spicy vegetable pizza and waited patiently outside for it to be cooked. A moment's silence crept upon us, which Bruce broke as soon as he could.

"Have you done much traveling around the world?" he quizzed me.

I shrugged. "Just Japan and a few places in Europe. What about you?"

"Nice, Japan looks stunning with all the cherry blossoms. I'd love to go," he said. "I've been all around Europe, South East Asia, Canada, and the US. And now, Australia."

He was a seasoned traveler and I loved that about him. "What's your favorite place so far?" I asked.

Before he could answer that, a screeching voice shouted, "Order for Thomas!"

Bruce chuckled. I walked over to the counter to collect the pizza. The face on the plump, sweaty middle-aged lady handing me the box was one of burnt-out exhaustion.

"Thank you," I said to her. "Have a good night."

"You too, darl," she grumbled.

Bruce and I ambled back to my car, continuing our conversation.

"Favourite place I've traveled to, I would probably have to say Hawaii, but maybe 'cause that was my latest trip," Bruce explained. "I spent two weeks there, and it was *just* amazin'. The hiking. The rugged landscapes. The surfing. Wow."

"You've really discovered a love for surfing, haven't you?" I questioned.

"Yeah, I have. It's hard to explain the feeling of it," he said. "Every surf is different. Every wave is unique. As you ride the face of the wave, you feel connected to something that you have no control over. But that's the beauty of it. You know, it's up to your creativity to feel as connected as you can to the board—to yourself, your weight, your motion—as you ride the wave. A bit like dancing. Both very fluid movements."

My mouth curved into a smile. "Wow. That's amazing!"

Bruce looked out to the ocean. "I usually feel at my most relaxed when I'm in the water."

"Kind of like a seal," I added.

We had arrived at my station wagon. Bruce met my gaze across the car. He beamed. "Exactly. Just like a seal."

I opened the car door swiftly.

"Have you ever surfed?" he asked me as we planted ourselves in the seats.

I shook my head. "No. Never."

He then said with a smile, "I could teach you someday."

He was trying to be cute, but I scoffed. "I think my terrible coordination would have something to say about that."

Bruce laughed. I then passed the pizza over for him to hold.

We parked up in a cul-de-sac by the water, to a secret little spot I'd brought only one date before. It hadn't lasted more than one night, unfortunately.

"I'm gonna go pee," Bruce announced.

I could *definitely* get used to that accent. It was refreshing, like home. But across the water from home. A beguiling mix of the familiar and the new. I folded the seats forward and constructed our bed in the back of the car with the vibrant blue blankets I brought with me. I had to make it comfortable for this presumed one-night stand, just like the one the week before. I wasn't getting déjà vu, though, which was strange. Maybe this time would be different.

Bruce soon returned from his tree urination. "Aw, the bed looks grand," he admired.

I winked. "Jump in."

He did so without hesitation, closing the car door behind him. It was cozy, just as I imagined on this chilly winter night by the calm waters. I flicked up my laptop and logged in.

"What do you feel like watching?" I asked him.

"Mmm, anything but a gory horror," he replied. "Oh wait, before I forget, I want to show you this video from Hawaii."

He stopped opening the pizza box and pulled his phone closer to me, loading up a video of him scuba diving amongst clusters of vibrant coral. A giant manta ray floated close above him near the water's surface. Bruce swam up to it, his GoPro clutched tight. It swam away to begin with, but soon returned and began wading in the water near him. It was the most majestic thing I had seen in a long time.

"It's beautiful," I said. "I bet that's something you'll never forget."

Bruce just smiled at me, and we drew our faces closer to one another.

Something felt different with him when we kissed for the first time, starting with the tingling sensation that spread over my entire body. The warmth of his lips and tongue against mine, I closed my eyes and he reached over, placing his hand upon the right side of my neck. I caressed his cheek with my right hand and then felt my way through his soft locks. We finally broke away, grinning at each other.

"Great kisser too," I added. "So, what brought you to Australia?"

He now stared at me even more intently, as if questioning my existence. "Honestly, I've been dreaming about going to Australia for years now, so I thought, why not go wander?"

"I'm the exact same. I finished my art degree back in London last year, and I just knew it was time to explore the world." I brushed the hairs on his arm, which resulted in a pulse from the front of my pants. "Australia was like my Argentina, if you get the *Dexter* reference."

Bruce chuckled. "I definitely get the *Dexter* reference."

He laughed playfully as he opened the pizza box and helped himself to a slice. I did the same. I was hungry, and content. And I loved the fact that we were eating pizza together in my car. Comfortable, at ease, and not in some restaurant or bar surrounded by a bunch of noisy people. Just *us*.

We cracked open a bottle of beer each and sucked it down with our food. The beers didn't last long, and neither did the pizza. We slipped the empty box and bottles into the front and cuddled up next to each other under the blankets. What followed was an all-consuming heat that nearly had me sweating.

"Just letting you know, I get *really* warm," he mentioned.

I chuckled. "Oh, don't worry, lad. I'm aware."

We began watching one of my favorite films of all time: *Into the Wild*. However, we only made it ten minutes into the movie before our cuddling turned into touching. That touching turned into Bruce biting my ear, and then my cock was rock hard. I grabbed at his crotch over his tight jeans. I couldn't feel much of a bulge just yet.

"I just get a little shy at first," he giggled diffidently, taking off his jeans. The more I grabbed his cock, the harder it got. Slowly, but surely.

His stomach was smooth like fresh leather. I peeled off my shirt, revealing my hairy chest. He grabbed my right pec.

"You're so fuckin' hot," he huffed, kissing me harder and climbing on top of me. We kissed passionately and I grabbed his hair.

He moved his head down my chest, kissing me all the way down. I lay there, flustered.

"Feels so good," I whispered.

He lifted his head back up and we made out again. I grasped his firm round butt and squeezed, reaching into his underwear. He not-so-subtly moved my hand away from his arse.

"Not tonight, mister," he chuckled.

I laughed. "Bit of an old-fashioned lad, are we?"

"Something like that," he mumbled, his face going red.

"That's okay with me," I said, kissing him some more.

The sticky silver mucus soon flowed, and we just lay there in each other's arms, staring up at the stars through a now partially fogged-up sunroof.

"That was hot," was all I managed to say in the aftermath. "It's so bad, though. After all that pizza and beer, now I really need to shit. And I know there's no toilet here. Got no toilet paper either."

Bruce laughed. "I need to shit too."

I sat up and spoke enthusiastically, "Well, let's go for a drive and go shit!"

He laughed again. "Sounds good."

What a first date it ended up being. Shitting side by side in a public toilet near the beach. Somehow, I just had this feeling, though, that perhaps this wasn't going to be a one-night stand.

We slept as best as we could in the car that night, but it would've been nice if we'd had a mattress at least. After watching the sun rise over the water from the back of my car, we decided to go to breakfast, bed hair be damned. I wanted to show him all my favourite spots around here, starting with the hip little café with the avocado wallpapered bathroom. It felt refreshing to sip coffee and eat a meal sitting across from him. The eggs benedict tasted better than ever that morning. And there was something about that drive back to Cooly that hit differently too.

I parked across from the hostel Bruce had booked the night before but didn't stay in.

"I had a great time last night," I said.

"Me too," he reciprocated.

"You said you were heading up to Noosa today, hey?"

"Yeah."

"Maybe I'll have to come check it out this weekend or something."

"Sure thing. I'll get the town warmed up for you."

He gave me that cheeky grin of his.

I wasn't letting this one get away, I decided. Noosa wasn't too far, and it meant I could enjoy a change of scenery. He kissed me, throwing his hands around my neck. I placed mine upon his face. He had already started growing stubble overnight in our slumber.

"See you soon, Thomas," he said, opening the door and waving goodbye.

I was pinching myself too, Bruce. Don't worry. I was right there with you, asking myself if this was too good to be true.

Oceans Away

I pretty much pranced into the house to refresh myself before starting work, singing in the shower loudly and proudly. I was on top of the world, so much so that I decided to ping him a message before work.

THOMAS
What an evening 😊

BRUCE
Yes, it was

THOMAS
What's your name on Facebook? We will talk there Mr
X

BRUCE
It's Bruce O'Brien. There's a fair few of us apparently...
Mine is the photo with the polka dot sweater and
    champagne bottle
If you can't find it just send on yours

He was right. There were a *lot* of Bruce O'Briens in the
world. But it didn't take much scrolling to find the one wearing
that sexy polka dot sweater and cheeky grin.

THOMAS
Found you!!
Thank god for the poker dots, otherwise it would've
    been hard 😉

BRUCE
Good job! The great gay detective, are we? 😉

THOMAS
Mwahahaha oh yeah, I forgot to tell you I actually am
    😂

BRUCE
Oh, you lead a dangerous and thrilling life, Mr Thomas
    🔥
Weird question, but what's your middle name?

THOMAS
Aha! It's Daniel. How about yours?

BRUCE
Jarrod 😬
Just a thought, but maybe

My first novel should be called "Call Me By Your Middle
    Name"

THOMAS
OMG! Imagine a parody! I'm in hysterics

BRUCE
It'd be amazing 😂 The crudeness would be next level
What could he fuck instead of a peach?

THOMAS
Some other mad fruit

BRUCE
Like a watermelon or something 😂

THOMAS
HAHAHA YES
Or like a big passionfruit

BRUCE
Bahahaha yes! We're onto something here
Okay so the protagonist
He could spend his days transcribing the lyrics of shitty
    rap songs

THOMAS
The dad is secretly a pimp
They're all part of like an Italian brothel
Instead of going to Rome they go and party in Ibiza

BRUCE
Yes to all of this!
Instead of that real classy intellectual Italian vibe

We go for trashy
An Italian *Shameless*
I see this going far

I snooped a few of his Facebook photos before work, and he seemed to have lived a fun life so far. He was truthful in saying that he loved the water, with numerous pictures of him snorkeling and scuba diving. He was twenty-seven and I was twenty-four.

I was never in a chipper mood when I first got into work, but today was different. I walked in smiling and greeted all my co-workers enthusiastically.

"What's the occasion, Tommy? You're pretty much glowing," Kat asked playfully, studying me while I made a coffee for myself.

Smiling, I blushed red.

"He had a hot date last night, that's why," Courtney answered for me while shaking up an espresso martini.

Good thing she did, because I couldn't *wait* to tell the girls about Bruce.

Courtney poured the martini into a shiny glass placed on the bar. Sebastian then collected it on a black serving tray and whisked it away to a table in the courtyard.

"I'm guessing it went well then?" Courtney assumed.

Courtney and Kat approached me from either side.

"It went really well," I blurted, sipping on my coffee. I told them all about it. "We're seeing each other again this weekend."

"That's really cute!" Kat cried. "Yo, I better go help Sebastian with some tables."

Kat left the bar, leaving Courtney and I to take care of drinks and coffees.

"A second date, Tommy boy," she teased. "I never thought I'd see the day."

I chuckled, cutting up limes. "Honestly, neither did I."

I talked to Bruce every day. He'd checked into a hostel in Noosa Heads and met a bunch of backpackers there. Looking at his photos on Facebook, he seemed to be having a good time. There were pictures of him drinking at beach fires, posing at hip cafés, and renting surfboards. I even got sent a photo of him stuffing as many tapioca balls into his mouth as he could. I adored Bruce's playfulness. He was my favorite kind of person, the way he'd be so mature but then regress to this state of childlike innocence and silliness. It was charming to say the least.

THOMAS
I want to go to the Glass House Mountains. They look amazing

BRUCE
Make sure you take me ☺

THOMAS
Of course. Maybe this weekend?

BRUCE
I'm down! My plan was just to hang around Noosa surfing this week

THOMAS
We shall organize something when I'm not so tired
Chat tomorrow handsome xx

BRUCE
Perf. Yeah, I'm goosed. Sweet dreams

About me 😊

THOMAS
Your slang is so different but it's something I could get used to

BRUCE
There's plenty more where that came from

THOMAS
Great! Ready to hear it all

BRUCE
Cultural exchanges all around

THOMAS
Goodnight Bruce

BRUCE
Night night Thomas

THOMAS
Call me by your middle name

BRUCE
Jarrod 💦

THOMAS
Oh, Daniel 💦

The following day, I received a phone call from Dad as I left work. I walked down the esplanade, the afternoon still and quiet.

"Hey, Dad!" I greeted him.

"Son," he began. I could feel his smile from halfway across the world. "How's that warm Australian sun going down? Bet it's done wonders for your skin tone."

"Ha!" I bellowed, glancing around to see if anyone heard me. "Well, it's actually been getting a little chilly now that winter's here. Only in the nights though, and nothing like England. How're things back at home?"

"Things are good. Just the same as usual. Work's starting to slow down now that summer's here."

Dad was a freelance graphic designer and worked from home. He used to work in a firm for several years, but finally took the leap of faith of starting his own business, which soared in the winter months and then slowed down during summer.

"How's things going in the land down under?" he asked me.

Was it too early to tell him about Bruce? Probably.

"Just been working in the café a lot still. Going on a few adventures here and there," I said. "Really loving it here in Coolangatta, Dad. It's relaxing."

"I bet," Dad replied. He sounded distant, like he was hiding something. "I've got some exciting news, Tom."

I grinned, letting the ocean breeze mess up my hair. "Ah, let me guess…you've decided to clean out all the junk you've been hoardin' in the house?"

Dad chuckled. "Ha! Not exactly. I mean, I wanted to surprise you, but I'm coming to Australia in a few weeks for a holiday. I booked it last night."

No way! The palest of the pale was coming to the land of sunshine. "You're kidding?" I blurted out. "What's the occasion? You never leave London."

It was true, and vastly out of character for my father to fly halfway across the world for a holiday. He traveled a little when he was younger but hadn't left London in the past few years. He always preferred the comfort of his own home.

"Well, business is good, and the car's been fixed, and I can do my work from a laptop, so I thought why not see where my son's set up shop," he explained. He seemed rather proud of himself for being able to do that, but then again, he'd worked hard to get where he was. "You've inspired me to travel again, Tom. I also need a bit of sunshine in my life."

"This is great news, Dad." Though, I was a little taken aback. "Not sure what to say. It'll be great to have you over here and show you around. Have you got much planned on your holiday? Not sure if I'll be able to get too much time off work to do any weeks away or anything with such short notice."

"That's fine, I wasn't expecting you to be able to do that," he responded gracefully. "As long as I get to see you and spend some quality time together when you're free, I'm fine with that. I've got a bit planned, like Uluru and The Great Barrier Reef. That brings me to the next thing I wanted to tell you."

Dad paused, as if a revelation was coming.

"Go on," I said bluntly, picking up on his hesitation right away.

He paused and sighed before continuing. "I didn't tell you yet because it's still early days, but Abigail, we've decided to ah—make things official. We'll be coming to Australia together and I—I'm buzzin' for you to finally meet her."

I wasn't sure why he hesitated, as if it would offend me or something. "That's great, Dad! I'm really happy for you. You deserve it. How long have you guys been together now again?"

"It'd be about three months now. She's really great, Tom."

Dad never dated, let alone left the house much after Mum passed away eight years ago. We grieved together for quite some time, until he had to be the strong one and be the rock for us both. I was only sixteen years old, and in the prime of puberty, when the teenage angst came rolling in like a bowling ball down a lane. But it felt like I was only hitting one pin at a time, especially when she was gone. My ball was deemed lighter, and my throw weaker. I learnt to live with it, though. I would never forget, which is okay.

"I'm keen to meet her, and to catch up with you, of course," I said, but I suddenly realized how nervous I would be. I wanted to tell him about Bruce so badly, but I still wasn't sure where me and the Irishman stood.

"What about you, son?" he asked. I knew where this was going. "Anyone special in your life I should know about?"

I had been well and truly sprung. "Well, there is this guy," I mentioned. "I only met him a few days ago, but we're spending this weekend together. He's from Ireland."

There was that dreamy tone in Dad's voice again. "Ah, the land of my favorite beer. Well, I hope it all goes well. Remember, patience is the key with these things. Just let it unfold."

I would try my very best, but it wouldn't stop me from checking my phone to see if he'd messaged me.

BRUCE
What are you up to handsome?

THOMAS
Just manifesting

BRUCE
What are you manifesting?

THOMAS
I want to go wherever I want when I want, but also have a stable home base

BRUCE
I'd love to manifest something similar
I just want to live a life worth writing about 😊

THOMAS
I journal a lot, but I've never written fiction

BRUCE
What kind of stuff do you write about in your journals?

THOMAS
Everything. Life, thoughts, my experiences, my
    memories, my reactions to things
Everything and anything

BRUCE
That's good, it means you always have something to
    look back on
Memory can be such a vague thing

THOMAS
I feel like it fosters self-awareness too
My memory can be quite shit sometimes
Imagine if we could play our memories back
Like that *Black Mirror* episode

BRUCE
It'd be terrible. It'd be so hard to forgive people. To get
    over things

THOMAS
It'd be so dangerous. We would get obsessive

BRUCE

You could spend your life analyzing them, fixating on
minor details

Sometimes I look back on my writing and the emotions
I felt

The surrounding, the atmosphere, all comes rushing
back

THOMAS

I get that if I look back on my journals.

That's why I try not to

I try to stay in the present as much as possible

BRUCE

When we live in the present, we are so much more
ourselves too

We thrive

If we live in the past everything becomes clunky

THOMAS

I've always struggled to think in the "now"

I've always had to be looking toward something, or a
goal to enjoy my present

But lately I've just been trying to be in the now and just
live simply

BRUCE

I think that goals can be good though

They can guide us to live a richer now

For me the problem is more to do with expectations

Goals are great if they aren't rigid

We just need to react to what's happening, and if need
be, adjust the goal

THOMAS

I've always wanted things to be done or go a certain
    way right now
But this year has really taught me to take a step back

BRUCE

I was just talking to a friend about this today
For a while I was pretty outcome-driven
I'd run to get fitter. Read books to get smarter
Now I just want to experience, and draw pleasure from
    the senses

THOMAS

Wow, lad, I'm really attracted to your outlook on life
I think it's so sexy
Go you, Brucey 😜

BRUCE

Right back at you Thomas x
I love that we can have these conversations
This is the stuff I write and think about everyday
And it's the type of thing we learn from living
Coupled with self-awareness
Fuck, you're so sexy

THOMAS

You too. I'm loving this

It was his thoughtful personality that reeled me in initially.
The way we could talk endlessly about life and what we thought
it meant, paired with the realization that there *was* no meaning,
only perspective. And although this kind of connection was
seldom seen by me, I wasn't completely convinced at first. I was
still busy doing life things of my own, like making drinks and

coffees for customers, and slapping paint onto more and more sheets of canvas. I'd nearly filled our garage with a collection of abstract pieces ranging in color, shape, and size. Even though I wasn't yet convinced that we might have a future, I felt no need to talk to any other lads, wondering if Bruce was feeling the same.

I planned to visit Noosa Heads for the first time that coming weekend.

It was a cloudy Saturday as gloomily predicted by my search engine weatherman, so the drive up was a little dim. I was excited to visit somewhere fresh, and to see Bruce. It had only been a week since we met, but it felt like I already knew him.

We booked an Airbnb in the small mountain town of Buderim. Bruce and I liked to call this chapter of our story "One Night in Buderim" as it really felt like the beginning of *us*. It was over that rainy weekend in the hills that our seeds were planted, soon to blossom from the winter drizzle.

I made it nine tenths of the way to Buderim without needing to pee. It wasn't until I was ten minutes from the town that I pulled into this small petrol station on the corner of the main road, before embarking up the hill. I jogged into the station and looked at the clerk.

"Is there a bathroom here?" I asked, uncomfortable and close to bursting. Why had I left it so long?

He pointed to the back of the store with a blank expression on his face. I rushed through the door, into the cubicle, unzipped my pants, and let it flow.

Oh, what a feeling, maybe I should call Bruce and let him know how good this feels.

I dialed his number as I left the station, waving a "thank you" to the clerk. Bruce picked up after two rings.

"Hello, handsome," he greeted, followed by that cheeky chuckle he always seemed to pull off.

"Oh, hey there, mister," I said, grinning and standing up against my car. "I thought I'd call for two reasons: one, I just had the best piss of my life, and two: I'm about ten minutes away."

He laughed. "I'm very happy about those two things. Good timing too. My bus just got in."

"That *is* good timing. Where did you want to meet?"

"Well, the bus just dropped me off outside IGA. There are some cafés around we could get lunch at? I don't know about you, but I'm starving."

My stomach grumbled. "I could definitely eat. And I'd *love* a coffee. I'll meet you outside IGA."

"Can't wait," he said, blowing a kiss through the phone. "See you soon."

I hopped into my car and ascended the hill. The scenic journey to the top stunned me, especially after rainfall. The trees and ferns glowed a fresh shade of lime. The hill kept on looping, and I was surprised my station wagon made it up without a fuss, or a full foot on the accelerator. A few coastal towns were in view through the gaps in the trees as I neared the crest. The town was more civilized than I imagined it would be, with a school and tennis court, various shops, and most interestingly, a slick black coffee shop housed in a shipping container at the lookout over the range.

I launched into the car park outside IGA and could already see him leaning up against a metal pole waiting for me. He noticed my car instantly. It began with a smile, and then a grin, which I returned through the windshield. I opened the door and hopped out.

You fell right into my arms, where you belonged.

Our eyes locked like they did every time our bodies were close, like magnets. I wrapped my arms around his neck as we kissed, not caring one little bit who was watching. This was *our* world. Our world of colliding comets and endless stars, and rays at our fingertips.

"How are you, handsome?" I asked him, looking into those almond eyes that seemed to glimmer on this dusky day.

"Absolutely great," he replied, shaking his head while his eyes didn't waste a glance. "Even better now that I'm with you again."

"It's been too long, hasn't it?" I joked, finally letting go of the embrace, as much as I enjoyed it.

"*Way* too long," he said, linking my hand with his as we strolled toward the assortment of cafés past the supermarket.

Coffee Cups

One thing Australians love is their cafés and their coffee. They have some of the best coffee in the whole world. And for someone who loves a good brew, I was in my element there. I mean, the UK would always be home, but their coffee was no match for the land down under. Something that made this experience even better was sitting across from Bruce in every café we visited, smiling at him and laughing. Most of the time we didn't even need to speak to communicate. Just being in each other's company was enough.

At this café in Buderim, we both ordered the vegan sweet potato and nut salad.

"How's the hostel going?" I questioned him.

"It's grand. Like, I've met a few nice peeps so far but I also wanna find somewhere a little more permanent." He started massaging his neck. "Noosa's so nice though, and the surfing has been class!"

I loved how passionate he spoke about things that interested him, especially at this hole in the wall. He linked his hands together and stuck his butt out on the seat as he moved his shoulders and chest forward as far as they would go. "It's such an achievement for me being in that environment, always aiming for the next wave," he explained. "A content achievement filled with bliss."

I raised a curious brow. "I'd love to watch you surf one day."

Bruce chuckled. "Maybe when the weather's a little better." He stroked my palm with his index finger. "What about you, how's the art going? Those photos you sent me were really great."

My lips curved upward. I was always fond of Bruce talking about my art, and I'd forgotten that I had sent a picture of my Cupid-like companion to him. "I guess I've been a little inspired lately," I mumbled, knowing quite well that my face now boasted patches of pink.

Bruce sure knew how to flirt. He just knew the way to get me going every single time. "I wonder what that inspiration is," he said shamelessly, arching a brow.

"I wonder…" I whispered seductively, stroking his finger against mine. "It's been good, though. I've just been working as well."

Even though my back faced the entrance to the café, I could suddenly see the whole shop light up from the ray of sun shining through. Several people gazed outside, including the barista and wait staff.

"What did you wanna do today?" I asked him, glancing down at the gold and brown watch I had been gifted for my last birthday. "We can't check into our Airbnb till two, and it's half eleven now."

"Well, it looks like the weather's clearing up. Maybe we can go for that hike we were planning after all."

Blue skies beckoned outside the café's doors.

"To the mountains we go," I declared in a deeper tone, taking my hand back. "Ready?"

"Aw, yes!" he piped up, sipping down the last few gulps of his decaffeinated long black. I did the same with my cappuccino.

We downed our glasses of water and left, ready to enjoy the sunshine. Ripping our sweaters off, we soaked up the rays. Even though it was meant to be winter here in Australia, the daytime temperatures and sun could still get quite warmer than a summer day at home.

The further we drove down the highway, the more prevalent the mountains in the distance became. The Glass House Mountains had a certain protruding structure about them that made us think we were immersed in the world of *Avatar* or something. Volcanic plug remnants beautifully sculptured by nature.

On route to Wild Horse Mountain Lookout, we listened to Lane 8 on the stereo and enjoyed the plugs and pine trees through the glass.

I started to rub Bruce's leg as we drove closer to Wild Horse Mountain. He had such solid legs and I could feel the muscle through his jeans. He rubbed mine and I was instantly rock hard the further I touched toward his thigh. I grabbed onto his cock through his tight jeans and massaged it. He chuckled and moaned a little.

"We've got ourselves into a little pickle, haven't we?" he teased, kneading my hard cock through my chinos.

"That we do, mister," I agreed, grabbing harder. "Feels so good."

"Is there somewhere we could pull over?"

There was, at a dirt road pull-off on the side of the road. I came to a stop and turned off the car. We gazed at each other and locked lips passionately, throwing ourselves at one another like the rugged comets we were. I grabbed onto his hair and pulled it, and he moaned. We unzipped each other's jeans, the feel of that aroused warm skin a welcome relief.

That empty coffee cup in the car came in handy, and it sure woke us up for our run up the cement trail to the top of Wild Horse Mountain.

"So, what do your parents do back in Ireland?" I quizzed him as we stopped on the ascent to catch our breath.

"My mum owns a crystal shop, and Dad's a mechanic. They're pretty much polar opposites," he huffed. "And you?"

I told him about Dad's profession, and then about Mum.

"Oh, Thomas, I'm sorry to hear that," Bruce said, scooping up my hand, softly.

"It was a long time ago," I admitted. "And it's something I've learnt to live with. She died of breast cancer. And she owned a beautiful little café in London. It's still there to this day— *Paula's.*" I laughed. "The name of the café has changed a few times, though. Not sure what it is now. I feel as if that's sometimes when the best partnerships form: polar opposites. I know that's what my parents were too."

"You can't be too similar otherwise you'd get sick and tired of one another." Bruce paused a beat. "How many siblings do you have?"

"I'm an only child actually," I revealed. "My parents lived really busy lives, so they could only really look after one of me. They gave me a good life, though, and Dad did his best guiding me through my late teenage years on his own. My best friend, Courtney, is like a sister to me too."

"That's the one you live with in Coolangatta, isn't it?"

I nodded. "Yep."

"I'd love to meet her and visit this café one day. It sounds great."

You sounded great, Bruce. Fantastic even.

"How many siblings do you have?" I asked him.

"I have two younger sisters and then two older brothers. Although, one of my brothers passed away a few years ago from a lung cyst operation."

"I'm sorry to hear that," I said, clasping his hand tighter.

Death was always so apologetic and sincere.

We reached the top of the hill, gasping for breath. It seemed as if we could both do with a bit more fitness.

"It's so beautiful," Bruce uttered in awe, staring off into the distance of the mountains from the edge of the gated lookout.

"You're beautiful." I snuck up behind him and grabbed him by the waist. He planted my hands around his hips. I kissed him on the neck.

He giggled. There was a young couple up there enjoying the view just like us. They left as soon as we arrived, having already basked in the beauty of the vistas themselves. The rugged volcanic plugs stood tall through the hazy plains in the distance.

"There's been a pretty bad fire up here on the coast the past few days," Bruce told me, pointing toward plumes of gray smoke beyond the pines.

"Yeah, I can smell it. Looks pretty bad too. They get a lot of bushfires in this area, I've been told."

"Climate change, hey?" he mentioned.

I sighed, shaking my head.

One Night in Buderim

The sun didn't stay long that afternoon. An overcast blanket folded back over the sky as we drove back to Buderim to check in to our Airbnb. The hillside house was held up by wooden planks overlooking the coast. We had the whole bottom of the house to ourselves, with a young Australian couple staying upstairs. It felt homely having our own space, and a large one at that. The downstairs suite was fit for a king. Or in this case, two kings.

"We're totally moving in, I hope you know that," I joshed, collapsing onto the bed, melting into the soft silky mattress.

"I wouldn't even be mad if we started living here now," Bruce admitted, shutting the door behind him and laying on top of me, showering me in kisses. "I just love kissing you," he whispered.

I loved him kissing him too, and I could've spent all afternoon here as the rain trickled again, onto the roof and down the window, lips locked with him, gazing into those almond eyes. The afternoon grew old, though, and so did we. He lay at my breast, stroking my pecs. I tickled his firm arse.

He giggled. "Soon, handsome. Very soon." He further nestled his head in my chest, a bit like a puppy burying its face in fresh sheets. He breathed out heavily. "*One Night in Buderim.* Sounds like the name of an amazing film."

"What's the ending going to be like?" I laughed. "Hope it's a good one."

He looked into my eyes and poked me on the nose. "It will be." I think I truly believed that, and fell deeper into those eyes, further into that touch. I hadn't felt this good in a long time. Bruce really did teach me to enjoy the moment even more, and I learnt to do that every second that we were together, especially in the beginning when we had limited time with each other. However, I already felt time slipping away from us.

"What should we get for dinner tonight?" he asked me. "We should go on a cute date."

"Well, as much as I love laying here with you listening to the rain, we do need to eat."

The light slowly faded outside.

"Should we get some wine?" I suggested after we showered.

"Absolutely." He smiled, kissing me up against the wardrobe mirror in our room. "You look great by the way."

I wore a blue shirt and cream chinos. I knew bringing my favorite button-up would come in handy that weekend. He wore a white shirt that paired perfectly with the same sexy black jeans he wore the night we met. "So handsome," I whispered. "Let's go."

Bruce and I loved our red, but we weren't fussy. I was glad he wasn't one of those people who only drank expensive wine. A fifteen-dollar bottle of Pinot Noir would do the trick. The Thai restaurant we ate at that night was even BYO alcohol.

"How's this for our first dinner date?" I laughed, pouring us both a glass while we waited for food. I ordered crispy sweet and sour tofu and Bruce went for a vegetable noodle stir-fry.

"One of many, I hope." He grinned, raising his glass. "And we'd just get better at it every time, so let's not think for a second that this is our best."

"Cheers to us moving into our first dream home," I joked, my glass meeting his. "In Buderim."

He laughed. "Cheers to that, and to Buderim. And to you, handsome."

"Right back at you."

It was raining when we woke up the next morning. This place was a dream I wished we never had to wake up from. Unfortunately, I only had a few more hours left with Bruce, and I didn't want to let him go. I was already scared of losing him. He could've just been lying when we said all those cute things to one another. That's why I kept standing on my own two feet and kept my love barrier up: the barrier preventing me from completely and utterly falling for someone. This had happened before, and it ended almost as soon as it had begun. I didn't want to make the same mistake again. I didn't know him. It felt like I knew him, but how much could I *really* know someone after a week?

We took a long while to get out of bed that morning. We both knew we had to say goodbye, but refused to at each chance.

"I don't want you to leave," he fake-cried, pulling the blankets over both of us and tangling himself within me and it.

"I don't want to leave Buderim, or you," I said. "I thought we lived here now."

"In a perfect world, handsome." A short comfortable silence rippled between us. He brushed my cheek. "When are you free next? I want to see you again as soon as possible, without sounding needy."

Remember when we said we wouldn't rush things, Bruce? We told each other that on the first night we spent in my car.

"Not needy at all. I feel the same way," was what I said. "Did you want to come down and stay with me next weekend? My dad and his new girlfriend are coming over to Australia and they're staying in Coolangatta. You could meet them, and Courtney."

"Ooooh," he hummed excitedly. Things were happening, and they were happening fast. "That could be fun. I'd like that."

"Good." I kissed him under the sheets, making every last moment count. Check-out was in half an hour.

One thing I didn't bring that weekend to the "Sunshine Coast" was a rain jacket. Neither did Bruce, funnily enough. It didn't bother us, though; I quite enjoyed walking around in the rain holding his hand, enjoying our sleepy Sunday. We started the day off with a coffee from the shipping container café overlooking the coast. It was there we sat and enjoyed our morning brew, eating our dinner leftovers out of plastic containers.

"What time do you need to be back in Coolangatta?" he asked me.

"Not until this afternoon, so we've got time to go to that waterfall in Buderim if you want?"

"Sounds grand. Forest bathing with you sounds like a great way to spend a Sunday." He planted a kiss upon my cheek, which was still wet from the rain. He massaged my wet hair, parting it to one side.

"Forest bathing, you say?" I chuckled. "I guess the more we walk in this rain, the more we will bathe."

He laughed, placing his hand on my shoulder. "Forest bathing isn't *actual* bathing, silly. It's a Japanese tradition and therapy of walking through a forest and becoming completely conscious of your surroundings. The smells, the textures, the sounds."

Everything he said made him sound even more special to me, extraordinary even.

"So, what are you looking for at the moment?" he asked me on our drive through the forest road to Serenity Falls. He didn't need to explain himself any further. I knew exactly where he was going with that.

"Uh, I don't know actually," I disclosed, my smile slipping. "I guess just someone I can do life with. That I can go adventuring with and love freely with. I want to take things super slow, though. I don't want to make the same mistakes from my last two relationships."

"And what were they?"

We parked the car at the waterfall trailhead. I turned the engine off, and we sat still as droplets of water made pitter-patter noises on the car.

"I feel as if they were both rushed," I admitted, eyeing the trees outside, "and I didn't get to know them enough before we both made each other such a huge part of each other's lives. It was like love at first sight both times, and then attachment, and then it fell apart really quickly."

"I can resonate with that," he replied with his eyes downcast. He was fiddling with his fingernails. "My only two relationships were the same. Very quick attachments, but, both fell apart slowly and painfully. I told myself that next time, I'd break the cycle."

He switched his gaze to me. "That I'd take things slow and get to know the person first."

"Well, let's do that then?" I suggested, meeting his eyes and massaging his hand. "Let's take things slow."

"Class!" He smiled at me.

We both looked at the digital clock on the dash of my car: 11:22.

"It's always those two numbers I see," he told me. "They come up everywhere."

"Now that you mention it, I've been seeing those two numbers a lot this week."

"They're my lucky numbers," said Bruce. "The number eleven was my brother's favorite number before he passed away. Twenty-two was my grandfather's. He's also gone."

I was surprised, but I also wasn't surprised at the same time. "No way! Both those numbers were my mother's favorite too," I said. "She was born at 11:22 a.m. actually. Fun fact."

We weren't aware of the true power of "eleven twenty-two" then, but we didn't need to be. We were just there to enjoy each other's company that day. Rain, muddy boots, and all. The forest glowed green, especially after all the rain. The earth smelt of pleasant petrichor, and a crystal-clear creek flowed alongside the trees. Stone steps lead down to a suspension bridge, overlooking the waterfall—the one we kissed under, and a place I'd never forget. Images that I could never delete from my memory. I didn't want to let him go, but life was working in our favor. If we wanted to take things slow, we had to take that time apart each week to live our own lives, only to be reunited the next week's end, ready for whatever life had in store for us.

The Broccoli Chronicles

Fifteen years old:

I sat in Mum's café, staring up at that black sign with the white illuminated writing: *Paula's*. I waited impatiently for Dad to pick me up, frantically checking my watch. He should've been here by now. I walked here after school every day and helped Mum pack up the shop. Courtney would usually help as well, but that day I strolled there alone and sat restlessly, zoning in on the elderly patrons around me. They regularly came to the café for their afternoon tea and cake. Two ladies behind me were discussing what they would usually eat for breakfast. One said porridge. The other eggs.

Sharon, a supervisor in the café, told me that Mum had gone to a doctor's appointment in a hurry and had left her in charge of closing that day. Dad just told me to wait, so I did. I waited and waited, and most of the diners had left their mahogany booths by the time Dad arrived. He didn't seem like himself. It might've been the blank, sullen stare he fixed onto the brick walls and not on me. For some reason, he couldn't even look me in the eye.

"Let's go, Tom," he ordered at once, his voice tinged with disappointment.

I followed him toward the front door.

"Thanks for closing up, Sharon," Dad called out upon exit. "Pauls will be in tomorrow."

"Not a problem, Harry!" Sharon called back, writing onto a notepad. "See you, guys!"

An awkward silence filtered through the air on the drive home. I knew Dad wanted to speak. He had something to get off his chest, but he just kept on sighing, and going to talk, but then stopping.

I had to say something. "Is everything okay?"

He huffed and slapped down on the steering wheel.

"It's your mother, Tom," he stuttered sadly. "The doctors found a lump on her breast and she found out. Ugh…" He sighed again. "She's got cancer, Tom."

I felt a sudden sense of urgency. "Shit. She's going to be okay though, right? They'll get it fixed—right?"

Dad sighed. It was at this moment that I knew it wasn't going to be okay. A cloud of anxiety folded over me like a melted marshmallow, consuming me and everything else in sight. I didn't quite understand it on that silent drive home that day, and I didn't fully comprehend that the next twelve months would be like a clock counting down. Counting down to her demise, and a loss that I would never regain.

Twenty-four years old:

The drive back to Coolangatta flew by in a flash. Every song on the radio reminded me of Bruce, and I caught myself smiling each and every time a song encapsulated our romance. I pretty much skipped into the house when I got home, knowing there was such a productive week ahead. Bruce didn't give me long to think about him when I got home. My phone rang. I beamed when I saw it was him.

"Hello, Jarrod," I said playfully, sinking back onto my bed.

"Daniel, how was the drive?" he asked me.

It had only been a few hours, but it felt so great to hear that voice. The voice of the best Irishman I had ever known.

"It went really quick," I replied. "Maybe because I had your face to think about, and every song that came on the radio, Bruce, it was just…I can't even describe it."

"Coincidental? Aligned? Perfect?"

"You're the writer, see? You can create words and I'll draw from what I see."

"That sounds quite poetic, Thomas. Are you sure you haven't been hanging out with me too much? Although, I feel that too. I thought about you that whole rainy bus ride back to Noosa."

"I don't think there's ever enough of us," I blurted out. "I want more."

"I hope there's much more to come." He then changed the subject rather quickly. "I wanted to call to see you got home safe. I already can't wait to come down this weekend. I'm hoping to get a job of some sort this week too."

"You shouldn't have a problem with that at all. A handsome boy like you, anyone would be silly not to hire you."

He chuckled. "I hope you're right there."

You should never have doubted yourself, Bruce. You were so much. A piece of art even.

"I'm craving broccoli so bad," was the conversation I started the next day.

"I am *so* glad you love broccoli as much as I do!" Bruce exclaimed.

"You know what, let's just go to music festivals dressed as heads of broccoli," I suggested.

"Thomas, you're a genius! If we ever got a place together, instead of the garden filled with plants, it'd just be a sea of broccoli growing fuckin' everywhere!"

We both laughed. I couldn't believe he was bringing up the idea of us getting a place together, not that I minded it. It stimulated me actually, because it felt right.

"Guinness World Record, handsome," was my response. "How many heads of broccoli can *you* grow in one spot?"

I was glad Bruce enjoyed my random humor. I knew I could be funny, but for someone to laugh at my jokes was one of the best feelings in the world.

"Challenge accepted," he announced after gathering himself. "You know how Australia has so many giant structures of vegetables?"

"Yeah. I'm kind of aware."

"Maybe we should put in a proposal to the local council to put in a broccoli structure, 'cause *obviously* it's the best vegetable."

I laughed. "You kill me. But, I'm also in full support."

We had all these beautiful, surreal plans. We even planned a possible trip to the Philippines to go swim with the whale sharks because well, why not? It had been on my bucket list for years, but to do it with Bruce just seemed like something that would happen. Because so far, he seemed like the type of guy that didn't go back on plans when he made them. He had an idea and stuck with it, no matter how obscure or difficult the journey was to get there.

"We're having a little work party here on Saturday night," I told him on Thursday. "So, I may be a little hungover when you get here on Sunday."

"Look, if I can't take you at your most hungover then I don't deserve you at your best. Let me tell you, though, I'd look after your hungover arse any day."

I worked until the end of the week, the honeymoon phase in full swing. Courtney could tell the difference in me, even if I couldn't. When love came, my surroundings disappeared. He became my sole priority. Courtney was only trying to protect me, but at the time, I couldn't see it.

It was a quiet day behind the bar, and we were polishing glasses together.

"Look, I'm not saying I'm not happy for you, mate," she began to lecture. "I'm just saying that this is exactly how you were acting when you first met Peter last year. And once that novelty wore off for you, it was too late. You were already living in Japan with the lad and had to fuck off back home."

My eyes began to narrow. "This is different, Court. Trust me," I stressed. "You'll realize once you meet him this weekend."

"I know, Tom. Don't worry, I know. I'm just saying, take it slow and don't make any sudden huge decisions. I'm not saying this because I don't want you to find someone over here. Hell, I'd love for you to fall in love with the right guy. But just take it slow. It's not a race."

"That's what we're doing, Court," I lied. "Taking things slow."

She was right. Were we really taking things slow even though we said we would? Fantasizing about curating gardens together and swimming with whale sharks in other countries? No, probably not. But I didn't care. I was in love, and that was all that mattered. I know my best friend was just trying to look out for me, but at this point in time, that's not what I needed to hear. I needed to hear how happy she was that I'd found this dreamy man who'd sprinted into my life ever-so unexpectedly.

I had Courtney's cautious opinion on the situation, but I also wanted to hear Dad's once he arrived.

Courtney and I drove up to Brisbane to pick him and Abigail up on Friday night. The anticipation to meet Abigail wasn't as I had expected. It hadn't really crossed my mind the whole week, especially being so invested in Bruce.

"How do you feel about meeting Abigail?" Courtney asked me. "It's like, you know, the first woman your dad's been with since your mum."

She knew me too well. I hadn't spoken much since passing the theme parks on the highway. I started biting my fingernails anxiously.

"I don't know," I admitted. "I guess I do feel a little weird about it now that I've had a chance to think about it."

"Yeah," she agreed. "It must be hard, Tommy. You never know, though. You might end up really liking her. She'll never replace Paula, like ever. But your dad must've seen something special in her, so don't get too anxious before you've seen the book's cover."

Duly noted, but also exactly what I needed to hear. "I know. You're right."

We pulled up at the airport. I received a message from Dad

saying they were already standing out in the public pick-up area. Dad was always efficient with time, ever since I could remember.

It was a shock to see how much Abigail looked like Mum—that thick brown hair and olive skin. Even the way she dressed was similar: the colors, the modern conservative style. It was almost as if I was picking up my father and my deceased mother. Whether it was coincidence or luck, I didn't know, as long as they were happy.

Courtney spoke about our adventures in Australia thus far the whole way home, and so did Dad and Abigail about their travels. I didn't speak much; only the occasional one-liner while I drove. I was still gobsmacked at Abigail's resemblance to Mum. She even spoke like her a bit. Her and Dad had gone traveling around Europe spontaneously since I had left London.

"Your dad tells me you're seeing an Irish fella?" Abigail piped up.

It took me a moment to comprehend what she was saying, and the whole car fell silent.

"Y-yeah, it's uh, going great so far," I stammered, feeling relieved that Coolangatta was now only a half hour away. "Just seeing how it goes, I guess."

"No expectation is a good expectation sometimes," Abigail explained. "When I met your dad, I didn't think in my wildest imagination that it would escalate to this. I'm very lucky."

"Aw, you both are!" Courtney chimed in, grinning.

I didn't have much to say about that. It was just too soon.

Courtney and I dropped them off at their hotel in Coolangatta, and after that, it felt like I could breathe properly again.

"She looks exactly like your mum?" Bruce asked on the phone

later that night, also bewildered. "That's some freaky universe synchronicity shite right there."

"Tell me about it!" I agreed. "Anyway, how's your night been? Have you been up to much?"

"Not a whole lot. Had a few beers and cooked dinner with the girls at the hostel. Wrote a little story."

"A story, eh? What kind of story?" I was genuinely intrigued by anything Bruce wrote.

"It's a silly one, handsome. I wrote it after having a few drinks." He paused a long beat. "Okay, would you like to hear?" I knew he wanted to read it to me.

"I'd *love* to hear it. Anything to relieve me from this weird night."

I couldn't keep the toothy grin off my face. This man was just melting my heart.

I loved every minute of his hilarious story about a broccoli tree that met up with a talking carrot and potato in a field. The three vegetables embarked on a bold quest to the "Golden Dinner Plate", to be enjoyed by a lucky one's appetite. I truly couldn't believe what I had just heard.

"I'm actually speechless," is what I said. "Just got this stupid big smile on my face."

He chuckled. "Good. That was my end goal: to make you smile."

I shook my head, laying there on my bed gazing up at the white ceiling, the grin still plastered across my face. "You have no idea how happy I am right now."

"I'm also really happy, Thomas. You're just, ah, *fantastic!*"

"I'm really looking forward to you being down."

"Me too. I can't wait."

• • •

Courtney worked the next day, and I was off to lunch with Dad and Abigail by the beach. We decided on the surf club. A meal with a view of the ocean sounded like something we all could use. Winters in this area of the coast seemed to enjoy endless sun. There wasn't a cloud in the sky and the blue hues of the ocean sparkled.

"I just can't believe how beautiful the beaches are here!" Dad said exuberantly, admiring the view out to the horizon from our ocean view table. "Nothing like this back home. Unless you're in Croatia or Greece or something, which was gorgeous by the way, Tom. Next time you travel around Europe, you'll have to visit some of the beaches there. We spent a bit of time there and it was great."

"Yeah, I bet. It's been super nice living here." I was still a little quiet and feeling a tad strange, especially with Abigail.

"You definitely got lucky, Tom," Abigail mentioned. "It's stunning! And the sunshine…"

I smiled awkwardly, folding myself into an even more uncomfortable silence.

"So, Harry tells me you're quite the artist?" she asked me. "He showed me some of your pieces and they're really beautiful." She beamed at Dad and then shifted her focus back to me. "Have you been working on any new pieces while you've been here?"

She seemed so interested in me which did make me warm up to her.

Before our lunch arrived, Abigail walked off to the bathroom. Dad and I didn't speak for a moment. We just stared off to the sea.

"I know what you've been thinking, son," he speculated. "She looks a lot like her, doesn't she?"

"Freakishly, Dad!" I cried out. "I've just been asking myself how it's even possible?"

"I ask myself that sometimes too. I occasionally still pinch myself to see if all of this is even real. I've accepted it, though, that it is quite real."

"I hope you don't think I'm going to start calling her Mum or anything," I muttered.

"No, Tom. I'd never ask you to do that. All I ask is that you give her a chance."

I drew a half-smile. "That I can do."

Dad rubbed me on my back and then gave it a friendly tap. "Good things are coming, Tom. I'm keen to meet Bruce tomorrow."

"I just don't want to get my hopes up too much, you know," I said glumly. "I've had a few flops in the past few years, and Courtney reminded me how rushed they were."

"We learn from relationships, though," he explained. Dad was just as wise as he was creative. "You know that as well as I do. You've learnt at a young age, whereas I learnt it when I was a little older, especially with the women before your mum. But just take it as it comes, son. And *enjoy*."

He lifted his beer glass. I did too in unison.

Abigail returned. A wholesome feeling of comfort washed right through me as I realized this was the closest I had been to my father in years. Things weren't always the case with Dad, especially after we lost my mother. Perhaps Abigail was the silver lining we both needed in our lives.

Mum fought for just over a year. And then it was just me and Dad.

Eight years ago:
I tip-toed into Dad's room one night, eggshells cracking beneath my feet. I felt so alone. She had been my main source of affection,

and the same for my dad. The room was dimly lit as if a romantic evening was playing out. A romantic evening for one. Dad sat on the bed, crying into a framed photo of her. He hadn't even noticed me enter.

"Dad…" I began, but my words became lost. I had so much to say but was unable to form words.

He sobbed harder. "I can't right now, Tom. Please."

I think that was the cue for me to leave. At the time, I just couldn't understand why he would push me away. But, he needed time to himself to reflect on the memory of her. I, on the other hand, was already in a spiral of teenage rebellion at this point. It wasn't that I had to rebel to relieve the grief. I had to rebel to become who I was. I came out not long after Mum's passing. I can remember the exact day in the car as if it were yesterday.

"Get in the car, Thomas!" Dad yelled at me when he pulled up at the shopping center.

He was fuming, but I was too high from the joint I smoked earlier to respond with much sense. I just hopped in the car sulkily like I always did. Dad shook his head as he sped out of the car park, bubbling with anger and frustration. However, I didn't care at the time.

"I just can't believe you, Thomas!" Dad growled. "You get caught stealing from the shopping center. You reek of weed. Your marks at school are going down the toilet…"

"You can blame Mum for that," I mumbled.

"Don't you dare put any blame on her," he ordered. "She didn't bring you up this way, and neither did I. God, Thomas, is there something you aren't telling me? We need to get you back on track."

Should I have told him about the lad I slept with at Courtney's house party on the weekend? Absolutely not. I just stared out the window. He didn't even know that I liked boys at this point, but I felt like maybe it was a good time he knew.

"Nothing," I lied.

"I'm so disappointed, Thomas," he said in a disgruntled tone, shaking his head. "And your mum…"

"Fuck off!" I snapped.

"Well, tell me why you're doing this then," he demanded.

"Fine!" I yelled. Here it came. "I'm gay. Are you happy? I'm gay, and no one will accept me when they find out. I get it."

He was speechless. I would've had to process that situation if I were him too.

My eyes pooled with tears, awareness of my actions in full swing. I turned away from him and stuck my forehead against the passenger window.

"Are you sure?" was his response.

I nodded. "I think so."

We pulled into the driveway and he turned his gaze to me before I reached for the door handle.

"Thomas, I accept you, no matter what, okay?" he assured me, putting his hand on my shoulder. "Look, I know the past few months have been tough. But we need to get through this together. I know I shut you out when we first lost her, and I'm sorry. But I need you to help me, by staying out of trouble."

"I will, Dad. I promise." Did I promise, though, or was it the weed talking?

Before I hopped out of the car he told me, "Just remember— people aren't going to automatically accept you out there in that big world. It doesn't matter whether you're gay or straight. You have to choose your friends wisely and cancel out all the negative bullshit. You'll be accepted by the right people. I promise you that, son."

"That's why I've got Courtney," I added, giving him a smile.

"And thank heavens for that," he said. "You've got a friend for life there."

I did, and a supporting father. I was lucky. One day, I hoped I'd be lucky enough to find that special man to spend my life with too.

Carbon Copies

When I picked up Bruce from the train station on Sunday afternoon, he strode toward my car, waving his hand about like a little kid on Christmas. He popped his small suitcase in the trunk and hopped in the passenger seat.

"Evening, handsome!" I greeted him.

Grinning at me, he grabbed me by the cheeks and pressed his lips hard against mine. I closed my eyes, surrendering to his touch.

"Boy, is it good to see you!" he rejoiced, relaxing back into his seat and folding his seat belt over.

I started driving. "How was the train?"

"It was fucking long," he admitted. "It's only meant to take two and a half hours by car, but this took, like, four."

I felt bad. "I'm glad you're here, though."

He massaged my leg. "So am I, you have no idea. I just think I'm definitely going to buy a car in the next few weeks."

"It's a good investment, especially around this area," I said. "The public transport isn't very good."

"It'll give me a lot more freedom too, which is what I need."

We sat in silence for a few moments.

"So how are you liking Noosa in general?" I asked him.

"It's pretty good. I mean, I'm still staying in the hostel which has its ups and downs, but I've met some really cool people there which is grand. I might look at moving into my own place soon."

I giggled. It really sounded like he was having fun up there, but obviously something was missing for him. Some*one* that resided in Coolangatta, perhaps?

"I joined this surfing group too," he continued excitedly. "And we've been meeting up a bit, which has been nice."

It made me excited to hear him achieve his goals. "Sounds like you've started getting a little life for yourself up there, handsome."

His love for surfing was inspiring, but it also made me look at my own fitness and feel like a failure. I wasn't exactly the fittest of all guys, but I did have definition, especially in my chest. Bruce worshipped my chest, and also had this way of discovering my special spots. He'd have his face buried in there, sucking away at my nipples. The oh-so-sensitive nipples. He knew what I liked and loved to please me. We both had our niche in the sheets. You know, that sweet spot. His was this little spot between his testicle and left thigh. A little tongue there and he'd shudder and roll his eyes.

He stood there naked after cleaning himself up that night, and I was still just laying before him, not wanting to move after the climax he had given me. He admired the blue and yellow cotton scarf my grandmother had knitted me when I was young.

"These are my county's colors back in Ireland," Bruce informed me, touching the scarf and smiling at how soft it was.

"No way! That's so strange," I exclaimed, eyeballing him. "But also, another nice coincidence."

We both stared at the black and white analogue clock ticking on my wall—11:22 p.m.—that time again. Our smiles disappeared for a moment in an eerie daze. He hopped back onto the bed on all fours and crawled back to me, not taking his eyes off mine.

"I'm not even surprised," he whispered, crawling closer. "About the colors." He massaged his hands up my thighs. "Or the time."

A bang from the front door made me jump and blink, ending the gaze. "Courtney must be home from her date."

"Well let's get changed and make a cup of hot water for bed," Bruce proposed, getting up and slipping into shorts and a T-shirt.

Bruce had introduced me to drinking hot water when we met. It helped with digestion, he would say. He gulped down a mug of it after almost every meal. I loved his outlook on life in that way. First the concept of forest bathing, and now drinking hot water as medicine for the body. This adventure to the kitchen would also be Bruce and Courtney's first time meeting each other.

Please go swimmingly.

Courtney sat on our navy-blue couch, sipping on a bottle of beer, eyes glued to her phone. She popped her head up the moment we walked into the kitchen.

"The famous Bruce!" she sang, hopping up from the couch.

"Nice to meet you, Courtney!" Bruce greeted eagerly, embracing her hug.

She finally broke away. "I've heard lots about you," she said, winking at me. I blushed.

Bruce chuckled. "All good things, I hope."

Courtney flicked her hand forward swiftly. "Of course. Of course."

"So, how was the date?" I asked her as Bruce filled the kettle.

Courtney took a generous swig of her beer. "It actually went really well. He's your typical Byron Bay boy: long sandy blonde hair, brown as fuck skin. So yeah, he's pretty hot."

"Are you going to see him again?" I quizzed her. "Sorry, I'm just doing the same interrogation you did to me after I met this one."

I grinned at Bruce, and it didn't take him long to catch it and wear it as his own.

"I might. He has a really cool van too that he wants to take me places in."

"Sounds like you've got yourself an adventure-seeker," Bruce mentioned, pouring him and I a mug of hot water. "That's what you want. Plus, you know, a man with a van can lead to endless possibilities."

Courtney chuckled. "Yeah, maybe. Anyhow, what are you guys up to tomorrow?"

"Well, Bruce here's got to face the wrath of Dad and Abigail," I said, sipping lightly on my scalding water so that it didn't burn my mouth.

"You're in for a real treat," Courtney joshed through peaked brows.

Bruce laughed awkwardly. "Should I be scared?"

Courtney replied, "No. They're completely harmless. Nothing to worry about. Also, we should all go for a few drinks tomorrow afternoon when I get off work."

"Yeah, for sure," Bruce said, deciding for the both of us.

"Wicked!" Courtney piped up, gulping down the rest of her beer. "Ah, bedtime. I'll see you both tomorrow. Oh, and I don't like being kept up by noisy sex, just FYI."

Bruce and I giggled. "We're very quiet. Don't worry, Court," I assured her, already loving the comfortable banter between the three of us. If this new lad of Court's fit into this wonderful jigsaw puzzle, then the four of us really could form a fun new group. If only it were that easy, though.

"Nothing's ever that easy," Abigail told me the following day when we mingled at a bar on the waterfront for lunch.

I peered over at Dad and Bruce, who were deep in conversation near us. Two peas in a pod. I mean, they were both Leos. They were bound to get along, but I didn't think it would be this instant. I could overhear some of their conversation. It was mainly about their family life growing up. They both shared their pasts, until I thought they wouldn't be able to share anymore. Fat chance. They kept on going, leaving Abigail and I to small talk. And that's what it was: small talk, until she broke the ice with me. I was glad she did, because there were moments where I still couldn't look her in the eye for long periods of time without wanting to cry. Every aspect of her reminded me of Mum.

"Relationships," she said, sipping on her espresso martini. "Nothing's ever easy. There'll be times when you really need to work for it."

I chuckled. "Yeah. I guess. Bruce and I haven't even got to that stage yet where we've made it official or anything."

"You will," she guaranteed me. "I can tell. You're both so compatible and you just *work*. It's only a matter of time before you both have that conversation. Might be in a week, might be in a month. Just depends on how long you both can keep your guard up. But yeah, love, it's a beautiful thing. I've finally found it again with your father. It's the best thing that's ever happened to me. I lost my husband three years ago in a car accident, and I wasn't sure if I was ready to date again. It felt like I was, betraying him or something. But Harry made me feel again, and I just knew it was okay to go down this path, not only for self-love, but that love shared with another person. I can see it between you and Bruce. I know love when I see it."

A smile worked its way across my face. She spoke about keeping guards up, and I think my guard for Abigail was let down that day. I realized she wasn't my mother and wasn't trying to be. She sure looked like her, but Abigail was a woman of her own, who had gone through a lot in the recent past, just like Dad had. I was glad the two had found each other.

"Just one little piece of advice," she went on. "Because my son's gay and he said it's quite common in gay relationships to rush things. Just let it unfold and enjoy the present. Don't jump into anything serious too quickly, because as much as you feel that those sudden actions are the right thing to do, sometimes they're out of fear of loss. My son learnt the hard way, multiple times. He's married now, though, because he was patient."

"You're right," I agreed, sipping down some mojito. "I think I've had a habit of doing that—falling in love too quickly. That's why I want it to be different this time."

We both passed a glance over to Dad and Bruce, who were still quite engrossed in each other's stories. Stopping their conversation for a moment, they beamed at us from afar before continuing.

"It's not about falling in love too quickly, I don't think," said Abigail. "Because that's what love is; it's uncontrollable. It's more about what you do with that love."

Feeling a little drunk now, I became more chatty than usual.

At the time, I wasn't ready to hear her advice on love, as I still wasn't sure where mine stood with Bruce. I guessed I would just have to wait and let it unfold. "Did Dad ever tell you that you look *identical* to my mother?" I asked.

She giggled. "Oh yes! I've seen photos. And it's rather crazy, isn't it? It's such a small world we live in. I was surprised when I saw the resemblance, but I also wasn't hugely surprised. Everything just felt like it was meant to be at that point, so I accepted it."

Abigail had that same twinkle in her eyes that my mother had. I cast a life-affirming gaze from her to Dad and Bruce. Everything in that moment felt right. It was everything I had been waiting for: every void filled, every missing piece of the puzzle slowly slotting into place.

By the looks of it, Dad and Bruce had gotten along far better than I thought they already would. Bruce mentioned to me a few times that he had always been closer with his mother than his father. His parents fought all the time when Bruce was growing up and things were rocky more often than not. Even though they had their special family time, things were still tense. As I watched him bond with my dad, I could feel that Bruce had longed for that his entire life. To have a close father figure that he could bond with and tell things to that he couldn't tell anyone else. Hell, he might've even told Dad things he wouldn't even tell me, and I was completely okay with that. In fact, it made me feel even more whole.

Before Bruce and I left that day, Dad told me that I'd found someone special. That also reassured me about the road us two star-crossed lovers were skipping down, hand in hand with nothing but a bag full of clothes and an adventurous heart. Dad had never said that about any of my partners. He had met Peter a few times and never really clicked with him. He also warned me when Peter and I moved to Japan together to work in a ski resort, that it was too soon, that I really needed to evaluate my actions. It didn't take long. It was a hard way to learn, and it only took two weeks for me to be on a one-way flight back to London.

"I had a great time down here," Bruce said as I pulled up to the train station to drop him off. Our few days together had gone too quickly, and now we had to say goodbye again.

I hoped that the time apart would fly by like it did the week before, and the week before that. Yet we weren't worried. About anything.

"You and Dad seemed to get on well," I mentioned. "He thinks you're a real special friend."

Bruce chuckled awkwardly, a tad taken aback. "*Friend?* Is that what we are, handsome?"

He wriggled closer to me, looking into my eyes. I wanted nothing more than to say, "No, you're my boyfriend and I can't wait to do all these incredible things together," but something stopped me, almost like an invisible wall.

"Well, yeah," I mumbled. "I just love how things are at the moment, and I don't wanna rush this because—I feel like it's something really special."

His head dropped in disappointment.

Letting you down was the last thing I wanted to do. But I just needed a little more time.

He sighed, but then he popped his head back up and managed a smile. "I understand, and I think you're right," he said. "I just want you to know, though, that I'm willing to wait however long for you. I know it's only been a few weeks, but ughh, you're just amazing, Thomas."

He planted a kiss upon me, and after a "see you next

weekend", he disappeared into the abyss of the train station, his small suitcase rolling behind him. I watched him walk away. He even waved back at me, as if to let me know that he was safe and that I could drive away now. I did, but something was different this time as I cruised down the highway back to Coolangatta. I felt a little lost without having him by my side. I even shed a tear but wasn't sure why I was crying. Was it because I was falling in love and I was so happy that I'd found someone like him? Or was it because I'd fallen in love with another lost soul? I guess I would find out in time. Unsure of what would happen, I sure was still enjoying it. The beginning of this love did that to me; it was a force that sugar-coated everything else in my life. Everything once dull was now shiny again.

10

Minus Two by The Lake

The week shot off on a good start. I was back to work, Dad and Abigail were getting ready for their adventures around the country in their camper van, and Courtney, well, I didn't see her much that week, only at work. She had been seeing this new lad from Byron almost every night. Perhaps she felt obligated to find someone to be intimate with, considering I was with Bruce a lot of the time, or at least talking to him on the phone. I didn't blame her, and I was happy for her just as I was happy with myself. I spent the first few days of the week entering my artwork into a few competitions and mentorship opportunities. Bruce had sent me a few links that he found in the depths of the net.

At the start of each week, we craved the weekend, where we could spend it entangled and happy, sharing and creating a love fit for, well, us.

"I feel like going camping this weekend," I said over the phone on Wednesday night.

He chuckled. "So, not like parked up in a cul-de-sac in your car?"

"Very funny. No, like an actual proper camping trip. In the wild."

"Are we going to recreate *Brokeback Mountain*?"

I giggled. "If anything, it'll be Brokeback Buderim, but yes. Are you down?"

"I think it'd be rude not to, especially when I think I've gotten myself a job today!"

My spirits rose like the aftermath of a double shot espresso. "Oh wow, handsome. That's so good! Where at?"

He had been asked to go in for a trial at an upmarket vegetarian restaurant in Noosa, which was definitely right up his alley being a meat-free man. He had also been looking at moving out of the hostel and into a house share of his own.

We'd chosen Lake Moogerah as our camping spot, nestled deeply in the Scenic Rim of South East Queensland. It was a two-hour drive from Coolangatta, and I was more than thrilled by the prospect of a weekend in a tent with this succulent shamrock of a lad. I just hoped our love would stay green and unwithered.

Said shamrock waited for me at Central Station in Brisbane on Saturday afternoon. I'd bought a cheap tent from Kmart, hoping that a two-man would be big enough for the both of us. The forecast for Lake Moogerah that weekend had temperatures at a low minus two in the early hours of the morning. I hadn't experienced that kind of cold since trips to Scotland to visit family in the wintertime. But as long as I had Bruce to cuddle up to, and the toasty flames of a fire, I'd be just fine. Surely.

Driving amongst the towering concrete of the city, I pulled

up in front of a tall limestone building. Bruce had arrived in Brisbane early, so he told me he would have a gander in the museum while he waited for me. He stood right out the front where he said he would be, wearing a yellow sweater and baggy blue jeans. He looked so comfortable that I just wanted to crawl inside his clothes and be next to him. He wheeled that petite suitcase and wore a smile of delight when he spotted my car pull up. I parked by the sidewalk, pressing the windows down. He yanked open the back door, planting his suitcase in the back. He then jumped in the passenger seat gracefully, pairing his entrance with a grin, a sigh, and then a kiss.

"Finally," he whispered flirtatiously.

"Touché."

"How was the drive up?"

"Easy. As usual. Not much traffic with it being a weekend."

I drove off out of the city, my hand massaging his thigh. We'd better not make each other too horny just yet. We could always save that for when we hit the country roads, a repeat of our lustful moment at Wild Horse Mountain, perhaps.

"How was your week?" he asked me.

"It was really good," I replied. "Saw Dad and Abigail set off. Worked. Waited for the weekend. You know how it is."

He laughed. "Yeah, that's just how we do these days, isn't it? Look forward to that weekend." He squeezed my hand on his leg.

"It's good you got a job!" I blurted out. "Congrats! How were the first few days?"

"I actually really like it. And the people I work with are grand. Amazing food too. I hadn't done too much hospitality work before, so it's been nice learning that side of the counter, you know."

I agreed completely. "Yeah. I feel as if a lot of people who haven't worked in hospitality at least once in their lives have no idea the process of how everything works when they dine in at a venue."

"Oh, one hundred percent!" he exclaimed. "I think I've found a car that I'm going to buy too. Was looking at second-hand ones on the train down."

"Ooooh," I sang. "What kind of car?"

"It's a Ford Falcon. Yellow."

I took a cheeky glance over at his phone while driving on the highway toward Ipswich. "Nice and bright, just like you," I flirted. "That's awesome, though. A car will be good for you. Think of all that freedom." I winked at him and he squeezed my hand again.

He then slumped back into his seat to relax. "I just can't wait to set up camp with you for the weekend. I looked up this place and it looks absolutely stunnin'."

"Beautiful, right? And there's some nice hikes to do around the area too. There's this one mountain called Greville that would be nice to do tomorrow. It's gonna be sunny all weekend too. But also fuckin' cold at night."

"Thank god we can have fires out here. Sounds so perfect, Thomas!"

"*You're* perfect, Bruce."

I turned the music up, and we enjoyed the country roads approaching. The further we drove from the highway, the more barren the landscape became. I was surprised that the lake sat only an hour and a half from Brisbane and boasted serene countryside hues, of oranges, yellows, and little spots of green. From the lush forest roads to the savannah-like plains, the contrast mesmerized us.

The closer we neared the lake, the more the day drew to an end, and the sun hid behind the rugged mountains. Bruce kept his hand entangled within mine until it became sweaty. We would keep our hands to ourselves for the moment, at least until we regained our normal temperatures. Then it was back to soft touches and strokes. I rubbed up his baggy jeans, massaging him. He did the same.

Ten minutes from the lake, and no obvious traffic on the road, I slowed down the car.

"Not this again," he giggled.

I chuckled, too, but didn't stop rubbing, and neither did he. Erect and horny, my mind was fixed on how great it felt with his hand down my pants and how the shape of his cock felt between my fingers. My vision shook. I wanted it out, in his hands or down his throat. Either one.

"You're gonna make me come soon," I huffed, panting deeply.

He jerked me faster. He wanted it. I wanted it. Oh, deary me, this was going to be a hot mess.

I finished first, all over his hands. He then rubbed himself and cleaned up.

"Less of a mess than you'd thought it'd be, babe?" he joked, catching his breath.

Did he just call me *babe?* I think he did, but I pretended that I wasn't hearing him say it for the first time. "Unfortunately not," I said, wiping my fingers with baby wipes.

I started driving the speed limit again and we sat in companionable silence.

"Oh, I think this is the place up ahead," I mentioned, slowing down as we approached the sign of the lake's caravan park. The sun struck its glow upon the lake, creating a still shimmer as we drove along the dirt road.

"I think it's safe to say we want the best spot, as close to the lake as we can," I said, admiring the glimmer beyond the trees.

"Abso-friggen-lutely," Bruce agreed. "As I've heard a few Aussies say."

"Or abso-fruitely," I added. "Or, *abso-fuckin'-lutely!*"

He chuckled. We collected our check-in sheet from the notice board outside the park office, which included a number we could call for firewood to be brought down to our campsite. We were definitely going to need it.

Driving towards the left side of the lake, we realized that the park wasn't crowded at all. And we would soon discover why. I threw on an extra layer of clothing the moment I jumped out of the car.

"Bit chilly already, isn't it?" I observed.

Bruce "brrrrrr'ed" in response, and I didn't blame him. "Let's get the tent up, and maybe some firewood burning."

I pulled out my phone and called the number provided for us. "Hey," I said as the man with the croaky voice answered my call. "It's Thomas here. We just checked into the park. Just wondering if we could get some firewood sent down. We're just at the far-left campsite as you drive in. Okay. Thanks. Yep. Sounds good. Okay. Bye."

Bruce had already started unpacking the tent and camp gear. With a little bit of teamwork, it didn't take long for us to set up our two-man house for the night. Though, once we pumped the blue inflatable mattress up and, somehow, fit it inside, it seemed there wasn't much room left for activities.

"It's a bit of a tight squeeze," I reported, hopping in to inspect some more.

He came in too, like a caterpillar pushing through its cocoon. When he said, "It just means I get to be as close as possible to you," I wished I was able to replay it over and over.

Actually, I wished I was able to play that whole weekend on repeat. From the red wine sipped around the raging campfire, huddling beside each other with a blanket connecting us, to trekking through the breathtaking gorges and mountain ridges on that crisp Sunday. There wasn't a cloud in the sky.

With many blankets and body warmth, we endured the coldest nights we had faced in a long while. Together, we'd created our own little lakeside paradise here. However, we seemed to do that wherever we went.

We pushed our bodies on the hike that next day. And by the time we had returned to camp, we desired nothing more than to pull up a picnic rug and rest by the water.

"Feels good to just sit down and relax," I noted.

"You'll feel even better after some of this," he winked, a bottle of red wine and two cups in hands.

We both said "Cheers", sipped, and popped our cups down, becoming horizontal on our backs. Bruce soon rolled onto his side and faced me, linking my hand in his. He did that laugh: the cheeky, playful, enticing laugh. Pulling the blanket over us both, I felt safe and content. I turned on my side, locking eyes with him; those almond galaxies. He kissed my lips softly like I was a delicate flower.

He then asked me that question, which felt much like a proposal would. "Are you my boyfriend?"

My lips curved upward, slowly. It was the moment, under that blanket, not needing light to see. I didn't need to think or ponder. I knew the answer.

"Yes. Abso-fuckin'-lutely," I announced.

He grinned and kissed me again, much harder this time, nestling himself into my chest. Weightlessly, I stroked his hair. "That's settled then," I whispered.

He was the first to say it. "I love you."

I kissed his forehead. "I love you too, mister."

The sun dipped behind the mountains and we lit the fire

early in preparation for the icy evening ahead. We had a bottle of wine to finish, and avocado, rice cakes, and dip to eat.

Lake Moogerah appeared purple at night and we weren't sure why. It might have been the moon's light mixed with the orange flame of the fire. We couldn't have known for sure.

Ajar

We almost slept on top of each other in that two-man tent. It felt even smaller than the night before.

The lower the temperature dropped, the more we entangled ourselves in one another for warmth. I struggled to roll over onto each side without balancing on the tent's walls, trying not to wake Bruce. Our blow-up mattress sunk during our slumber, leaving a thin layer of plastic between us and the ground. It was far too cold to get up and fix it, so we just dealt with it. I was cuddled up to my boyfriend, so it didn't matter too much to me. Gosh it felt good to say that: *my boyfriend.*

It was the crack of dawn when we left the lake the following morning. A thin layer of icy frost caked the grass and my car. It was like we'd breathed out bong smoke at each exhale. The lack of sleep or cold didn't bother us, though. Before we knew it, we were back on the road with a steaming hot coffee in hand.

"Next time you see me, I should have a car," he claimed as we cruised into civilization.

It was strange being back around cars zooming in every direction, and people, and traffic lights.

"I wish everyday was like that weekend we just had," I said. "As cold as it was."

"Me too, babe. Plenty more weekends to come, though," he ensured. "Don't you worry." He grabbed me by the waist and kissed me in the crowded car park, his suitcase by his side. "It's my birthday next weekend. Let's plan something like what we just did. But even better!"

"And possibly a new tent," I added.

Bruce nodded. "Agreed. That tent was not meant for two people. Imagine if it were two people that actually didn't want to be on top of each other!"

"You know, my car would do well with that blow-up mattress in it, just like the night we met, but much more comfortable."

"One of my fondest memories," he mentioned. "All right. I'd better get going. Don't want to be late meeting the guy with the car."

"I love you," I said, beating him to it this time.

"Love you too, babe."

After a kiss goodbye, he walked away with that suitcase again. I wanted nothing more than to run after him and tell him that he wasn't going anywhere without me, to maybe even kidnap him and take him down the coast with me. I glanced down at my watch. Of course, it was 11:22.

Everyone had told me to take baby steps with him. I guess I wasn't as good at that as I hoped, even if the intention was there.

Neither was Bruce, and we didn't even know it at this point. We were in love and that was all that mattered.

I worked a lot the following week, so it went by as fast as I'd hoped.

"I can't believe you and Bruce are in a proper relationship now!" Courtney exclaimed on Monday over a post-work wine. I could tell she was pleased for me but also had a tang of sarcasm in her voice. "Congrats, though. I bet the sex life is going well, then?"

She winked. I dropped my head down.

"Wait, you guys haven't had sex yet?" she asked, rather curiously.

"Depends what you define as sex, but intercourse, no. I've tried a few times, but I don't know, he seems to want to wait," I admitted awkwardly.

Courtney sipped her wine, intrigued. "What do you think about that?"

"I'm honestly fine with it," I revealed. "He just says he's not ready yet."

"And do you believe that?"

"Well…yeah. I do trust him."

"And he's probably being somewhat truthful, but like—"

"What do you mean?"

"I just mean, I think there might something he's not telling you about that," Courtney said in a matter-of-fact tone. "I dunno, there was just something about him when I first met him. It's not like, bad vibes or anything, cause he's a lovely guy. But I dunno, it's something. I dunno, I could just be crazy too. Not the first time that's been the case."

What could it possibly be? I couldn't stop thinking about it over the next few days. I bought myself a new indoor plant for my room to distract myself. A beautiful bright fern, in fact. My bedroom was now blooming with bright baby blue sheets, but I thought I needed some more life in the space. I sent a photo to Bruce of the fern sitting in a white vase on my mahogany bedside table.

THOMAS
This be my new child

He sent a photo back of an old yellow Ford Falcon.

BRUCE
This be mine hahaha

My smile widened, which was hard after a day of standing on my feet mixing cocktails and making espresso.

"You got the car!" I exclaimed into my phone.

"I did, babe!" He was equally as enthused. "Got it for a good price too. Look at us go. You got a plant today and I got a car."

"We're just treating ourselves, aren't we?"

"It's just how we do."

"So, your birthday's this weekend," I mentioned. "What do you want to do?"

"Anything really…" he answered. "As long as I get to spend it somewhere pretty, with someone pretty like you."

Oh, Bruce. You always knew what to say to melt me like a chocolate fondue.

I left it to him to decide. He did, and little did I know that he'd chosen one of the lushest locations I would have been to yet. He had attended yoga classes run by an instructor named Linda a few times since he had been in Noosa, and the two had formed a somewhat fruitful friendship. Linda and her husband owned a two-hundred-acre property in the forests of the hinterland and rented out the land to campers. It sounded like the perfect place to spend Bruce's twenty-eighth birthday. They were a lovely couple, with the kind of life I aspired to have one day: a home of my own, surrounded with self-sufficient gardens. The only person I could imagine by my side, picking herbs and vegetables for our meals, was Bruce. We would lay down a rug and make love under the mango tree. Perhaps have a few kids of our own running around.

We drove along a dirt road, following the directions Linda had given us.

Bruce frowned. "This place doesn't look like the photos on her website."

It really didn't. I remember him showing me the photos and there were no rolling green hills in these woods we'd just driven into, just an old shabby white cabin. A few vibrant decorations were planted on the veranda, so I didn't sense a crazy serial killer vibe quite yet. Though, from nowhere, a deep booming bark jolted the both of us. A fully-grown German Shepherd ran from the house and darted at my car. It came to the driver's side and tried to jump up to my window, which was completely wound down. An old man wearing blue jeans and a plaid shirt emerged from the house the same side the dog did. I had seen too many horror movies to know how these kinds of situations end up: two backpackers go for a scenic escape in the woods, only to be held prisoner, tortured and fed to the dogs by hillbillies. The man ambled over to my car.

"Hey, mate, we're just looking for Linda Cooper's place if you know where that is?" I told him as he stood by my window.

"Ah, Linda!" he said gleefully, his furrowed brows now replaced with a smile. "My daughter. I'm guessing you're both camping for the weekend?"

"Yeah, the map kind of led us here," Bruce chimed in.

He then explained, "Linda and Carl live at the little turn-off to the left as you go back down the road. People miss it all the time and end up here." He chuckled. "Not that I don't enjoy talking to people. I don't speak to many people these days, except for my daughter and grandson."

I felt empathy toward the man, and I knew for a fact that Bruce did too.

"Hey, would you fellas like to pop in for a cuppa or something?" the man asked us.

"Uh…" I began.

Bruce interrupted. "We'd love to, but we should set up camp before dark."

"Good thinking! It's gonna be cold tonight, so you'll want to get the fire going," he said, peering through the window at Bruce. "Have a good weekend, fellas."

I reversed and maneuvred a three-pointed turn to drive back the way we came. The man was right. The turn-off to Linda and Carl's part of the property was quite hidden, but there was a wooden sign a little further up written in red paint: Cooper Retreat. The dirt road dipped into a valley and into a clearing with a lush creek and vast open areas. Presumably for camping.

We parked in front of the ashes of an expired fire pit. I hopped out of the car to a waft of fresh hinterland leaves. There was a plethora of green at each turn of the head out here. Across the clearing, three cows stood like statues, staring warily at us. A white and brown dog shot out of nowhere and jumped up on us for pats. She must've come from beyond the brook. A woman with curly ginger hair and bright green eyes approached us. She wore a vivid red jumpsuit, with natural beauty seeping through her luminescent skin. Bruce had told me Linda was in her forties, but her shimmering glow made her look much younger, angelic even.

"Libby can hear the cars a mile away," Linda called out. She grinned at her dog, who sat at her feet obediently as she stood before us. "Means I know when people are arriving so I can greet them too. How are you, Bruce? Oh, and you must be the famous Tom!"

Her energy was contagious. She approached me for a hug and I returned the favor with a warm embrace.

"I've heard a lot about you," she continued.

I turned to Bruce, blushing. "All good things I hope."

"Oh, of course, darling!" she ensured.

Linda looked from me to Bruce. "Glad you guys made it out. We haven't got anyone booked at all this weekend, so you've pretty much got the whole place to yourselves."

"So much room for activities," Bruce announced in a child-like voice, looking around in awe.

Linda didn't get the joke, but I sure did and chuckled discreetly. We followed her past the fire pit, studying one of the cows staring at us. As we approached, it ran off behind the trees.

"I think there must be a broken fence somewhere, 'cause our neighbor's cows and alpacas always seem to come over here to snack on our grass," Linda explained.

Bruce gaped. "Oh, I love alpacas!"

"Well, you're in luck cause a whole pack of them come into this field every morning," Linda said. "The campers love it because they can sit and have breakfast in the shelter with a family of them. It's quite gorgeous actually."

She led us past a little shack toward the back of the valley. "So, this is the compost toilet. Unfortunately, the shower isn't working at the moment because it's been so dry, and we rely on rainwater."

Come to think of it, it had rained very little since I'd been in Australia. "You're more than welcome to bathe in the little creek," she added. "It's actually quite refreshing."

"Such a beautiful spot you've got here, Linda," Bruce admired. "So happy I get to spend my birthday here."

Linda beamed. "We're happy to have you here. It's a great spot to reconnect with nature, to be free. And you both get to share it together. How good is that!"

Bruce and I exchanged glances and smiled.

"Well, the sun's going down," Linda then said, scanning the sky. "I'll grab some firewood and start the fire. You two should set up your tent."

"Are you sure you don't want help collecting firewood?" I asked her.

She flicked her hand forward. "No, don't be silly!"

Linda disappeared behind some trees to gather some wood from a pile sitting behind them. Bruce and I dragged out our tiny tent, both sighing when we realized that we completely forgot to buy a bigger one.

"Maybe we should just sleep in the car instead?" Bruce suggested, "and put the mattress in there."

It was a much better idea. We could actually roll from side to side without landing on top of one another. That evening, the car was even steamier than the first time we'd met.

I woke up in the middle of the night, though, suddenly very aware that I couldn't breathe properly. Actually, it turns out I was breathing so heavily that I became starved of oxygen. I shook Bruce's body in panic. I pinched myself to make sure I wasn't dreaming. Unfortunately, this was very real.

"Babe, I can't breathe properly," I wheezed.

He sat up, breathing as heavy as I was. "Neither can I," he gasped.

Bruce and I simultaneously tried to open the doors on either side of us.

"It won't open for some reason," Bruce fretted.

He was right. I tried to unlock and push open all the doors, but they wouldn't budge.

Fuck. Where were the keys? I could feel myself losing breath fast and panicking more. I tore into the central console and rummaged through it, digging through all sorts of belongings. Receipts and wallets, but no keys.

Bruce drew a shallow breath. "Can you feel them?" he asked with a worried tone.

I dug deeper and heard the keys scratch against the side of the console. I tried fishing them out with my fingers, but it wasn't until the key ring attached to them fell from my finger that I knew we might be in some trouble. They crashed into the abyss between the console and the passenger seat. The abyss that subsequently consumed things, only for them to never return again. I stuck my hands down the tight crevasse, already seeing a news report pop up in a local newspaper: *Two Young Travelers Die in Car from Oxygen Deprivation.* Was this *it*? Was this our destiny? I always knew we were meant to meet for a reason, but I didn't know it could be this. To die out here like tragic star-crossed lovers, surrounded by the winter dew and alpacas. Then, just when all hope seemed lost, I started using my pointer and middle finger as chopsticks to try and retrieve the keys. My phone light came in handy. And the moment I fished the keys out, I unlocked the car in an instant. Gasping for air, we opened the doors on either side of us and just lay there, allowing the icy cold air to softly blow through the car. I could've sworn it was the freshest air I'd ever breathed.

I finally said, "Thank fuck for that," regathering my regular breathing cycle.

"Babe...did we nearly just die?" Bruce asked me, staring up at the ceiling of the car.

"I don't know..." I admitted, but I was pretty sure we did.

"But I'm glad we didn't. I was about to smash one of the windows."

"That was going to be my next suggestion after you couldn't get the keys. Phew."

"The only thing I could think of is the hammer, but that's next to the fire."

"Well, that definitely answers the question then," Bruce said. "We *did* nearly just die."

Even though the air was cold, we left the windows ajar for the rest of the night.

I Fell for You Like a Waterfall

When the sun peeked through the hills, I woke Bruce up. I massaged his chest and stroked his hair. He groaned playfully.

"Hey," I whispered in his ear. "Morning, birthday boy."

He turned to face me, wrapping his arms around me and yawning. "Thanks, babe. Love you," he whispered back, tickling my arm. "Even after our near-death experience, I still slept better than we did in that tent."

Laying on my back, I tucked my hands behind my neck. "Tell me about it."

Linda was right about the family of alpacas. They scattered the field to grace us as we hopped out of the car, in all shades and sizes, from black to white to brown. Bruce was mesmerized, like a playful kid. He even tried to speak to them. It made me never want to grow old and to enjoy moments in life without the overwhelming sense that I should "have everything together".

The property was beautifully misty and moist from the morning dew. It cleared out swiftly as the sun rose. Another cloudless day in the hinterland, with a charming boy that I now called mine. We grew closer after moments like this, through each bite of food, through each kiss, through each glance at the clock. It was always 11:22 and I now believed in magic. Whatever that was.

With him, it was easy from the very beginning. We were in our own little world and we thought nothing could taint it. But from every light comes dark, and little did we know that this world we tried so hard to create would soon come crashing down. Our comet's edges would crumble, leaving us to pick up the pieces floating through the atmosphere.

The alpacas wandered in our view while we ate burritos for breakfast. We smiled and laughed at each other like we always did while we shared food. He didn't have to say it, but I knew this was one of the most special birthday mornings of his life, something I hoped he would never forget. It was just as memorable for me as it was for him.

We spent the day ambling around the old town near Linda's property. The streets were stacked with old wooden terrace shops and enough historic memorabilia to satisfy the birthday boy. I saw Bruce eyeing off this blue and black Baja poncho in a little store near the park. While he went to the bathroom, I decided to buy it for him as a surprise. When I spotted him across the road, I did my best to hide it from him. He was on the phone and waved over to me to excuse himself. It didn't surprise me. It was his birthday after all and he probably had loved ones from back home eager to get in touch.

I sat down on a curb-side wooden bench. Everyone smiled

at me as they walked past. In that moment I felt completely accepted, and even more when I felt Bruce's hands grip and massage my shoulders. I grinned and tilted my head up to face him.

"I got you something," I said, pulling out the poncho.

His eyes lit up. "Babe! You didn't need to do that!"

"But I wanted to," was my argument, not taking his "you didn't need to buy me a birthday present" bollocks.

"I love it," he purred, kissing me numerous times. "You saw me eyeing it up, didn't you?"

"What can I say...I'm an artist with an eye for detail."

"And an artist whose masterpieces are gonna be in all the big art galleries someday," he added, pulling me close to him.

"We're just the perfect creative duo, aren't we?"

"You know it! How did I get so lucky to spend my birthday with you?" He shook his head and smiled with twinkles in his eyes.

"We're both lucky," I corrected him.

"I got a message from Linda," Bruce said as we walked back to the car. "Her and Carl are heading out for the night, so we've got the property to ourselves. I've also got a few things to show you too, so it's perfect."

What things did he have to show me? He was being mysterious, and it made me a little worried. I didn't like surprises, especially when I knew they were coming.

Later, we lay naked by the fresh-flowing brook, drying off in the winter sun after our chilly swim. He fished into his backpack and pulled out a cream-colored piece of paper neatly folded in a square. The piece of paper that I would hold dear to me forever.

"I wrote you something last week," he told me. "I was waiting till the right time to give it to you."

A chill trickled down my spine and into my hips, and it wasn't just from the cold water dripping down my back.

"What is it?" I asked before he unfolded it.

"It's a poem I wrote for you. But before I read it, there's something I gotta tell you."

Confrontation was difficult for me sometimes. I'm glad he felt comfortable enough to tell me, though—to answer the questions I'd been asking myself.

"You've probably been wondering why we haven't had sex yet," he said, his eyes fixed on the water. "Like, *really why.*"

"A little, yeah," I admitted, my smile fading. "But it's fine."

He sighed, lifting his knees and hugging them. He shifted his gaze up to the clear afternoon sky. I placed my hand on his shoulder. I could tell whatever this was, it was hard for him.

Bruce exhaled heavily and began to speak. "Before I moved over to Australia, I was living in Dublin and working as an editor for a media firm. It was grand, being around all these other writers. I was also in a relationship with this guy named Joe. We'd been together over a year, and it was going good, it seemed."

"Seemed?" I interrupted.

Sadness dawned on Bruce's face. "Joe and I hadn't always had the smoothest of relationships," he went on. "We argued a lot. He was a little older than me. Muscly guy, worked in construction. I mean, should've left him much sooner, but he had this, power over me that I still can't explain. It was like he made me believe that I was nothing without him. Shit, he even shouted those exact words to me at the top of his lungs during one of our arguments. And I believed him. We were in this toxic, fucked up love and I felt as if I couldn't leave him." Bruce paused a beat. "Things got a lot worse after we moved in together. I realized how controlling he actually was."

Empathy surged through me onto Bruce. Our rugged comet

edges felt rougher than ever right now. He didn't say anything for a moment, and then he sighed. I swallowed, hard.

"After we moved in with each other, the arguments soon turned physical," he then told me. "He began to beat me. Most of the time until I was bruised and bleeding. It got so bad that I was too afraid to go into work with my face looking like a swelled-up balloon. He also forced me into sex toward the end." Bruce's voice began to tremble, and his eyes became glassy. "Every time he hit me, he would blame it on me, tell me it was my fault and that I made him do it. And that I couldn't survive on my own and had to do everything he said. I let it go on for a year and a half."

I softly placed my hand on Bruce's bare thigh. He flinched a little. This boy was hurt, and I wanted nothing more than to save him. I didn't care about the sex. As long as I had him. I could help him through this, I thought.

"Bruce, I'm so sorry," I said, trying to be strong enough for the both of us. "What happened? Did you report him to the police?"

He shook his head. "No. I didn't tell anyone. My family was back at home and I didn't have many friends in the city. I packed all my stuff and booked a flight to Hawaii and Australia. Left while he was at work. Blocked him on every platform. I couldn't deal with it. I'd been wanting to come here for so long. It's just shit that it took something like that to happen to take me here. I still have nightmares about him. That he's gonna find me." A pause. "I'm sorry, Thomas, I—you're probably thinking 'what the fuck' right now. I just knew I had to tell you the truth. I couldn't run from you as well. And I can understand if you don't want to deal with the repercussions of what happened to me. I know it's something I still have to process myself."

"No. Babe, I'm here for whatever you need. And trust me, I'm not gonna let anything happen to you," I assured him, kissing the knuckles on his hand. "We're in this together, okay? Please let me know if you need anything."

He drew a teary-eyed smile. "I love you, Thomas. I really do."

"I love you too, Bruce. I mean that."

"Now, let me read you this thing," he then said, wiping his eyes and unfolding the piece of paper. "I'm probably going to get emotional all over again. I hope that's okay."

No one had ever written a poem about me. Words that were not just said but remained on paper; a warm reminder on a cold winter night without him.

"Babe, read it to me," I encouraged him. "Everything's okay."

You etched those words on me, my dear. And they would stay engraved in my heart for the rest of my goddamned days.

He nodded, pausing as he gathered his words. Then he began, like a serenade from the voice of a soothing angel. I closed down my eyelids as I was taken away:

"I fell for you like a waterfall," he said. "Like the one we kissed under."
"In a forest that smelt of earth,
And glistened as if by the tears.
Of love lived and lost.
Said we wouldn't make the same mistakes,
Said we wouldn't jump.
Said we would take it slow.
Was it lying if we believed it was truth?
Overlooking water and under-looking stars,
You painted yourself onto my heart.
And there with you on my chest,
Your head rising and falling to the tide of my breath,
I wondered to the dark…"

Both of our eyes pooled with tears.

"…Will this script become scar?
I've barely said hello,
But I'm already afraid of goodbye.
Because I'm falling, jumping, racing
At what we're making.
I want to laugh at night with you,
Chase away the day.
Roll in dewy grass.
Blanketed by the stars,
Dizzy but unafraid.
Hell would be worth it,
If the devil had your smile.

No point in waiting for heaven,
When I'm already at your side."

He looked at me with those passionate almond eyes of his, now beaming under the sun's gaze. I grabbed his hand, to let him know that everything was going to be all right. That I knew loving again and letting go of the past was easier said than done.

"Let's create memories,
Fit for the immortals.
Let's do life things,
You and I.
Let's create,
Us."

One word could warm three months of winter, and that word was "us".

The Power of Water

After Bruce's birthday, the days we spent apart were the hardest yet. We spoke on the phone during lunch breaks and whenever we had a moment free.

I'd been drawing and painting more that week too. A new morning ritual had taken shape, just like having a cup of coffee. I would draw cartoon versions of him and I, doing different domestic things, like cooking in the kitchen, and sitting on the roof of our dream home, stargazing into the night. I even concocted a sketch of us getting married at Linda's property next to all the alpacas. I didn't show Bruce these drawings, and I promised myself I wouldn't until if and when the time was right. I didn't want to scare the lad off.

A few weeks passed, and my drawings began to manifest themselves. Bruce and I relaxed by the beach now that the weather was getting warmer. He'd moved into a quaint share house in Noosa. We cooked food when we were tired of the waves. We obsessed over plant-based burger patties, determined to find the best in the world. Everything was just as it should have been and how I wanted it to be.

I finally got to see him surf too. He slipped through those waves exactly as he had described. There was a true connection between him and those crashing masses of foam and water. I couldn't lie and say I didn't think about Bruce's horrid experience back in Dublin, and it came to me in times I wished it wouldn't, like when we were touching, when I gazed into those almond eyes of his, when he whipped out a poem to read to me before bed. Or when he'd bust a wine-induced dance move to an upbeat tune. I could see through his mask. He was fractured but I hoped that my presence could heal him, or at least soothe the wound.

"A grade-A surfer, a wordsmith, and a dancer. What aren't you good at?" I once said playfully.

He simply replied, "I can't draw like you can, Thomas. We all have our gifts."

In retrospect, he was right.

Bruce's little blue and white house was just a stone's throw from Noosa's rolling waves of salt. The shack never fully rid itself of sand, and that was just how we liked it. He lived with a lovely French couple whom I barely saw. They were never home. However, they surfed just as much as Bruce did, so it made sense.

The beginning of August greeted us with some rich, warm days. Every time I arrived on the curb of his street, those two aqua numbers stared at me, bold and glowing: twenty-two. If this were *The Matrix*, we sure had hit a major glitch. Or was this just the way life was, those numbers, everywhere we went, assuring us that we were right where we were meant to be?

He stood shirtless in the front yard, waxing a surfboard a tad taller than him. A wetsuit covered him from the waist-down. If it weren't for his neighbor pulling out weeds in the garden next door, I would've tackled him right there and then. He looked extremely dashing, glowing in the sun like a fiery flame. I would've covered him in dirt and made him cum in it to make mud. But instead, I peered down at the second surfboard lying flat on the grass, a black wetsuit folded on top of it.

"Have I been replaced by a new surfing buddy of yours?" I joked, arching my brows.

He lent me a cheeky smile, meeting me at the white wooden gate. He opened it for me with a kiss. He then distracted my question with some irresistible lip locking, but I soon grew concerned again.

"Do you remember when we first met, when I told you I could teach you how to surf?" he asked.

I shrugged sarcastically. "Nope. I don't remember that." There was no way. This couldn't be happening. Nothing frightened me more in this moment than standing up on a board in the ocean. As fun as it looked from afar, it was another thing to embark on that moist quest in real life.

"Well, today's the day I show you the world of being a seal," he said confidently, gifting a wink.

There was nothing I could do but shake my head and gravitate back toward him and say, "You're fucking crazy."

And before I knew it, I was consumed by a thick wetsuit, giant board under my armpit, as we trundled down to the ocean. The beach was only a few streets away, but I could already smell the salt and faint waft of fish. The board wasn't extremely heavy, more awkward if anything. Bruce seemed to pull off the look just splendidly. Me; I just couldn't help but think what lurked in the deep blue. Sharks were the first thing I thought of. Knowing me, I would be that unlucky one whom a Great White would think was a seal, on his first surf that wasn't planned at all. I'd heard a stack of tales about the barbaric wildlife in Australia and how deadly it could be. Most Australians would tell me that it's completely overexaggerated, though. That there *was* deadly wildlife here, but the chances of having an encounter were quite slim.

The water was still chilly as I dipped my feet in. I hadn't gone for many ocean swims since I had set foot in Australia.

Bruce grinned at me as we placed our boards in the shallows. "Are you ready?"

I wanted to shiver. "Ready as I'll ever be, babe."

He winked. "It'll be fun, I promise. The swell isn't too rough today. Perfect for a little introduction. Now, strap the rope to your ankle."

We both did just that. A set of waves hit us softly. I nearly tripped into the water. We were off to a greaaaaaaat start. I attached the rope tightly.

"Alright, let's go," he ushered, becoming horizontal on his board and paddling.

I followed his lead. We crashed over a few small waves before reaching the larger ones. I pulled up next to him while we waited for the next set. He dunked his head under the water and gave me a wet kiss.

"So, we'll start off with a smaller one," he told me, spinning me around so I couldn't see the waves behind me. "When it comes, I'm gonna push you. The wave will take you, and once it does, and you have momentum, stand on the lower end of the board, with your feet a little to the right. About here."

He pointed. I nodded, taking a few deep breaths.

The faint whooshing sound of the wave behind me grew louder. My heart raced, a bit like my first phone call with Bruce. I was in safe hands, right?

"All right, it's coming," he said.

With a whoosh, I was off faster than I imagined I'd be, the barrel of the wave enclosing me. Is this the moment I had to stand up? I slowly lifted myself off the board, standing in the same spot Bruce told me to. And just like that, the wave dumped me harder than my first boyfriend. I was trapped under, unable to reach the surface for a few seconds. It made me think how truly powerful water was, that it could keep you entangled within its force for however long it wanted.

It finally let go, and I rose to the top, coughing the saltwater out of my mouth. It trickled out of my nose. It was in my eyes. I wiped them, the piercing sun blinding me. I finally regained vision and blurrily looked around for him. Bruce wasn't far behind me, gracefully gliding in on a wave, laughing.

I groaned. "Told you my balance is terrible."

"You took that a lot better than my first wave in Hawaii," he giggled. "I literally received a mouthful of sand, and I think a few shells. It was nasty. Want to go again?"

I wanted to say no, but I knew he was having fun, so I agreed. Perhaps I would eventually enjoy this. I did, but boy, did I suck. Like, I really sucked. Fell nearly every time. I did stand up on a baby wave, though. Bruce congratulated me with a kiss, and we eventually ditched the boards and wetsuits and lay on our towels on the sand. The sun's rays glowed upon us. If this were August, I wondered what summer would be like.

"Fucking hot," Bruce answered for me. "Like Hawaii. I was there just before their summer, and it was *sweltering*. Couldn't walk around outside without sweating, but it was still class. Spent every day at the beach."

I hoped we'd be laying in this same spot four months from now.

I wanted nothing more than to sweat with you. To bask in that sweet, sweet humidity. But life had something in store for us that we didn't see coming.

That night, I reeled out Bruce's pain that he kept so deep in the abyss. Behind every smile of his, there was a voice in his head telling him he didn't deserve any good that came to him, including me. Bruce had always been good at hiding things, and the closer I got to him, that hiding would be laid out onto the table to dry. The excretion would be so loud, and so painful, that the whole surface would be covered in dark oozing shame.

We cooked dinner as usual. Watched Netflix as usual. A brilliant new detective show had us hooked from the first episode. We binged, until we became horny, which was typical, our naked bodies tangled yet again. Sweat formed, followed by subtle bites on the neck. Then, Bruce was on top of me, grasping both our throbbing cocks together and jerking them soft and slow. He seemed like he was ready, his bare arse massaging my hard-on like a hand changing gear. The tip of my finger poked inside. He moaned the further I got, biting his bottom lip, gazing at me seductively without a blink. As soon as my finger touched inside, he suddenly switched like a traffic light. He quickly hopped off me and put his underwear back on, catching his breath back. He sat on the edge of the bed, his back facing me, his fearful eyes glued to the wall. I was speechless.

I never, never, never, ever, wanted to hurt you.

"I'm sorry, Thomas," he sighed. "Fuck, you shouldn't have to deal with this. I'm trying."

I was swift to comfort him, with a soft hand on his back. I didn't want to get too close to him in case it was triggering for him. "No. Don't be sorry, babe. Don't ever be sorry for something like that."

He sighed again. "Just sucks because like, I am so attracted to you, you know that. It's just sometimes, when anything goes down there, I see him. And it takes me back to…"

I kissed him on the shoulder. "I know, but don't think that you *need* to please me in that way. If you're not ready, you're not ready. And who knows, maybe you won't be ready for a long time. But I don't care about that. As long as I get to be in your company, that's enough for me."

He smiled. "I want you to make love to me someday, Thomas, because I know it will feel so good when the time comes. But it also scares the hell out of me."

I didn't want to ask him, but I did. "I don't want you to take this the wrong way, because I'm not trying to be intrusive, but have you thought of maybe talking to someone about what happened? Just to like, get it all off your chest."

He was quick to say, "I'm honestly okay, babe." I didn't believe him one bit, but the words he spoke were his truth. "It's just something I have to put behind me. And it's gonna take time to accept and overcome, I know that. I've been doing everything I can to fill my life with good things: surfing, yoga, you. I think I'm doing the right thing."

It was his life, and I couldn't force him to seek therapy; that had to be his choice. I couldn't hear his thoughts. I didn't know what was really going on up in that intelligent, pierced brain of his. And that was the beauty of it all. He would continue to hide, and I would continue to seek, until we came crashing down to solid ground.

A Long Way to Go

Courtney sauntered into my bedroom while I was sketching. She wasn't home much these days, so we'd barely spoken that week. I had so much to tell her, and her I, especially about her tanned boy with the long locks.

"How's it going with ah…" I had already forgotten his name.

"Jake?" Courtney said in a corrective tone, arching a brow. I'd missed her daily sass these past few weeks. "It's going well. I was always told that the Bay was just a big overrated hub drowning in tourists, but Jake's been taking me to all the secret spots. I think it's starting to get—somewhat serious between us."

My jaw dropped. It had been years since Courtney had had a boyfriend, and to hear her talk about this guy in that way made me happy. She never got into relationships easily in the past, always palming the lads off before they got remotely close to her.

I didn't blame her, though. Courtney deserved the best of the best.

"Aw, Court! I'm thrilled for you!" I exclaimed. "You've been over there quite a bit lately. It's good you both live so close to each other."

"Yeah, I thought the Bay was far away, but you and Bruce live like over two hours from each other." She shook her head. "I don't know how you do it."

I smiled. "Love or something."

She gifted me a warm, lengthy smile. "Oh, Tommy…" she said, snuggling up next to me on my bed. "It's been so long since I've caught feelings for someone, and I *love* this feeling. I never want it to end."

"It doesn't have to," I added.

Her grin faded and she sighed. "But it usually does eventually, especially with people our age. When it comes to dating, it's like we have all these choices right at our fingertips. And people wanna seem to try them all. They can't stay fixed on one person a lot of the time."

I wondered whether I should tell her the truth about Bruce. I had to tell someone. If it was going to be anyone, it would be her.

"I found out the truth about why Bruce and I haven't had sex yet. Don't freak out when I tell you, though, promise?"

"Of course, Tommy," Courtney said sincerely.

I told her what had happened to him. Although, she wasn't as shocked as I thought she would be.

"I weirdly had a feeling something had happened to him," she admitted. "I just didn't want to worry you with my theories, in case I was wrong."

"I want to do something for him, but I know he'd just smile and tell me not to," I told her.

"Tommy. You know you can't fix him, right?" It wasn't what I wanted to hear.

"I can always try," I protested.

"You can, but sometimes it doesn't work like that."

What would she know? My eyes narrowed. "I can see myself marrying Bruce," I argued.

"C'mon lad, it hasn't even been two months," she reminded me. "Don't get ahead of yourself."

I sighed. "Why do you have to rain on my parade?" I snapped.

Courtney sat up. "That's not what I'm trying to do. I just don't want you to get hurt, okay? It's only early days between you and him, and anything could happen, honestly. And I'm here to make sure you keep your feet on the ground, which you know I don't mind doing; you're my best friend."

I didn't listen to her. "We're going traveling around the country together soon."

Courtney nodded, not in agreement but in mockery. "This sounds a bit familiar."

I couldn't believe her. Why did she need to bring up my ex? Why couldn't she just be happy for me?

"This is different from Peter," I said, raising my voice. "You should know that."

She gave in. "Okay. Look, I'm sorry. You know, maybe it will be different this time and it will work out long-term. Just...don't ignore the red flags. I mean, he does seem like he's got his shit together a little more than your past boyfriends."

"He does, Court," I assured her.

But did he really? Did I? Or were we just two lost souls who had found each other in a hopeless wide atmosphere, shining our bright beams of light from flaming rugged edges? We were now inseparable, floating through the universe together. Nothing could disrupt the bond we'd forged, or so I assumed.

Bruce's friends from Ireland were visiting Australia, and he suggested that we go out for a night in Noosa and book a hotel room. He really wanted them to meet me, which made things feel even more real and wholesome. They were friends of his from back in high school, and he described them as quite the cheery bunch.

"They love to party," he explained to me as we lay on this comfy creaseless hotel room bed.

I shrugged. "That's fine by me," I said, winking.

I was the kind of person that could go weeks without partying, but there came a time that the dancing shoes turned dusty, and I had to drag them out of the cupboard and slip them on.

"Sounds like it's been a while since both of us have let off some well-deserved steam," Bruce laughed.

I couldn't wait to dance with him. I imagined what it would be like, and it scared me a little. I hoped he wasn't a different person when he was drunk like we were to be that weekend. I had been with guys before back home that were decent lads sober, but when they were partying, I couldn't stand them.

We had to christen that cloud of a hotel bed. Both now naked in embrace, Bruce slung a surprise my way that I wasn't expecting. It was just five simple words.

"I think I'm ready, babe," he said, massaging my pulsing cock as I grinded on top of him. I shifted my gaze down to his butt retracting, and those muscly legs wrapped around me.

When he unleashed those words on me, I was a little skeptical at first. I had been quite happy exploring ourselves at a nice pace in this relationship. But I could tell he wanted it as he bent his legs further back toward his shoulders. My penis was now rock-hard just watching him, his firm arse exposed. I'll never forget that seductive glance he gave me, biting his lip tenderly.

"Are you sure you're ready?" I asked him. I wanted to make sure I was absorbing the impression he was giving me.

He nodded. "I want you to make love to me, Thomas."

I was a little hesitant at first from what had happened the weekend prior. But then again, it couldn't have been more perfect timing. I hovered over him, grinding up and down against his body, kissing him avidly. He gasped. Using lube from my backpack, I fingered his ass and it loosened to my sticky touch. His cock stood to attention. He moaned softly. My dick was pre-cumming like crazy. I lubed it up. He shuddered as I entered slowly to begin. He pulled me in tighter with each slow thrust. His mouth widened with a mix of shock and pleasure.

"I love you," he whispered.

"I love you too, baby," I groaned, sweating a little on my forehead.

I didn't want to hurt him. I tried to be gentle, but he wouldn't let me. He wouldn't even let me pull out, nor did I want to. It didn't take very long, especially it being our first time together.

We soon lay back in a daze of euphoria. It took me a minute to gather my breath and for my heart rate to decline.

"That was—amazing," he gasped, kissing me on the cheek.

"Was I okay?" I asked him, yearning for positive feedback.

"Were you *okay!*" he teased. "You made me cum in like three minutes."

I kissed him, stroking his stubbly cheek. "And I loved every minute of it. Seeing you come, feeling you come, makes me come."

"One of us always waits for the other," he added. "It's good we seem to take it in turns."

"It's just how we do," I said. "Tell you what, though: I think it's time we checked out this rooftop hot tub before it gets dark."

The hotel we stayed in had a far better view than either of us expected, with sweeping views of the coastline, all the way over to the *Avatar*-esque Glass House Mountains. The sun began to set to the west and the rooftop had not a soul in sight. The hot tub bubbled just for us, lightly emitting steam from its warm waters. I drew goose bumps and hard nipples the moment I took off my shirt. We couldn't hop into the tub quicker, immersing ourselves completely. The sunset was stunning that afternoon; maybe one of the best I'd ever seen, from such a picturesque vantage point, with such a catch of a lad.

"Let's plan out the rest of our year together," Bruce said, wading through the water, holding on to me by my thighs.

"We're going traveling at some point, aren't we?"

"Yeah, but after that. When we run out of money, we'll have to stop travelling at some point."

"We could always come back here and do the same we're doing now?" I suggested.

"Yeah, but, by then, don't you think we'd want to move in with each other, babe?"

He was getting ahead of himself, and I could see it in his starstruck eyes. I didn't say anything at first, I just smiled. But inside, a slight anxiety rolled over me. Was I *really* ready to commit this early? I sure thought I was, but when it was finally discussed, a part of me pulled back a little.

"That'd be nice," I mentioned, stroking his hand.

The sunset faded. Twilight approached.

"We could have a nice veggie garden, maybe start a food truck, or a café together," he fantasized out loud.

Okay, now he was *really* getting ahead of himself. Was it just me being scared to talk about these things so early on? He was definitely going back on his vow of taking things slow with me, and I was falling for it. I don't blame myself for diving into the pool of the unknown with him, though, nor do I regret the decision I made to push against the anxious voice in my head that night: the voice telling me to run far, far away from him, and from love.

We ate out at a wicked burger joint on the beach that night, and then walked to the supermarket to buy food for breakfast the following morning.

"How much were the groceries?" I asked, crawling into bed.

Bruce unraveled the receipt and instantly smiled.

"I bet you can guess how much the total was," he said playfully.

I ripped it from his hands: $11.22. Was I even surprised anymore?

Dewy Grass and Shutter Vision

My teeth sunk into one of Bruce's famous tortilla and egg breakfast burritos, jam-packed with avocado, tomato, and Mexican beans. The rain had set in overnight, and we sat at the kitchen table of our now gloomy hotel room, gazing out the window as we chewed down our food. I spent an hour or so drawing in my sketchbook while Bruce read the first volume of *Heartstopper*. Procrastinating, I watched water droplets plummet down the glass.

"This weather makes me just want to stay in bed all day," I said dreamily. The wind outside howled ferociously.

Bruce kissed me on the forehead. "We totally can stay in bed all day, babe. My friends aren't getting here until late this afternoon. Until then, we can do whatever we want."

Our idea of "whatever we want" involved sex and Netflix all

day long. I mean, in this wild weather there wasn't much else to do besides that. Let's just say we were well-rested by late afternoon. We'd already been out to buy alcohol before his friends arrived at the hotel at four. By then, it had ceased raining and the blue sky even poked its face out to conclude the day. Bruce was a little nervous about his friends arriving and kept checking his phone. I asked him if he was okay, and he assured me he was. He just hadn't seen these friends in what seemed like forever and was excited about them meeting me. It was adorable actually, to see him fussing over me like that.

"Well, you've met my dad already," I said, putting things into perspective. "How do you think that made me feel?"

"Yeah..." he agreed. "You're right. I need to stop worrying."

I winked at him. "It is cute, though."

I've always been terrible at remembering people's names, especially when I first meet them. Bruce reminded me of his mates' names several times on our lift ride down to the foyer where we were to meet them. Laura, Eric and Natalie. *Laura, Eric and Natalie.* I swore I would remember. Laura was one of Bruce's friends I would never forget, starting with her vibrant green hair and glowing eyes to match. She had that type of personality that just radiated with humor and fun. I could tell why they were best friends. Their friendship reminded me of mine and Courtney's. The way they laughed without a filter, and all their inside jokes. It made me wish Court was here meeting Bruce's friends and enjoying a night of letting our hair down. Eric and Natalie were a quiet-natured couple who spent most of their time asking me questions and telling Laura and Bruce to quieten down in the hotel. I just presumed this was a regular occurrence in their friendship group.

"So, Bruce tells me that you and he are going to go traveling soon?" Laura said to me.

We had spoken about it but hadn't organized a single thing. I glanced at him after a sip of vodka and orange juice. He gave me a cheeky smile, as if to say, "Yes, I've been boasting about you to my friends."

I then said, "It's definitely on the cards. I've got this café job on the Gold Coast and a bit of a life down there, though."

"Guys, c'mon. You don't know how long you're going to be in Australia for," Laura piped up, "and this is the *best* time to be seeing the Top End." She was a little drunk, and loud. "Café jobs are totally replaceable. But I tell you what isn't replaceable? Amazing memories!"

"Gosh, Laura, leave the poor lads alone," Natalie interrupted, tapping her lightly on the shoulder with her backhand. "Let them get there on their own terms."

Laura shook her head and took a generous swig from her glass of vodka coke. "Look, Nat. I'm just telling the lads what's good for 'em. No harm in that."

She did prove a point. A lot of the places I did want to see in the northern parts of Australia often experienced wild, rainy weather in the summer months. The cooler months, like now, were the best time to go if you wanted a getaway full of dry, sunny and pleasant weather. Maybe that's what we were missing on this gloomy, rainy day: a glimmer of sunshine, a palm tree, maybe a swimming hole tucked away between sandstone cliffs. The sun-kissed country we came here for. Perhaps meeting Bruce was a sign I hadn't seen yet. A message, per se, telling me to cut ties with this job I didn't really like, and to experience Australia for real. I took a calming gulp of my drink. An untamed morsel lay in the palm of Laura's hand. It was a bag of five capsules.

"Laura…someone might see that," Eric hissed.

"Fuck off, Eric," Laura laughed. "There's no one up here. I already checked."

"The good ol' love buzz I'm guessing?" I asked her, curious. She winked. "But of course."

The night escalated before the sun even completely set. Our conversations became elevated, from light to full-blown banter as everyone's caps kicked in. We'd decided on a club for the night. I wanted to dance, and I could tell Bruce did too. I felt like I was floating on pure euphoria, without a worry in the world. Nothing else mattered but being here.

Laura, Eric and Natalie stumbled down to their hotel rooms to get ready, leaving Bruce and I on the rooftop. He latched onto me from behind. It felt better than ever to be touching him, wrapped up in his embrace, as if the skin from my hands were now a part of his.

"I forgot how good this felt," I said, casting my gaze at the vivid building lights from above, which were a little blurred but still shining bright.

"You're telling me," Bruce giggled. "We deserve a night to run wild, I think. We deserve to travel to the nooks and crannies of this country too."

"I want to travel with you so bad, Bruce," I told him, desperation in my voice.

"Let's just go then," he mentioned without hesitation. "I mean it."

I turned around and looked at him. The almond in his eyes had been clouded with something darker.

"What do you mean?" I asked, not taking my eyes off him. "We can't just *go.*"

"Why the hell not? Let's just pack everything up and get out of here after this weekend," he suggested impulsively. He tempted me further with every word. "Live life on the road. I know we've got enough money to keep us going for a while at least. What do we have to lose? A shitty job? To stay in one place? Is that really what we came to Australia for?"

He was right. So, so very right. I shook my head, musing at him like he was one of the wonders of the world. "Who *are you?*" I fantasized, pausing a moment. "Fuck it. Let's go."

He kissed me so hard I could've fallen back. We knew what we were ready for, and it wasn't in one place right now. It was life behind the wheel, where we were our happiest and free. We would hold on stubbornly until our voices croaked, and our feet hurt from the gravel upon our bare feet, in search of the ultimate freedom.

Was this our perfect chance to create "us", Bruce? I hoped so, because there was no end in my eyes, or my heart for that matter. I knew you just wanted to make that poem a reality.

Even I didn't think we would roll in dewy grass that moist night on the coast, on a love buzz that neither of us could shake, unless it was our hips in the club.

Why had the grass felt so good as we played in it like wild dogs, laughing and howling into the darkness? It should've been colder. In fact, it was cold, but we couldn't feel it.

We raced each other back to the hotel, knowing quite well that our time here was numbered. We showered and tumbled into the sheets, making memories that would last an eternity. Or at least until new, more iconic memories came to the fore, boasting their importance on a brain so selective, so complex.

16

Crocodile Schnitzels

Harrygreengraphics@gmail.com
11/08 11:22am
To: You

Hey Thomas,

Sorry I haven't been in contact since we left on our travels in Australia. Abigail and I have been trying to not be on our phones as much as possible so that we can experience this beautiful country to its fullest. We have done just that. We began our journey in the Great Barrier Reef, where we stayed on this gorgeous island just off Gladstone called Heron Island. It took two hours on a boat to get there. There were rough seas and I was a little seasick.

That grueling first experience of the reef was soon forgotten though once we stepped off the boat. The island was surrounded by the bluest water I had ever seen. You and Bruce would love it there. We spent three days snorkeling and fishing. It really was amazing. The chefs at the restaurant even cooked up the Redthroat Emperor fish we caught that day. There were also these strange black birds on the island that would howl at night like demonic screaming babies! They're called Shearwaters A.K.A Mutton Birds.

We couldn't believe our experience on Heron Island was just the beginning of our travels in Australia. From there, we flew up to Cairns, where we took a road trip through the Daintree Rainforest. Crocodiles are known to inhabit beaches up there, so we weren't game enough swim. We found a few creeks and waterfalls to swim at though.

Our last destination was Uluru, the most intriguing place of all. I know you plan to travel there at some point, so I won't reveal too much. I will just say that I cannot recommend it enough! It's blooming with culture and it is just the vastest landscape I've ever stepped foot on.

Anyhow, we are heading back to London tonight so I will give you a call once we are back and settled.

Looking forward to hearing about how you, Bruce and Courtney are going.

Cheers,

Dad

Thomasgreenfinearts@gmail.com
11/08 10:11pm
To: Harry Green

Hey Dad,

Good to hear from you! Not going to lie, I was getting a little worried about you guys, somewhere between your lack of social media updates and that you didn't reply to my Facebook message a few days ago. Good to know you haven't gotten yourselves in a Wolf Creek-esque situation. It sounds like you've had a great trip though.

Everything is going well on this end. Our favorite lass, Courtney, has gotten herself a boyfriend which is exciting for her. By the sounds of it, he seems just as crazy as she is, which is what she needs. Bruce and I are going well. We're actually setting off on a road trip through the Northern Territory in eleven days. It was a spontaneous idea from the Irishman himself. It made me realize how much I have been working, and that this "working holiday" in Australia needs some more holiday to it. We don't have much of a plan, but I don't think we need to. I think we are going to do what you and Abigail did, and just figure it out as we go. I can't wait though. Let the adventure begin!

Hope you and Abigail have a safe trip back to the mother country. Maybe it will be our turn to visit next.

Cheers,

Your Amazing Offspring

Courtney wasn't as thrilled as Dad was when I told her about my upcoming expedition. I didn't understand at the time that she probably felt a little abandoned by me. Her best friend had moved over to Australia with her, fallen in love, and now he was going on a road trip with his new boyfriend. He didn't know when he was coming back, or where he would end up. Even though I'd agreed to pay the rent until I returned, I knew she felt a little lost and hurt. She wouldn't admit it, though.

"I'm glad you've found someone you're happy with," she did

say. "I'm happy too, I just wish I was the one traveling with you, like we planned."

I felt bad. "Maybe we could do a trip together when Bruce and I get back," I suggested.

She sighed. "*If* you come back."

As salty as she may have been, Courtney knew that I would be back by her side soon enough. As far and wide that I traversed, her and I would always end up back together, no matter what. It had always been that way, like when we lived separately while I went to university in Bath, and when I left London on that not-so-romantic Japanese escapade with Peter.

I didn't hesitate when quitting my job at the café, nor did my boss expect much from me being on a work visa without any responsibility or places to be held down by. The travel planning was mapped out over the next couple of weeks, with our scheduled departure day on August twenty-second.

Bruce and I sat at my place on the couch after cooking up a breakfast quiche, brainstorming ideas for our road trip. Everlasting destinations sparkled at our fingertips, with no time limit on discovery. At this moment in time, we were still grasping our spontaneity.

"We could either fly directly to Alice Springs or..." Bruce trailed off.

"Or what?" I asked him, keen to hear what he was to suggest.

"We could buy a car in Darwin and drive down the center of Australia." Bruce's eyes lit up like a chandelier. "How cool would that be!"

"Oh my god, that would actually be so much fun," I beamed, my eyes lit up in sync with his. "I gotta say, maybe you should be the planner in this relationship."

He giggled. "I'll happily take those reins."

Before we knew it, we were booking flights from Brisbane

to Darwin. By this time, the early hours of the morning had struck upon us and we were celebrating at a cocktail bar in Coolangatta. We'd eaten pasta, drank wine and discussed many ideas and the places we wanted to go on our outback adventure. The bartenders even had to ask us to leave because they were closing for the night. Time flew by when planning travels, I guessed. But now that we had begun, would we ever stop, or would we just be on this non-stop journey for the rest of our lives? Only time could tell. Right now, time told a fantastic story of me jumping on a plane in two days to the Northern Territory with this man I loved. The Top End of Australia eagerly awaited us.

"You're crazy," Courtney said on the night before our departure, "but, I'm happy for you."

Those were the exact words I needed to hear, because it reassured me even more that this spontaneous decision was somewhat the right one. I had met her in the kitchen after packing a suitcase and backpack full of most of my belongings. My bags were perched in the living room, a little like they had when I was leaving London to come to Australia.

The excitement was different this time, though. Perhaps because I waited so long before coming to Australia. It was like counting down the days, months in advance, everything planned. This time, I was still grasping the reality of the situation.

"You've got the house to yourself for a while," I said with a wink, trying to bring every inch of positivity to the party. "What are you gonna do?"

"Oh, probably start a meth lab in your art studio," she replied, ever-so casually.

We exchanged silent eye contact for a moment, and then burst out into a fit of laughter. Both hunched over the kitchen bench to try and control our sore stomachs, we refrained from looking at each other in case the laughter fit started again.

We took some deep breaths. And still not looking at each other, we shook our shoulders.

"So, what time am I dropping you off at the airport tomorrow morning?" Courtney then asked, pouring herself a glass of wine.

"Our flight is at half eleven, so maybe we aim to get there around ten-ish so I can meet Bruce and check in and stuff?"

"Sounds good." Courtney lifted the bottle of pinot grigio up to me. "Mmm?" was all that came from her mouth.

I nodded an "mmmm" back and she poured me a glass.

Sitting outside on the balcony, Courtney and I basked in the last few rays that hit our house. As we gazed out to the little strip of blue in the distance, it really hit me. That, as excited as I was, I was going to miss the east coast ocean. Indeed, I knew I'd be back. I wasn't sure when, though.

"Whatcha thinkin, Tommy?" Courtney asked me.

I had just been sitting there, taking sips of wine, lost in the sound of the waves.

"I was just thinking that," I began, "things have been quite unexpected since we got to Australia, haven't they?"

Courtney took a generous swig. "You can say that again. And again, and again."

We both chuckled.

Courtney turned and faced me. "Did you guys end up finding a car for the trip?"

"Yeah," I answered. "We've been talking to this lad on a Darwin Buy Swap and Sell Page. He's got this vintage gold station wagon that he wants to sell, and it's pretty cheap as well. So we can just buy it and sell it once we're done traveling."

Courtney winked. "We all know you and Bruce looooove your station wagons."

I thought back to the night we'd met and how impetuous we'd been then. Now look at us.

"It's good that you guys are leaving your cars here on the east coast," Courtney explained. "It would suck driving your car all the way out there and it blowing up or something."

"You're not wrong," I agreed.

We sat in silence for a beat. I began daydreaming again. The sun started to set, releasing a radiant glow over the ocean, houses, and high-rises.

"Things are going really fast," I blurted out, biting my lip, my smile fading a little. "I'm going to fucking Darwin tomorrow, which is over three thousand kilometers away."

I wasn't getting cold feet as such, but they certainly weren't as warm as they'd been when Bruce and I first organized all of this.

"Australia really is a big country," I then said. "I calculated the distance we're going tomorrow, and it's similar to going from London to Turkey."

"That's so weird to think about. You guys are gonna have so much fun, though," Courtney assured me, clinging her glass softly against mine. "Just enjoy it, it's gonna be an unforgettable trip. You'll be fine."

"Are you sure you're fine?" I queried Bruce once we settled into our seats on the plane.

"I'm fine," Bruce confirmed, his eyes noticeably red. "I just didn't sleep that great last night. I was so excited, and then having to get up early to catch the train to the airport."

He had been quiet ever since Courtney dropped me off at

the airport. He slept nearly the whole four-hour flight, his head resting on my shoulder as I listened to music. I even managed to snap a cute photo of him asleep with his mouth open. Perhaps that would have to be released on his birthday the following year. Maybe, just maybe.

As soon as he and I stepped off that plane at our destination, a huge cloud of humidity smacked us straight in the face, like stepping into a sauna after hopping out of the hot tub. The Gold Coast was warm, but wow, Darwin was *fucking* hot. Towering palm trees welcomed us at the airport. I felt like one of Tony Montana's henchmen from *Scarface* rolling into Cuba to deliver important packages. I was here, free, ready for this unknown affair ahead of us. This included eating a crocodile schnitzel at a pub that first night in Darwin. Whoever thought these prehistoric creatures would taste so tender. A striking mix between chicken and fish. The otherwise vegetarians had to try the local cuisine, of course.

"This fishbowl will be the death of me," Bruce huffed while we sat at the pub, chewing off a piece of orange from his oversized glass filled with bright green and blue liquor. It was more like a small bowl filled with alcohol rather than a drinking glass. Good on you, Darwin. I hardly touched mine, which was orange and red in color. I was still recovering from my croc schnitzel meal which I never finished. A few stray hot chips lay on my plate soaked in a pool of balsamic salad dressing.

"I don't think I've ever been so full in my entire life," I finally said.

Bruce slunk back in his chair. "I feel you there, babe. I'm floored."

I observed the other patrons in the pub. Most of them were far more energetic than us right now; chatting away, cackling to jokes we wished they wouldn't, drunk men screaming, "Go, son!" at the rugby players on the television.

I sat back into the cushion of the booth. "Honestly, I could pass out right here."

We planned to stay out much longer that night, to perhaps see what nightlife Darwin had to offer, but our bodies told us differently. We were back in our hostel room by nine, and asleep a half hour later.

We slept well most of the night. However, when two backpackers busted into the room in the early hours of the morning babbling in Swedish, a not-so-glorious early rise followed. And before we knew it, it was time to check out the golden station wagon.

I'd never seen anything like this station wagon. Maybe in movies from the 70s but that was about it.

"It's a little old, but it'll get you from A to B," was the guy's selling point when we went to take a look. "I'm moving to Melbourne soon, so I won't really need a car there for a while. Until I get myself sorted."

I cast a glance at Bruce, waiting for his opinion. I shrugged. "I like it. Our Insta grids will look pretty fuckin' sexy too."

Bruce grinned. "Let's do it."

And so, windows down, breeze through our hair, we left Darwin in a whirlwind of glee, ready for our first stop: a swim in a waterfall. We had been recommended this little slice of paradise by a European couple we'd met at the hostel the afternoon prior.

After a few hours' drive onto the straight stretch of the Stuart Highway, the heat became drier and the roads dustier as the aridness of the Territory crept in. The roads were stained with sandstone dirt and the terrain faded to amber with a tinge of spotted green.

We officially named our new car "The Golden Gal", and

after we parked her, we proceeded along a narrow dirt path. The company of several grasshoppers joined us, squealing throughout the trees. They seemed to keep flying into Bruce and not me, which irritated him as I suppressed my laughter.

By the time we reached the lookout, a magnificent view of army green mountains welcomed us. The top of a waterfall roared off the cliff above us. And it didn't take us long to rip our clothes off—down to our swimwear—and jump into the crystal-clear plunge pool that led up to the flow of the falls.

"Brrr..." Bruce shivered. "It's so fucking hot outside. How is it so cold in here?"

He wasn't wrong. The water was freezing. And yet, we didn't care. Not one bit. The fresh spring water instantly cooled us down as we waded in it.

"Now, this is class!" Bruce winked after grabbing me by the waist and kissing me.

We were surprised there weren't any other tourists around. I wasn't complaining at all, though. It meant that I could canoodle with Bruce all I wanted without us being disturbed. And that's what we did. But just as I felt his hard-on rub up against me, we were interrupted by a loud splash in the water before us. Pulling away from each other, we glanced to our right. The water seemed calm, but we were ever-so on edge.

"It was probably just a fish," Bruce said, grabbing me again and kissing me. He pecked my neck and rubbed my crotch.

Gosh, I was so ready to get you going in that fresh water, with that pristine view.

That is when I saw it: those beady green eyes, dark spotted scaly skin, and razor-sharp teeth attached to its long snout.

My mouth agape, I pulled away from Bruce slowly. The crocodile stayed still, its territorial glare stabbing me some twenty meters away.

"What's wrong, babe?" Bruce asked me.

"Shhhh," I whispered, frightened with shock. "I-I don't want to alarm you, but t-there's a crocodile behind you."

Bruce's eyes bulged. We stayed completely still standing waist deep in the water, eyeballing each other, still unsure of our next move. "F-Fuck," he gasped.

The crocodile stayed just above the water in the same spot, still staring at us. It then sunk beneath the surface.

"Go!" I boomed, breaking away from Bruce.

We both tore out of the plunge pool onto the sandstone shore, a split-second adrenaline injection keeping us going. As we ran out of the water dripping wet, the crocodile splashed out after us. We dived over the metal fence of the lookout track before it snapped its long jaws. I let out another bellow as Bruce and I tripped onto the dirt after diving over the fence. The crocodile tried to follow but was unable to get over, under, or through the fence. And we just lay there in the dirt, huffing and puffing in shock, the croc on the other side of the fence as it growled at us aggressively. It didn't take long for more tourists to venture up the walking track. We warned them of the croc, and they turned around.

Before reaching the car park, we were accompanied by several tourists who were all intrigued to hear the story of the crocodile. One of them called the rangers. The rangers immediately called in for back-up and closed off the walking track to the falls. They then informed us that the falls would be closed until the crocodile was professionally removed.

As the afternoon approached, dark, flocculent clouds grew in the distance, followed by faint groans from the sky. It then began to rain hard, and for a long time. We ran back to our car when the torrential downpour began. Thankfully our mattress was already set up as a bed in the back of the station wagon. We lay there, appreciating the dry, and sighing with relief.

"Wow, what a fucking day," Bruce said.

I put my head into his chest on the car bed. "Bruce?"

"Yeah?"

"Fuck, I love you."

"I love you too, babe. Shite, we nearly lost our lives today. First we nearly suffocate in the car at Linda's property and now we nearly get eaten by a crocodile? The universe *clearly* wants us dead."

"Or it's just creating great content for your book," I corrected, dripping over his face.

Bruce licked his lips, kissing my forehead resting on his chest. "You might be right there," he said.

I hoped so. I really, really did.

Surrender

Rain poured all night, our first sleep in the Golden Gal moist but soothing. It cleared toward the early hours of the morning, bringing another hot sunny day. In just a night of torrential rain, the neighboring roads became slightly flooded. We hoped that the crocodile incident would be our last complication on our quest to the Red Center.

After we left the rugged cliffs and swimming holes of Kakadu, we continued along the Stuart Highway eastbound, planning our next overnight stop to be Daly Waters. This would be after a full day's worth of driving. But not all plans go smoothly, and sometimes life just comes in and changes everything. After passing the town of Katherine, we realized we had forgotten to fill up with petrol for the Golden Gal. She became hungry, *real* hungry. Indeed, it wasn't long before the empty fuel light lit up orange for us both to see.

"Surely there'll be a gas station coming up soon," I said optimistically.

Wrong. No gas stations until a town called Mataranka from what I could see on the map.

"Ugh, how could we be so stupid?" Bruce muttered, hitting the steering wheel fiercely.

He stopped the car. I peered at the time on the digital dash clock. 11:22 shone lime green.

"What should we do? Should we turn around or keep going?" I panicked.

"I don't know, babe," Bruce sighed. "How far are we from Mataranka?"

I looked down at the map in front of me. "About fifty kilometers away."

"Well fuck," Bruce winced. "I guess we'll just have to keep going and hope for the best."

Hoping for the best got us nowhere that day. The Golden Gal ran out of fuel ten kilometers before we reached Mataranka. We were now left on the side of the highway in the middle of a stinking hot desert day.

Just our luck, Bruce. Just our luck.

"Fuck," Bruce swore, burying his head in his hands. "We should've been more prepared for something like this."

I pursed my lips, before saying, "Absolutely noted, mister."

As soon as we hopped out of the car, we spotted two kangaroos hopping through a field near the road, which for a moment, garnered our attention.

Thankfully, it only took a minute or so for another vehicle to emerge from the west. We waved our hands in the air as it approached. The cream-colored van slowed down when they saw us. A man and a woman sat in the front seat, sweat-kissed but calm. The brunette woman, who looked perhaps a decade older than us, wore a rainbow head band around her forehead, and the guy a bandana in his long curly golden hair.

"Hi!" Bruce blurted out with a sigh of relief.

"Y'all having some car troubles?" the guy asked us. He had a strong accent. At first, I couldn't tell whether he was American or Canadian.

I nodded awkwardly. "We ran out of fuel."

They both giggled.

"Guys, c'mon, you're in the Australian outback," the woman said. "You should be stocking extra fuel just in case."

Bruce and I both glanced at each other in embarrassment.

"Jump in," the guy told us. "We'll take you to Mataranka to get a barrel of fuel to bring to your car."

We jumped in the back of their van eagerly. The back seats had been taken out of it, replacing them with a bed and shelves. We lay on the mattress, trying not to get too much sweat on their pride and joy.

"My name's Marcus, and this is Cheyanne. We're from Oregon in the U.S. What brings you guys along the Stuart Highway, apart from being a source of moisture for the flies?" He laughed.

Bruce went red. "This is definitely our first time in the outback," he confessed sheepishly. "I'm Bruce, and this is Thomas. Ireland and England."

Cheyanne chuckled. "We all learn lessons when we travel. It's what makes it beautiful."

"Where are you guys headed?" I asked them.

"Well, we started in Byron Bay two months ago, and we traveled along the coastline," Cheyanne explained proudly. "We went down to Sydney and Melbourne first, then drove across

South Australia to Perth and then up through Western Australia. Now we're driving back across to the East Coast to visit the Great Barrier Reef." She smiled over at Marcus. "It's been amazing."

"We were living not too far from Byron before we came out here," I said. "We felt like we needed to go exploring, though, instead of settling down in one place too long."

Marcus chuckled. "Oh, we had a great time in Byron. Didn't we, babe?"

Cheyanne giggled. Say no more.

It wasn't long before we reached Mataranka, a small town known for its lagoon-like thermal pool in the forest.

"We're planning on staying at the campground in Mataranka tonight," said Marcus.

"Yeah, you guys are welcome to join us there," Cheyanne added.

Even though our original plan was to keep driving, we agreed to camp with them. And so, after filling a jerry can from the petrol station in Mataranka, we were driven back to our car to refuel. We then convoyed back to town and parked at the campground in the national park. After a short walk around the area, there wasn't much daylight left, so we took out our camp chairs and started preparing the food we had bought at the roadhouse. This campground made for a good barbecue, and fantastic company to top it off.

"Apparently there's this beautiful natural hot spring in the national park," Cheyanne told us. "Crystal clear mineral hot springs. Ahh, reminds me of home."

This certainly intrigued us. And even though getting stranded on the side of a highway in the Australian outback wasn't exactly ideal, we were glad to have met Marcus and Cheyanne. If we hadn't, we wouldn't have discovered the magical Bitter Springs. The water was so clear that a mask and snorkel came in handy to observe the underwater forest beneath the surface.

"Life on the road really seems like *the life*," I said the next day, drying off on the bank by the springs, Cheyanne sitting next to me. The turquoise hues of the water sparkled in the sun before us.

She laughed. "Oh, it's great, but it's not like it doesn't come with its downside."

"What's that?"

"It's just not sunshine and rainbows all the time like some people think. And especially if you're sharing it with someone, you really have to work out your differences quickly."

My stomach dropped a little. Bruce and I had never had a fight since we met, not even an argument. If play arguments that led to sex counted, then I could boldly tick that box.

"Do you guys have a plan or are you two just going to be spontaneous sailors like Marcus and I?" she asked.

Did we have a plan? That was a great question.

I shrugged. "Spontaneous sailors."

Cheyanne giggled. "It's called surrendering to the lack of control you have over your life. Both of your lives," she explained. "A lot of people live in fear. Fear of the past catching up with them, fear of what the future holds. But when you don't have a plan for so long, that fear of the unknown seems to diminish."

I chuckled. "I think that might be my problem sometimes. I think too far into the future, of this reality that I don't even know is gonna happen or not."

She tapped me on the shoulder. "Don't worry, Tommy. We've all been there. You're young. You're on the road. Stop trying to grow up so quickly." She laughed, shifting her gaze to me.

Our eyes linked, and I caught her laughs contagiously. She

had her eyes: Mum's eyes. "C'mon," she soon said, looking away and scrambling up from the bank. "Let's get back in that divine water."

It was a shame we had to part ways with Marcus and Cheyanne so soon the following day. They were to commence eastbound along the Carpentaria Highway while we continued along the Stuart. Cheyanne gave me a book to read.

"There's some cool info in there about the hiking trails in Central Australia," she explained. "I've already read it, and think you'll like it."

I smiled. "Thank you."

Transitions

It was 11:22 a.m. when we stopped at the petrol station to fill up. Our surroundings dried even more, the dirt color changing from a cream beige to a dark orange red. In the book Cheyanne gifted me, I read about some of the hiking trails in the Central Australian desert, imagining myself at all the lookouts, Bruce by my side, accomplishment plastered over both of our sweaty faces.

Upon looking up, the Stuart Highway appeared endless. It was just one long straight strip of road, surrounded by vast arid plains on either side. But there was also a certain beauty to the empty-seeming land we were seeing.

"I can't believe we're actually here," I said after a prolonged and peaceful silence of staring out the window.

Bruce rubbed my leg, his other hand on the wheel. "It's crazy, isn't it?" He then chuckled. "I'm also keen to get to some sort of a town, though, especially when it gets dark. Deserted barren places like this, they're pretty, but they're also the reason why I'm terrible with scary movies."

I tickled the back of his neck. "I'd protect you."

Bruce gave me a cheeky side glance. "Thomas, my hero," he said, his mouth quirking into a smirk.

We took turns driving for the day, stopping every couple of hours to switch. The desert seemed to inspire Bruce when he was planted in the passenger seat. Perhaps because he had a document open on his laptop to dive into a planet of words with. He typed away while I focused on the road, envisioning what my next art piece could entail. The images that came to mind were of Bruce and I wandering down the middle of the Stuart Highway, walking in the direction of a UFO in the distance, which hovered in level with our foreheads.

"If you could describe me in three words, what would they be?" Bruce asked, rather randomly.

The UFO quickly disappeared from my mind. I chuckled. "Um, interruptive for one. Can't you see I'm thinking about aliens over here."

Bruce narrowed his eyes on me for a moment and then laughed. "I mean, if we were going to be abducted by aliens, this would be the place."

How on Earth could I really describe you in just three words, Bruce?

"Three words," I began. "Hmm." I had to think about this one. "Um, creative. You know, your writing and stuff is pretty wicked. Handsome, because well, look at you. And, uh, magical, because I think you're some sort of wizard and you're not telling me. P.s. please don't judge me for my lack of knowledge for big words."

Bruce beamed, raising his eyebrows. "You know I'm a wizard."

"Okay, your turn for the three words," I then said, eagerly.

Bruce looked at his laptop. "Actually, I already have mine written down."

I hit him lightly on the leg. "Well, that's cheating now, isn't it? If I would've gotten time to think, I probably would've been able to at least come up with some better words."

"Oh, c'mon, I thought your words were cute."

"Fine. I'll take that. Now, what are yours?"

He began to read from a notebook next to his laptop. "Okay, number one: zany."

"What now?" I chimed in.

"Zany," he repeated. "It basically means that you're an amusing weirdo."

"Zany," I said, nodding my head. "I love it."

"And number two," Bruce went on. "Talented, because well, your art is class and you deserve all the praise for it."

I didn't even need to look in a mirror to know that my cheeks were glowing pink.

"And three, empathetic, because you just get me, and I get you."

A smile formed on my face. To me, his words held undenying power. So much so that I could feel the moisture in my eyes multiply.

"Who *are you*?" was all that left my mouth.

We held each other's gaze for a short moment. I could've kept it for a lot longer, but I had to watch the road, even though there weren't going to be any bends or turns for quite some time. I asked Bruce what had inspired the three words game, to which he said that he'd been writing and got bored, so he thought it would be fun.

We spent the next few hours loudly singing along to a noughties playlist Bruce had downloaded to his phone while we were in Mataranka. It certainly made the time pass with ease.

The sun set elegantly that evening, the moon rising by the time we reached the small town of Tennant Creek.

"I'm so hungry I can barely function," Bruce mentioned, frantically studying every shop that seemed open as we drove through town.

I yawned, slowing down the car so I could peek out the window myself. "Me too. I could honestly do anything at this stage."

"Pizza?" Bruce called out as soon as he spotted the sign.

"Sold!"

Pizza it was. However, it was nowhere near as good as the last vegetarian takeaway pizza we'd eaten, on the night we first met. What was better, though, was the sleeping arrangement. Because as soon as we'd eaten, we were bedding down for the night in the Golden Gal in the town's caravan park.

The earthy smell of wind-swept dust welcomed us the next morning, paired with cloudless skies and the relentless flies of the sunshine, endlessly searching for their taste of moisture. The buzzing critters would usually find what they were looking for in our ears, nose, mouth or eyes. And unfortunately, there were even more of the buzzing critters as we entered the Red Center.

The road from Tennant Creek to Alice Springs had very little bends, just clear open stretches of tar. Bruce volunteered to drive the first stretch, which meant I could read my newly acquired book. Every time I put it down, the environment's greenery faded away like a paint palette, to a light brown and gray floras with vast masses of red dirt. The more I stared at it, the more I became used to it.

"How's the book going, babe?" Bruce asked me while I looked out the window, daydreaming as the afternoon sun crept through the windshield.

It took me a moment to process his question. "Oh…sorry. Yeah, it's good," I said, sending him a half-smile.

"You seem a bit dazed. You okay?" he mentioned, placing his hand on my thigh.

"Yeah, I've just been reading for too long," I admitted with a laugh. "Can I drive?"

Bruce nodded and pulled over to the side of the road. He kissed me on the cheek before I hopped in the driver's seat. I drove the rest of the way to Alice while he napped.

I cast a glance over at him from time to time, thinking how cute he looked while he slept, those bold eyelashes twinkling in the sun. I thought about where I was at this point in time, and how lucky I was to have met someone this special who had brought me on this amazing journey.

But as they say, all good things come crashing down eventually, just like life itself. I couldn't possibly have something so good for so long and have it stay the same forever. I guess I just never wanted the euphoria to end.

Alice Springs was lively, homely too, with people scattered everywhere. We booked ourselves into a hotel and then decided on a pub for dinner. Well, Bruce seemed to have already decided for us. He said he'd been searching for places in the car when he wasn't asleep. It was a nice little place, with a long bar and buzzing atmosphere. We even dressed up a little, as we had been living like barefoot bushmen for the past few days on our road trip. We shared a generous plate of nachos, followed by a beer from the tap.

"Am I a true Aussie yet with my VB?" I asked Bruce cheekily.

He giggled and snapped a photo of me on his phone, and the evening reeled on. Pints kept pouring and live music roared. I'd never sat in a room and listened to country music for so long and actually liked it. Bruce hadn't either. Some songs we even knew the words to. A little dance floor had formed in front of the shaggy man playing his guitar and singing with a growl. At this point, Bruce and I were well into our second pint. He gave me that look, with his butt sticking out, and a toothy playful grin on his face.

"What?" I questioned, smirking.

He reached into his pocket. "I have a surprise for you."

I wondered what it could possibly be. But before he could say anything else, a plethora of claps filled the room. The man with the guitar started talking over the microphone.

"Thank you! Thank you. That's it from me, folks," he groaned. "For the next hour, we've got our weekly poetry night before our resident singer songwriter, Claire, takes over for the rest of the night."

Poetry night? How did we not know this? Well, by the excitement in Bruce's grin, he definitely seemed to be aware. I observed a large poster on the wall signifying the event. But I was still more interested in the surprise he had for me. A far more well-dressed and younger lad stepped up on the stage as the shaggy man departed with a stumble.

"Wow, full house again tonight. That's great," he called out to the crowd. "Thank you all for coming. We've had some great submissions for tonight's poetry and we're keen to share them with you all. Tonight's theme is Environmental Issues, as some of you may know. And first up we have 'Forest Bathe by Face' by Bruce O'Brien."

The blithesome lad stuttered as he said Bruce's last name, but I wasn't too fussed on that. I was too busy gaping at the fact that Bruce was literally walking up to the stage with a piece of paper. He winked at me, my eyes following him as they often did. *You've got to be kidding me.*

This guy was full of surprises. My eyes lit up as he smiled at me through the lights on the stage, his face blotched with patches of pink. The crowd fell silent.

"Hello." Oh gosh, his voice sounded astonishing over a microphone too. "I'm Bruce, and I'm from Ireland. This is something I wrote here on my road trip through the outback."

I shook my head in disbelief, unaware that he wrote this in the car, by my side.

He took a deep breath.

You took it away, handsome. You really did.

"Have you ever sat back in your seat,
Basking in the coarse ray's heat,
And realized that you have at least something you
    wanted a year ago?
A lot can happen in a year,
Perhaps half of those days living in fear,
Fear of what the world holds for us.
Will the storm bring rain or dust?
Will our leaders take heed,
Or will they ignore the pleads?
But there's one thing we all know,
Something that lives high and low:
It's you,
Every shade, every turquoise hue.
Your skies bring clouds and rain on a cold winter's day,
But when your smile radiates,
The wet mud around you turns into clay.

When green turns to red and red turns to blue,
Where the bloody hell in the Territory are you?"

The crowd—including Bruce and I—giggled in unison.

"It doesn't matter, you're here.
You're those flies buzzin',
And those pints gluggin'.
You're those strands of spinifex waving in the afternoon wind,
And the moment you draw a loved one's grin.
I am me,
You are you.
We…are we.
The forest has its own face,
Within your mirror, a soft embrace."

Your eyes were like a frozen glacier lake and so were mine, Bruce. And I wouldn't have had it any other way.

The crowd clapped, and Bruce said, "Thank you," before stepping off stage. I shook my head at him as he returned to our table.

"I can't believe you," is all that I said. "You're amazing."

He winked. "That's two poems now inspired by you. How does that make you feel?"

I laughed. I wanted to say that it made me feel like the luckiest man alive, but the next speaker was ready to begin. I didn't feel the need to answer him. He already knew.

We snuck off for more pints during the remaining four speakers, and then it was soon time for more live music. I officially loved Alice Springs. And I knew Bruce was drunk when he grabbed my hand and said, "Dance with me."

Not letting go, I followed him as he skipped over to the

dance floor. A woman sang on stage. *Take Me Home, Country Roads.* I bellowed at the top of my lungs with pride and beamed with limerence as I watched Bruce shake his shoulders and grin.

We didn't stay out super late that night. Especially after driving five hours during the day. The hotel bed seemed much more enticing than any beers or music did. We had drunk a fair amount of beer, though, and we had a feeling that we might have to pay for that in the morning.

19

The Blue Bar

Bruce and I spent most of the next day laying around in bed, serving out our hangover sentences. Before we knew it, the night was young, and we were strolling to this quaint bar-slash- hotel hidden in town. Some locals had told us about it the night before at the spoken word event. They said that the place didn't even come up on search engines. And they were *absolutely* correct about the hidden part. The bar was tucked away up an alleyway in town. We were told to look out for the turquoise door. Even then, it just looked like the entrance to an apartment or something. But once we opened the door, we were instantly baffled by the pastel blue-hued interior. A handsome man wearing an all-cobalt suit greeted us as we ambled in. He stood behind a desk, a downward flight of stairs behind him.

"Good evening, gentlemen," he greeted us. "If I could just see your I.D please?"

We whipped out our passports and handed them over to him.

"Long way from home," the man mentioned with a curious smile, studying our booklets.

Bruce and I both went red. This guy was gorgeous, with a dramatic jawline and bold eyes. I wasn't sure if he had penciled on eyeliner or if his eyes were naturally that dark.

He soon flicked our passports back to us. "Enjoy your time down there, gentlemen."

I grabbed Bruce by the arm, the long flight of stairs leading us down to a short corridor. A faint ambient sound crept through the walls as we followed the lights. Mesmerizing tiles in all shades of blue lined the corridor. Bruce stopped and dug out his phone, facing it to the wall for a photo.

Blue had always been my favorite color, and I never thought I'd be in a venue that showcased every single shade. Even the waiters wore blue vests and bow ties.

Very few people dined at The Blue Bar that night. Tables circled the room, most unoccupied. A breeze of subtle laughter wafted from the tables that were tenanted as they told stories amongst themselves.

Bruce and I claimed seats at the bar. Countless glasses and bottles sparkled before us. The bartender was equally as attractive as the man we had met in the reception. He smiled at us as we sat down and asked if we wanted a drink. I realized that I had never drunk a dry martini before. One with a singular olive swimming in it. And after a few sips, it seemed as if I was already conditioned to that potent salty aftertaste. Something about this bar gave me the chills, as if we'd just discovered some sort of fantasy dreamland. One that soon became my idea of the ultimate gay club.

"This has gotta be the most amazing venue I've ever been to," I mentioned, picking the olive from my glass and nibbling on it. I then left the seed on a napkin beside me.

"Makes you feel like you're part of something real special, doesn't it?" a deep voice echoed from my right.

A muscular, well-built man now sat next to me. I hadn't even noticed him there. Might've been the almost-straight vodka I was sipping back. He wore a navy button-up shirt that looked as if it would burst any second from his bulging pecs and biceps. His brown stubble was perfectly sculptured across his cheeks and chin. That rugged model look.

"I mean, sure," I said half-sarcastically.

Bruce peered over at the man and instantly fell silent. The man seemed a little older than us. Perhaps in his mid-thirties, but doing splendidly for his age.

"What's your poison of choice tonight, boys?" he asked.

Bruce shrugged, gripping his martini glass. The man shifted his gaze across me to him.

"Maybe a shot?" I suggested awkwardly, saving Bruce from his stare.

The man waved to the bartender, who was polishing glasses calmly.

"Can we get four shots of absinthe?" he requested from the bartender.

"*Absinthe?*" Bruce piped up.

"I honestly haven't had absinthe since I was like nineteen," I said.

The man winked at me. "Well, for old time's sake then."

"Why four shots?" asked Bruce. "Is there someone joining us? Or are you shotting two of them?"

The man chuckled. He then looked beyond us. I turned around. It was the guy from the front door with the cobalt suit.

"Hey, honey. You're just in time," the man next to me said. "Guys, this is my partner Lochie. I assume you've already met. Oh, and where are my manners? I'm Alvaro."

Lochie took a seat on the left side of Bruce. Alvaro held out his hand to me. Bruce and I took turns in shaking their hands. A warm burn spread through my esophagus and chest like wildfire as the absinthe cascaded down it. The more drinks Alvaro and Lochie bought us, the more chatty we became. They asked how Bruce and I had met, and we were more than eager to tell them. We then reciprocated the question. They had been together for four years. Lochie's father owned the bar. But now that his dad was growing older, Lochie managed it for him. Their relationship inspired me. I hoped that Bruce and I would be together that long and still be happy, and not want to kill each other.

After my second absinthe shot, I stumbled to the bathroom to pee. I stared into the circular mirror between the male and female bathrooms—at the pale British boy amongst a sea of baby blues. I turned my gaze to the neon digital clock glistening above the mirror. *Eleven twenty-fucking-two.* It seemed as if the absinthe had gone straight to my head, because for some reason, I could hear a familiar voice begin to chant into my ear. It took me a moment to realize where I'd heard that voice before. Indeed, it was the soft voice of my mother.

"It's all about the numbers, and the timing, my son," she whispered. I could almost feel her lips brush against my earlobe. "If you think this is some coincidence, you are clearly mistaken."

I fixed my gaze into the mirror. She stood beside me, wearing a silky turquoise dress. Ummmm, did Alvaro or Lochie put something in my drink?

"What do you mean?" I asked her.

"Look at yourself in the mirror," she said. I did. "Do you truly love that man staring back at you?"

Before I could answer that question, Bruce burst through the door. My mother and the turquoise dress disappeared.

"Oh my god, babe, you've gotta come save me out there," Bruce blurted out, his face a tad sweaty.

"Why? What's going on?"

Bruce sighed energetically. "Okay, so. Turns out Alvaro and Lochie are *open.*" He lifted up his fingers to impersonate quotation marks.

"And? What do you think about that?" I was slightly offended and I wasn't sure why.

"I mean, I dunno. That's why I wanted to see what you thought about it. They openly told me they want a foursome. I said I wasn't sure but they kinda persuaded me to come talk to you about it."

I pictured the four of us in bed together and it did turn me on. But I was also protective over Bruce and didn't want anyone else touching him in that way.

I smirked. "Hmm."

"I mean, we don't have to if you don't want to," Bruce said, "but, like, it's not like we're ever going to see them again. Could be fun."

My smirk soon turned into a devilish grin. I pushed Bruce up against the wall next to the mirror and kissed him hard. He surrendered, softly biting my lip. I bit back, my penis pulsing through my jeans. I don't remember it becoming fully flaccid again before the four of us wandered to that room behind the bar. Or when we laid on that lush king bed, our clothes sprawled on the floor. Lochie wrapped his arms around me, slamming me down on the right side of the bed, climbing on top of me and kissing me hard. I soon took control and forced myself onto him, our bodies roughly rubbing against one another. I peered over at Bruce and Alvaro. Alvaro had him pinned down. Bruce's legs were jacked up and wrapped around his hips. He began to gaze into Alvaro's eyes.

It was only then that Bruce pushed Alvaro off him in a panic. Lochie and I stopped.

"Woah." Alvaro was taken aback, his hands up as if a gun was pointed at him.

Bruce scrambled off the bed, gathering his clothes. "I'm sorry. I can't do this. Can we go, Thomas?"

I hopped off Lochie. The couple's smiles faded. They were concerned and so was I.

"Are you okay, babe?" I asked Bruce.

"Yeah, I'm just not feeling too well," he said with a sense of urgency. "Can we go back to the hotel, please?"

"Yeah of course," I agreed, slipping my clothes on.

"Too much absinthe, Bruce?" Alvaro asked.

Bruce didn't reply. He didn't even look at Alvaro. He just left the room in a hurry.

"Thanks for the hospitality, lads," I said to the naked men.

Alvaro nodded. Lochie gave me an *eye eye, captain,* and I left too, power walking to keep up with Bruce.

We walked back to the hotel in silence. It was a fair journey to the other side of town. I went to speak but then stopped a few times. "You wanna talk about it?" I then asked.

Bruce exhaled heavily into a deep sigh. "He just reminded me so much of Joe, and I think that's why when I was drunk, I was so...intrigued by what would happen if I went back there. Because that's what I would do back in Dublin. He would abuse me, and then I'd realize that I had no one else, so I'd always go back to him. But it was never grand when I did that. It would always end up worse."

I sighed, stepping in front of him and catching his cheeks in my hands. "Why would you wanna go back there?"

He gazed right into my eyes. "I dunno," he confessed, pausing for a long moment. I freed his face from my grip.

"Maybe, as scared as I am of him, a little part of me still hasn't fully let him go," he then revealed. "Even after all the terrible things he did to me. We were together for a year and a half. I guess it's just easier said than done to forget about it."

We sat down against a mural in front of a stone wall. The streets were quiet, and a misty haze of fog drifted through the air.

"There's something I've also been thinking about," he added. "The way you walked into my life, it reminds me of when Joe and I first fell in love. And it scares the shit out of me sometimes."

I squeezed his hand. "Hey, look. I would *never* hurt you like he did."

"Deep down, I know that," he admitted before smiling cheekily. "I think it's safe to say the foursome was a really bad idea on my front."

I chuckled. "I mean, it definitely wasn't your best. I only agreed to do it because you suggested it, you know."

He nodded. "I know."

I put my arm around him. He rested his head on my shoulder. After a moment, I nudged him gently. "C'mon, mister. Let's get you to bed." I forced myself from the ground, lifting my hands up in the air for a stretch.

Bruce yawned. "Bed is amazing. I love bed."

I drew my hand out to help him up. "Are you sure you're okay?" I had to ask.

He quickly avoided my eye contact and just said, "Yeah."

Red Dirt and Dusty Boots

I lay helpless on the ground in the dusty red dirt, surrounded by spinifex. I was injured, tired, legless to carry on any longer through this scorched desert. A familiar face towered over me. It was Bruce. Weak and alone, I was thrilled to see that he had come to my rescue. I dragged myself along the dry ground to try and reach his legs to latch myself on. But when I spotted the sharp blade of the knife in his hand reflecting the sun's rays, I felt my stomach churn.

"I'm sorry, Thomas. This isn't gonna work out anymore," he said, imposter-like, shaking his head. He placed his hands over his face for a moment. "Everything just happened too quickly. I don't know if I'm ready for this."

Bruce approached me with the pocket knife, his expression hardening. And without another word, he plunged the blade straight into me without hesitation. A wet sound of lacerated flesh followed. He shed a tear.

"I'm sorry," he apologized.

I woke up with a fright. An overwhelming feeling of fear and anxiety clouded me. My heavy breathing woke Bruce. He kissed me on the cheek and asked if I was okay.

It was just a dream, I reminded myself over and over.

"I'm fine," I said, smiling at him.

He smiled back. "Today's the day. Kings Canyon for a few days, and then the Rock after that."

I soon forgot all about my horrid dream after some great morning sex on that rickety hotel bed. And before I knew it, we were packed up and back in the car driving, ready for our four-hour journey further into the remote wilderness. We didn't speak about what happened at The Blue Bar. To Bruce, it was like it never happened.

Kings Canyon was an exciting prospect as we left Alice Springs. It was the thought of somewhere we hadn't previously explored yet. Bruce volunteered to drive the whole way there.

"I'm just really keen to be behind the wheel," he repeated.

I didn't mind at all, as long as you didn't have that blade handy.

Driving through the towering beige sandstone ranges was overwhelming; it really felt like we were in the outback now. Kings Canyon's rugged sandstone towers gaped between the West MacDonnell Ranges and the George Gill Ranges. I thought about the books I had read, and the films I'd watched. Where the protagonist soul-searched for the ultimate freedom. The quests of Cheryl Strayed and Christopher McCandless came to mind, inspiring me more than ever on that day in the desert.

Bruce and I arrived at the roadhouse that we would call

home for the next two nights. As we stepped out of the car, we were welcomed by the area's other natives: the many fucking flies. Several of them buzzed around our faces as we walked toward the roadhouse reception.

Dusk drew close, and a warm breeze rolled in. The blonde receptionist at the roadhouse showed us to our room, which was a short walk down a dirt track.

"So, this is what real outback living is…class!" Bruce said energetically, falling backward onto the double bed.

"As long as our bed is comfy?" I winked at him.

"Oh babe, just you wait," Bruce teased.

We laid back on the bed. The only sound we could hear was the faint intermittent howls from dingoes. Our sanctuary there in the outback quickly became a little slice of home. And it was ours for what seemed like a comfortable forever.

We spent the next morning hiking the famous Rim Walk, trekking along sheer cliff canyons and through beehive sandstone domes. It really did feel like we'd just stepped foot on a whole new planet. Along the walk, Bruce and I pinched our sweaty selves several times, making sure that all of this was real.

After a post-hike coffee, Bruce took a nap in our room while I took a stroll to the roadhouse art gallery. It was filled with some of the most incredible Indigenous-made art pieces; mostly dot paintings, but ones ever-so detailed. A dot painting of a dolphin caught my eye the moment I walked past it. My mother loved dolphins. They were her favorite. She always made this known, mostly by filling our childhood home with dolphin-dedicated decor. There were ornaments, paintings, even a glass table in honor of her spirit animal.

As I stood smiling in front of the dolphin painting, I thought about the other night, when I was in the The Blue Bar bathroom. Was she really there, I kept wondering, or was it just a hallucination, and I was in fact a little crazy?

After opening the door to our room, I was welcomed to a cool breeze from the air-conditioner. But I was also welcomed to Bruce, who had obviously woken up from his nap. He was talking to somebody, but stopped—mid-sentence— the moment I walked in. He looked up at me, wide-eyed in shock, like I'd just caught him doing something he shouldn't. He wasn't on the phone, though, so it struck me as odd.

My eyes narrowed. "Who were you talking to?" I closed the door.

He chuckled awkwardly, going red in the face. "Oh, uh, no one. I was just talking to myself. Relaying a scene for a novel idea I have."

"Oh yeah?" I asked. Honestly, I would've loved to hear any ideas he had with his creative projects.

"It's nothing," he excused himself. "Just something possibly in development. How was your walk?"

"It was good. How was your nap?"

"Good."

"Good." I paused. "So, I was thinking…if we wanted to stay another day in Kings Canyon, we could do the Giles Track tomorrow," I suggested. "It's this twenty-two-kilometer track that connects Kathleen Springs to the Rim Walk."

"Babe, I'm exhausted," Bruce protested, flicking through photos from that day's hike on his phone. "I think I'm gonna pass on that one."

"Oh, c'mon, when are we going to be out here next?" I persisted.

"I know. I just feel like I got everything I needed from Kings Canyon today," he told me. "Flies and all."

"Where's the macho Bruce who goes surfing for three hours every day?" I mocked.

This is when he snapped. "Just because I surf nearly every day, doesn't mean I want to do every hike. We're meant to be on a holiday. I just wanna chill out. Why don't you do the hike and I'll chill by the pool tomorrow?"

"I don't want to do the hike on my own." I didn't. I wanted Bruce to come with me, just like we'd experienced everything else together so far.

"Well, I don't wanna do the hike. I do have a say in what I do."

"I know you have a say, but I *really* wanna do it," I whined. "Can't you just come?"

"No, Thomas. I don't want to!" he shouted, his eyes expanding.

"Fine!" I yelled back. "We won't go."

He chuckled. "You can still go if you really want to do it, babe."

I brushed him off with a cold shoulder. "No. It's fine. Let's just go to Uluru tomorrow like we planned."

"Are you sure?"

"Yeah."

"Come here."

I did. He hugged me.

"Let's not fight about stupid stuff like this," he said. "Just remember, we both have a voice and sometimes we aren't going to agree on things. But what we can do is compromise."

I should've just gone on the hike, because after we left Kings Canyon, I wondered what the Giles Track would've been like. I had read all about it in the book Cheyanne gave me. Guess I would never know.

Crumbling Exteriors

It seemed as if Bruce had woken up on the wrong side of the bed. He had become snappy with me all morning. Was it that argument we had the day before? Surely it couldn't have been. I thought we were past that.

That morning, all I did was politely tell him that he smelt of B.O, and suggested he put more deodorant on. This led to him thinking of every opportunity where he could fault me. Telling me to hurry up, telling me not to pack the car that way.

"I'm sorry, let's not argue," I said. But why was I the one that had to resolve the argument? "You smell very pretty now, by the way."

He cast his unimpressed gaze at me, and I drew a slight smile out of him. Alas, he didn't speak much on the three-and-a-half-hour drive to Uluru.

• • •

Some say that Uluru holds an eerie but inspiring presence, and they're right. It's an all-encompassing thing that can make one speechless.

The pre-eminent sandstone rock stood tall before us.

"My parents always dreamed of taking our family here," Bruce mentioned, as awed as I was at the towering formation in the distance. "It never happened. Money always got in the way. I'm so glad I get to experience it for them."

"I'm sure they'd be very proud," I said, kissing him on the cheek.

A fellow tourist used my phone to take a photo of Bruce and I with Uluru in the background. It would become a photo that I'd never forget. Lips locked in front of Australia's rugged heart. It looked like it should be on a postcard or something. Maybe it would be, in my art and in his stories.

Bruce was bewitched by the rock and kept staring at it. I wanted to know what was going through his head. I grabbed him from behind, but he didn't reciprocate much energy at all. Something was up, I knew it.

I finally asked, "Is everything okay, babe?", kissing the back of his neck. Still no reciprocation.

"Yeah."

I wasn't convinced. "Are you sure?"

He sighed. "I just pinch myself sometimes, that I got so lucky to be able to experience this, but my family never got to."

"Hey, you worked hard to get here," I told him. "Some might say it's luck, but I also think you can earn what you get. You deserve it."

He nodded. "I guess I'm just feeling a little homesick is all."

Bruce didn't look at me as he turned around from the rock.

I grabbed him and forced him to lock eyes with me. "Hey, we can take a trip back to our neck of the woods soon, if you want."

He smiled at me and stroked my cheek. "No. It's okay. I'm just having a moment. Thanks for thinking of me, though."

He walked in front of me on our stroll back to the car. I wanted nothing more than to be beside him, but I knew he needed a moment to just think and feel. I hoped none of this was to do with me, that perhaps he was having second thoughts about us. No, this was too perfect for him to give up. He wouldn't do that, I thought. Not after this amazing journey we'd been on. I truly believed we could achieve great things together. But the faster he walked in front of me, the more I struggled to keep up.

I wanted to say "I love you" over and over, but it felt like you were too far from my call.

As uncertainty bubbled, I needed to hear those three words more than ever.

"I love you," I told him as we drove further south in the Golden Gal.

He gave me an uncomfortable smile as he held my hand loosely. No grip. No energy. "You too," he said.

He couldn't even say the real words, and a voice in my head screamed things at me I wished it wouldn't. It told me that it was time to let him go soon. It also told me that Bruce, under the mask of new and exciting experiences, was broken, and there was no one that could fix him other than himself. But what did this mean for us? Was I too attached to leave him? Or was Courtney truly right—that I couldn't be Bruce's savior, his knight in dust-caked armor? I sighed and pulled my hand away. "Should I be worried?" I asked.

"What do you mean?"

"Something's going on. I can feel it."

He sighed. "I don't know. I just...I just feel off. I don't know why. I never thought you'd see me like this."

I grabbed his hand, his deep breaths elevating. He stroked my knuckle with his finger. I began telling him about Cheyanne and I's conversation back in Mataranka about how working through each other's differences while traveling was crucial.

"What if I don't want to live life on the road, Thomas?" Bruce argued, narrowing his eyes at me.

Now I was angry. "Hey, this was your idea! You just wanted to up and leave our lives back on the coast..."

"I know, but now that it's actually happened, I just don't know if this is the life for me," Bruce said sporadically. "Plus, we're gonna have to go back eventually. I'm running out of money."

I hit the steering wheel hard. "When were you gonna tell me this?"

"I'm telling you now," he mumbled.

I shook my head, fuming. "So, before we left when you said you had enough money to last a few months..."

"I just wanted to explore Australia right there and then, I wasn't thinking. I wanted to tell you back in Alice, but I was a little embarrassed."

I couldn't stay mad with him, nor did I want things to get any weirder. What happened to carefree Thomas and Bruce, mesmerized by the twinkle in each other's eyes?

"Looks like Adelaide will be our last stop then," I told him bluntly.

"You can keep traveling if you want," he suggested. "It seems like you've got a taste for it now."

Was he just trying to set my anger off, or was it my short-tempered reactions that were the problem?

"What do you mean?" I snapped. "It seems as if you're just trying to get away from me or something now."

He grumbled. "Gosh, Thomas. No, that's not what I'm saying. I'm just…saying what I see and what we both seem to want."

This knife hit harder than the one in my dream. "I just want us to be together. Isn't that what you want too?"

"Yes, Thomas. It is." He sighed, gazing out the window. "I'm just trying to work out what we both want."

"I know what I want!" I yelled. "But do you know what you want?"

He didn't say anything.

"I can't believe this," I said. "What is wrong with you?"

Like the crack of a whip, it hit my eardrums at a decibel I never knew possible from him. "Everything is wrong with me!" His bellow of words rumbled my insides in a way I would never forget.

In shock, I pulled the car over to a halt, skidding through the dirt and ploughing into a bush of spinifex. We sat in silence for a moment. He huffed and puffed with anger out of the corner of my eye.

Bruce cracked the door open, jumped out, and slammed it hard behind him. I shuddered, breathing heavy. We were now on the side of a remote desert highway, nothing but coarse plains and a grim tension that I didn't know would pass. Bruce stalked off up the side of the highway. He stopped about fifty meters from the car.

I hopped out slowly, crouching and sitting up against the bonnet, pondering while I stroked my lips. I was never the best at solving confrontation, or even approaching it for that matter. So, I just stayed where I was.

Bruce screamed deeply into the sky. My eyes extended, his

roars booming louder before they got any quieter. It lasted for a few minutes before he fell silent. I sat up against one of the tires of the Golden Gal, breaking twigs in my hand and holding back tears. That never worked. I could hear his footsteps crunching through the gravel as I broke down.

He sighed when he saw me, sitting down next to me. I sobbed harder when he put his head on my shoulder.

"I'm sorry," he apologized. "What happened to me, really fucked me up. And it keeps coming back."

He squeezed my hand. We both cried. It felt nice to let it rain in this barren desert. "I need help," he confessed. "I know that, and I'm going to get it when we get back to the coast. I promise."

I nodded. He tilted my head to face him, kissing me softly.

"Do you wanna talk about anything before we keep going?" I asked him.

He shook his head. "No. It's okay."

"Are you sure?"

He quickly avoided my eye contact, just like he had that night in Alice Springs, and just said, "Yeah. I'm fine. Let's go."

When There's Nowhere Else to Go

I asked Bruce if he wanted to drive back to Alice Springs, somehow sell the car and then fly back to Brisbane. But he suggested that we tackle the fourteen-hour drive down to Adelaide and go from there instead. After driving further south and crossing the state border into South Australia, we stopped in Marla for the night, which was just over five hours from Uluru. There wasn't much there, except a roadhouse and caravan park. We were both tired from driving and from our mental breakdowns earlier, so it was a matter of having an early dinner and heading to sleep in the Golden Gal. If there was one thing I was going to miss about the desert, though, it was the sunsets. And the one in Marla was no different that night.

The following morning, I awoke, early, to the sound of soft weeping. Staying completely still, I was quick to realize that it was Bruce from behind me. My back faced him. He had his arm draped over my belly, and it was clear that he trying to control his tears in case it would wake me. I wanted to turn around and hold him, let him know that I was here and awake and that he was safe and okay and everything in between. But for some reason, my body was frozen, so I couldn't even do that. He stopped crying after a few minutes, sniffling quietly as he gathered himself. Once he had, I stretched my legs out and rolled onto my back, opening my eyes as if it was for the first time that day.

"Morning." I cleared my throat, rolling over some more and kissing him on the cheek.

He scrolled on his phone, hardly returning my affection.

"What time is it?" I asked him.

"Oh, sorry, morning. It's six forty-five," he finally replied, dropping his phone down before saying, "Let's watch the sunrise, so?"

"It's so cold, though," I groaned, curling further into the blanket as he sat up.

The cold didn't seem to bother him right now, among the things that did. And so, he slipped his shoes on and crawled out of the car. I stayed for a moment after the door closed, sighing a few times, before sitting up. The windows of the car were all fogged up and I felt a little queasy, something that seldom happened to me first thing in the morning. My stomach churned and shot off some explosion sounds. My head started spinning a little. Ultimately, I opened the door and braved the cold, the fresh air already making me feel better.

My stomach did still feel a tad uncomfortable, though, even when I walked over to Bruce, who was sitting on a picnic bench, looking out to the sun popping up in the distance. I planted myself next to him.

"I feel sick," I said grumpily.

Bruce turned to me slightly. "What kind of sick?"

"Stomach."

He sighed. "That's no good."

"Mmm," I groaned, putting my head on his shoulder. "Feels like I've got a little alien growing inside me."

"Might've been all the shite food we've been eating the past week," he guessed. "You usually eat pretty healthy."

I nodded my head. "Yeah, honestly, why didn't we buy a van instead, with a little kitchen so we could cook in it?"

Bruce shrugged.

"Because we're rookies, that's why," I concluded, lifting my head up. "We really need to upgrade next time."

Bruce managed a half-smile, which meant my deed that morning was done. That, and to find some ginger tea to settle my stomach, which I sipped on at the roadhouse before we hit the road.

It was an eleven-hour drive to Adelaide, and we wanted to make it in one day, especially since we'd woken up so early. I drove the first stretch as my stomach continued to settle, and I kept thinking how much a do-over wouldn't go astray. If I could just acquire a time machine of some sort so that I could go back and make sure Bruce never meets Joe, as well as ensure that Bruce and I buy a van for our Australian road trip. I could even go further back and see if I could save Mum. Not sure how I would do that, though.

We stopped in the town of Coober Pedy to pick up some snacks, refuel, get a coffee hit, and take photos of the car to post on an Adelaide Buy Swap and Sell page. I drove most of the way as my stomach still wasn't feeling the best and being in the passenger seat made it worse. As disappointed as I was that we were cutting our road trip short, and probably missing a lot of the sights on this long haul to the city, I was, however, rather eager to eat some healthy food once we reached civilization.

Bruce posted pictures of the car, and we agreed that we would try and sell it for a little cheaper than what we paid for it. The car was in high demand, it seemed, because Bruce's inbox was inundated with messages from people wanting to come check it out. Bruce replied to a few of the first people who expressed their interest, telling them that the car would be available for viewing the next day and that we would message them the address later on.

As the hours passed, the red dirt began to disappear, swapped out for floras far greener. The closer we neared Adelaide, as well, the shorter the distance became in between towns. When we were about two hours away, I asked Bruce to find a hotel in the city for us to stay at that night, something we should've done much earlier that day.

"I'll pay for it since you're a little short on money," I told him, pointing down to my wallet in the center console. "You can use my bank card to book it."

"It's okay, I just did it on mine and you can transfer me," he said casually after a yawn.

It was then that I was plagued with the most intrusive of all thoughts, one of which had me questioning whether Bruce was lying about running out of money. I wondered if that was just an excuse for him to escape from our road trip because he was having serious second thoughts about us. Fuck, I hated it when my brain did this. It was as if, even for a brief moment, that I couldn't find the truth throughout the noise in my head.

But this time, the chatter overstayed its welcome, because even once we reached the Adelaide, it hadn't settled down. And even though it was refreshing being back where the lights were bright, I couldn't exactly enjoy it as much as I wanted to when we arrived.

As soon as we checked into our hotel room, which, to make things even more coincidental, was number 1122, I had to go for a walk to clear my head. Anywhere. It didn't matter. I let my breathing elevate even more once I left the hotel room. I then hopped into the elevator, realizing I had no destination in mind. And so, after staring aimlessly for a few moments at the gold numbered buttons on the wall, I hit number thirteen and the elevator started going up.

By then, more thoughts were arising: if Bruce was lying about not having any money— which, I wasn't sure if he was or not—was he lying all those times he said "I love you"?

You most certainly had been lying when you told me you were fine, but even I'd been guilty of that.

The elevator dinged at the thirteenth floor. I stepped out of it as a young couple stepped in. They looked like they were dressed to hit the town, whereas my attire still had dust on it. Thankfully, there was no one on the thirteenth floor, so I could sit on the couch and dial Courtney's number, taking deep breaths while I was at it.

She picked up after a few rings. "Tommy!" She sounded drunk, and there was a wave of indistinct chatter and music in the background.

"Hey," I said crestfallenly, scratching at the material of my chinos.

"How's the road trip, lad?" she pretty much yelled into the phone. "I've been seeing your pics and damn, I am one jealous best friend."

I didn't respond for a moment, just sitting there, thinking of what to say, and how to say it.

"Tommy? You there?" Courtney asked, the chatter and music subsiding.

I sighed. "Yeah. I'm here." I couldn't hold it in anymore. "It's not going too good, Court."

I then cried into the phone, hoping that no one came out of their rooms to see me in tears by their floor's only way out.

"Oh, Tommy, what happened?"

Once I could actually speak, I relayed everything, all the while trying to grasp the reality of it myself. The reality that, when we got back to the East Coast, I didn't have a clue what was going to happen.

"I'm sorry to hear that, Tommy," Courtney said sincerely. "It's so sad to see him suffer like this. And it seems to be taking its toll on you too, which isn't good, mate."

"Court, when I saw him on the side of the highway, my heart just broke."

"Trauma can really hurt people, Tommy. And everyone feels it differently."

"I know, I just wished it wasn't happening, that's all. I don't know what to do anymore."

"You both just need to get back here," Courtney told me. "A little bit of familiarity will do you both good, I think."

My phone buzzed. I put Courtney on loudspeaker. Messages from Bruce:

Hey where did you go?
I'm going to head to bed. So tired.

Come to think of it, I was exhausted.

"Tommy?"

I clicked back into the call. "Yeah, sorry. I agree."

"Go and get some sleep, okay?" Courtney suggested. "You sound like you need lots of that."

"Yeah, you're right." I yawned.

"Let me know how it goes with trying to sell the car tomorrow, okay?"

"Will do. Thanks for the chat, Court. I really needed it."

"Don't be silly. I'm always here for you, anytime. You know that. Even when I'm at a party."

"I wish I was at a party right now," I then said. But, did I really?

"No, you don't, Tommy. You want to be at bedtime sleepy land."

"Okay, I'm gonna go do that."

"Good."

"Have fun," I said. "Love ya."

"Love you too, lad. Bye."

She'd hung up before I could say goodbye back, but I said it anyway.

My breath had returned to a somewhat normal rhythm after my phone call with Courtney. And as I stepped back into the elevator, I felt better than when I was in there last, at least. Darkness welcomed me upon entering our hotel room. Bruce popped his head up from the blankets on the bed, realized it was me, and then fell back asleep. I went straight for the bathroom and into the shower. It was finally time to wash the desert off me. Hopefully not for the last time, but for now. Then, I tip-toed onto the balcony, where I stood and overlooked the city. For some reason, I missed the outback already. It felt like our road trip flew by too quickly to even comprehend.

We'd literally just driven three thousand kilometers down the center of Australia.

My eyes grew heavy the longer I gazed at the twinkling lights of the buildings. It was time to take my best friend's advice and head to the place I could visit when there was nowhere else to go.

The bed was the comfiest I'd layed on since my own back in Coolangatta. Even through the darkness, I could see Bruce's tanned bare back. I went to stroke his shoulder, but then stopped, inches from his skin. I sighed softly, before putting my arm down, rolling over, and falling asleep within minutes.

Tripping Point

When I flicked open my eyelids the following morning, the first thing I realized was that Bruce wasn't next to me. Upon clicking open my phone, my eyes blew up at the sight of the time. How on Earth did I sleep in until eleven in the morning without being woken up by A. my boyfriend, or B. a hotel worker informing me that I was late to check out?

Bruce's suitcase and other belongings were still in the room, so at least it was safe to say that he hadn't done a runner on me while I was sleeping. A vague memory popped into my head, of Bruce telling me that we had people looking at the car early that morning. I messaged him: hey, where are you? Better yet, why am I only just waking up.

He replied almost instantly: right here.

As his messaged popped up, the door to our room swung

open. He was truthful in what he said, because there he was, walking through the door, holding a cardboard tray with two cups of coffee in it, wearing the brightest smile I'd seen on him in a couple of days.

"Good morning, beautiful," he chirped, striding right up to me and planting a big long kiss on my lips.

"Morning," I replied with a slight frown. Had I missed something major? Was there another glitch in the simulation and the world had completely changed overnight?

Not that I was complaining one bit to see my boyfriend in a good mood, but I must admit it was a tad strange to see his emotions take a sharp U-turn in the past twelve hours.

That was just the beginning of Bruce's drastic highs and lows, though. After jokingly telling me he could taste my morning breath, he handed me one of the coffees and ambled out onto the balcony.

Before I could ask him where he'd been or what was going on with the car, he called out, "So, do you want to hear the good news or the bad news?"

I glugged back a generous sip of my warm morning nectar. "Uh, bad news first."

"Okay, bad news is that I have to start work again on Monday. I called the vegetarian restaurant in Noosa to see if they'd take me back, and they were a bit hesitant at first but then they did."

I rolled my eyes, joining him on the balcony. "I should probably do the same with my job at the café. I just can't be fucked yet." I paused before asking, "So, you're going back to Noosa?"

"Yeah, for the time being. I'm still renting that place, so."

"I was gonna say, you could move down to Coolangatta," I suggested.

He completely ignored my comment. "Okay, wanna hear the good news?"

I wanted to ask him why he completely brushed off the conversation as soon as I mentioned us being closer to each other on the east coast. But I did like good mood Bruce on that day, so I surrendered to his infectious sentiments.

"Please, we love good news around here," I answered, my lips curving upward.

"While you sleeping this morning, I went and sold the car," Bruce piped up, lifting his coffee cup to mine for a "cheers".

"No way! So quick!" I exclaimed, stroking his hair. "Good job."

"Yeah," he went on, "Your man who bought it said it was a super rare model and wanted to snap it up as soon as he looked at it. Had to tell the other people wanting to look at it that it'd been sold already."

"That is good news," I confirmed, kissing him on the cheek.

It really was. It meant Bruce and I had more money now. Bruce, most importantly. Turns out he wasn't lying when he said that he was running out of money, because he showed me his bank account and then proceeded to tell me that he was going to have to pay for things with the bundle of cash the guy gave him for the car. At least until he could go to a bank to deposit it into his account.

We had one more night in Adelaide and then we were hopping on a plane back to Brisbane the next morning. Bruce's good mood didn't last long at all, and he spent most of the afternoon writing on the balcony. He was even quiet when we ordered our decadent room service dinner of spiced tofu steaks, mashed potato, and vegetables. He continued to be quiet throughout the evening as we watched movies.

For it being the last stretch of our adventure, it wasn't

upbeat, nor was it awkward or tense. It was just mellow. A tired, dreary mellow.

We both took turns looking pensively out the plane window the next morning. Even though I wished we could travel more, at the end of the day, I just wanted the best for Bruce, even if I feared that he could break my heart at any moment. When he hadn't spoken to me much during the whole flight, I asked if he wanted to save up money to fly back to our home countries.

"We can go back if you want soon," I offered, anything to make him feel better. "I'd feel complete leaving Australia having seen all the places we've been to."

"No. It's okay, Tom," he said miserably. "I'll be fine."

A few weeks passed. He wasn't coping. We spoke less every day now that he was back up in Noosa. He told me there was a wait to see a psychologist. Had I done something wrong for him to become so distant all of a sudden? The cold silence felt all-consuming. I started to become annoyed, so I promised myself I wouldn't message him at all on Thursday, in hope that maybe he would contact me.

He didn't, and then Friday came. Still nothing. I called, still hopeful. He answered almost immediately, with a croaky voice. Something really wasn't right.

"Hey. How are you, babe?" I asked.

"I don't know. I feel like shit," he groaned glumly. "I'm just rundown. I have no motivation to surf. Work is pretty intense, too, back at the restaurant. Sorry I haven't called."

Where had you gone, Bruce?

"It's okay," I said. Whatever he was going through, I just wanted to be there for him.

He sighed. "How are you?"

"I'm okay," I lied. I was far from okay right now. He knew it, I knew it. "I miss you."

"I know. I miss you too," he reciprocated. I could tell he was holding back tears. "My head's just all over the place right now."

"I feel like you don't want this anymore. Us, I mean."

He began to cry. "I don't know what I want. But I know I need help. You're right. And it's probably not making it any easier that I've taken on so much stuff in my life and gone straight back to working so much. I'm just exhausted. I've got a consultation next week, though."

"Don't push yourself," I told him. "I know you like to keep busy, but it's not worth damaging your mental health for."

He kept crying for a few moments. "I know. Thanks, Thomas. I'm sorry that I've been distant. I just—I'm trying to process all my emotions and it's hit me all at once."

"We can fix that with some fun at the doof on Saturday," I said, trying to sprinkle some positivity over the phone like confetti.

He wasn't convinced. Nor had he called me "babe" since we'd left Adelaide. Mackenzie messaged me that week though, a lot. He was the one who told me about the doof that weekend. And, in my desperation, I wanted nothing more than to let off some steam. Mackenzie had finally broken up with Stu and seemed a lot happier than he had on that frosty morning in the grass those months ago. I wish I could've said the same about Bruce. He was morose and silent most of the drive out. We had taken his car, and I agreed to drive as Bruce mentioned he was tired from the journey down to Coolangatta. The rave was at the same property as the one back in June, the sun much warmer now in October, and the air far more humid.

"Where's your friend, uh…Courtney, was it?" Mackenzie

mentioned, zestfully popping his head between Bruce and I from the backseat.

"I think she might be coming out with her Byron boyfriend," I replied. "She said he's really into raves, so I wouldn't be surprised if we see her out. Although, I haven't seen her in a few days, so who knows."

"So, you're from Ireland, aren't you?" Mackenzie asked Bruce, tapping him on his shoulder.

Bruce stared aimlessly out the window. It took him a few moments to respond. I even had to place my hand on his leg. He peevishly moved and wriggled it, finally glancing over.

"Sorry…uh, yeah. In the flesh," Bruce said sullenly.

Mackenzie laughed. "I am a strong fan of Guinness."

Bruce shrugged, his lips quirking upward, but only slightly. "It is the world's best beer."

He then went back to gazing out the window, at the trees flickering by like a camera's shutter. I just wanted to know what was truly circling that brain of his. I had asked, but I wasn't getting any answers. Not the answers I wanted anyway. I knew that whatever it was, I was going to find out one way or another. I just wished it would've been over a Guinness at an Irish pub, so that Bruce would've felt more comfortable than he did.

The heat rose the further we ventured inland. I turned on the air conditioner, something I hadn't done in a hot minute, even in my own car.

"There's no ocean breeze out here," Mackenzie noted.

"Reminds me of Central Australia a bit, hey, babe?" I asked Bruce. "Except, I feel as if the air is warmer out here, and not as many flies, of course."

"Central Australia seemed like more of a dry heat," Bruce added.

Even if it was something simple like talking about the

weather, I was glad I could get some words and a smile out of him, no matter how forced it might have been.

We played Eye Spy on the last stretch of tar before the lengthy dirt road, although there wasn't much around to work with. I would always swamp people when it was my turn with this game.

"Eye spy with my little eye, something beginning with T," I would always say. No one would get it.

"Tree?"

"Nope."

"Tractor?"

"Nope."

"Ticket?"

"Nope."

"Tree...trunk?"

I laughed. "No."

"All right. We give up."

"Tar!" I piped up.

Bruce and Mackenzie both laughed.

"How did we not get that?" Mackenzie exclaimed, whacking Bruce on the shoulder.

"It's literally everywhere," Bruce observed.

And that was how I fooled people every single time. A simple thing like tar got overlooked, but it was everywhere on the road. I mean, it *was* the road. I too had been guilty of overlooking the simple things in life that were prevalent around me; like my loved ones, and the way food tastes.

Within the first half of setting up camp at the doof, we ate magic mushrooms. A tanned Dutch man with dreadlocks approached us at our campsite asking if we wanted to buy some, and it felt rude not to. It might've been the pirate attire he wore that was the selling point. I had done mushrooms back in the UK with Courtney at Boomtown. Mackenzie had taken them a bunch of times too, but it was Bruce's first experience. I told him we didn't have to do them if he wasn't feeling up to it. But he insisted we do it, and after twenty minutes, I could feel it in my entire body: a tingling feeling that was unshakeable.

By late afternoon, the psilocybin had completely taken over. The trees began to breathe in the direction of the wind, and even though there were plenty of people around, it felt like we were inside our own little bubble. Our sanctuary. For someone who had never done mushrooms before, Bruce was handling it splendidly. His hearty giggles made me gleeful, like when he would get excited over the smallest things, like how delicious the market stall food tasted, and when a ground-rumbling bass drop erupted on the dance floor. It was great to see that smile back on his face. Or was it just the drugs doing this?

We locked eyes at the front of the sound system several times, intertwining under the vibrant purple and blue shade sails. Maybe he did need that serotonin boost, or perhaps this was just what he needed to crawl himself out for a while.

Mackenzie had disappeared with a few of his friends, leaving Bruce and I to trundle through the campsites, uncontrollable laughter in our trippy state. We touched a leaf from every tree along our walk, each as green as the last.

"Tommy!" called out a familiar voice from behind me.

It was Courtney and her boyfriend, whom I hadn't met yet. He wore an open button-up shirt, revealing several tattoos on his chest. We weren't sure if they were tripping or not, so it was difficult to reel ourselves out of the world we were in to converse normally with them.

"Hello, my dear sister," I greeted Courtney merrily, skipping to her. Bruce followed behind me.

"Jeez, what are you two suspects up to? I saw you both touching every tree you walked past just now like it was a furry fuckin' wall or something," Courtney chuckled, raising her eyebrows.

I told her about the mushrooms.

"Yeah, that makes total sense now," she said. She turned her gaze to Bruce. "How are you, Bruce? Haven't seen you around in a bit."

His goofy smile faded. He had to think about this one. "Yeah, I've been okay."

He sank his head dejectedly. An awkward silence swept itself from under the rug, into the open air.

"That's good to hear, lad," Courtney smiled. "I know it might not be my place, but if you ever need to talk, I'm here." She then turned to me.

"Uh…yeah, thanks. I'm just gonna…" He looked distressed. "I'm just gonna go for a walk."

Bruce trudged off, alone. Courtney and I locked eyes, to give each other that indication that something wasn't okay. Bruce was sometimes like a flame, warming himself and those around him. But even the best blazes were put out eventually. And his, well, it was nearly extinguished. I knew he was fragile right now, but I didn't comprehend just how much so, especially after that dance floor energy he sprayed me with; like sprinklers on a scorching day.

"Tommy, I didn't mean to offend him," Courtney excused. "I was just trying to help."

I put my hand on her shoulder. "I know. I'd better go see what's up with him. He'll be okay. It was nice to finally meet you, Jake."

Before I could run off, Courtney grabbed me. "Tommy, you

need to watch out for him here, especially when he's tripping. He doesn't seem right."

"I will. Thanks, Court."

I couldn't see Bruce anywhere. I checked the bathroom block. I checked the swimming hole, where Mackenzie and his friends were skinny dipping. They asked me to join them, but I had my boyfriend to find. I checked the campsite, but he wasn't there either. The sun was already starting to set.

I sat in the tent, looking out to the field. The breeze had subdued, and I sighed.

Where was he? He couldn't have gone far. I scanned the tent, sifting through our scattered belongings. His backpack was still there, which was a great sign that he hadn't up and left. His journal lay in front of his bag. It teased me to flick it open, even though I knew that journals were extremely personal. I wanted to know the true fragments that made up the whole of Bruce's mind by now. If he was going to bring me along this journey with him, it wouldn't hurt to read the latest entry, I thought. At least then I could more clearly know what was going on here. I had been told before that the way people project themselves toward us could be extremely different than how they feel inside. And as I began to read, I felt the tingles elevate. Even the black words scribbled on the page looked like they were dancing:

20/09

I woke up today feeling exasperated and I don't know why, but I hope these words on this page help with becoming aware of how I am truly feeling, and why I might be feeling this way. I feel encased to the point where it's like I can't breathe sometimes. I don't know what it is, but it clouds me like the plague. It's a feeling that shrouds me in darkness. I do not feel worthy. I feel powerless, just like I had in Dublin when I was trapped by Joe. How could someone hold such power over me? Thomas is right. I do need professional help so that I can at least live with what happened and manage my emotions. I'm glad I've got this consultation next week, and I do hope that things will get better. I feel unable to get any closer to Thomas, and I don't know why. Ever since we visited Uluru, I've been riddled with anxiety. Something just doesn't feel right. A few months ago, he was the love of my life, but now, I feel as if I'm not worthy of the love he gives to me. I don't want to disappoint him if, for some reason, I don't get better. He deserves the world, and I'm afraid that I won't be able to give that to him, because I don't even love my world. I thought it was fate. We saw those numbers everywhere. Magic, signs from the universe, whatever you'd like to call it. But maybe it was a message, telling us that if we wanted to ever share this kind of love with someone, we first had to love ourselves. I don't know. I'm holding on, but I don't know what I'm holding onto. Something needs to change, because I don't want to feel this way anymore.

I wanted to hold him, to somehow tell him, scream at him, that he was worthy of all of this. But I knew he wouldn't listen; he was too far gone. We had been covered in thick, oozing slime, and our rugged comet edges were far too slippery to grasp. I closed his journal. I sighed, placing it back where I found it. He couldn't discover that I had read it. Not yet anyway.

The sun had disappeared, and things were becoming dark. Laser lights started to spray across the campsites and through the trees. Vibrant glows lit up the branches and leaves, revealing their true broccoli-like outlines. Blurry vision came-a-knocking, followed by racing thoughts. I had to find him. It was his first time on mushrooms, and I couldn't possibly know how it was affecting him. He seemed fine, and then he didn't. That was just how temperamental psychedelics could be I guessed: euphoria to impending doom within the split of a second.

He couldn't have gone far. The car was still here, Mackenzie was still here, Courtney was still here. We were all still *here.* Maybe I was overthinking things, and he just needed some time to cool off. Or maybe these mushrooms were starting to affect me badly. No, I couldn't start thinking like that. But I was, and the thoughts were beginning to take over. Thoughts that he could have hurt himself on purpose, that he was going to break up with me soon, and so on.

I silenced my mind and power-walked toward the flashing lights and the music. It grumbled the closer I got. Everyone glowed pink, red and green, with warped and pixelated faces everywhere I looked. The bass was so strong that I couldn't not welcome it into every inch of my body, projecting it back out through my arms and legs. The crowd of ravers seemed like one big ball of energy, flowing and bouncing from person to person. A bonfire raged in the middle of the dancefloor, people dancing around it like a shrine.

I knew you would be there. Where else would you be?

We locked eyes across the crowd. I breathed deeply, his force strong as he approached. Courtney watched on from the back of the dance floor, having a boogie with Jake. She smiled. Bruce put his head close to mine.

"I've been waiting for you," he whispered in my ear as he kissed it. I felt his tongue lick my lobe, followed by his heavy breath.

His face appeared bolded and outlined. I smiled, and he smiled. We kissed, and I could feel it within my whole body. My skin got the tingles, it felt like I'd just downed pre-workout. At least Bruce was happy and dancing again, though, in my arms.

We slept only a few hours that night, which was better than none. Sex on psychedelics was like whipping up a snack in the kitchen, especially in that darkened tent. When the cock was like a caramel eclair, and its semen an exploded packet of rainbow sprinkles.

The sun woke us up just after dawn. Why was Mackenzie's voice so loud at this time in the morning? Oh yeah, that was right, he hadn't slept yet. I didn't know how he could push on until the next day and act like he hadn't rested. I mean, I knew how, because I used to do that when I was younger. But why would I stay up all night when I had this gorgeous lad next to me? Bruce rustled within the blankets as I sat up.

"I feel surprisingly not fucked this morning," he grumbled.

I chuckled. "Yeah. That's 'cause we didn't take any M last night."

Mackenzie was deep in conversation with an older lad who was shirtless and probably in his mid-thirties. They both sat in camp chairs, sipping on beers, laughing throughout the chatter.

"Morning, sleepy head," the man smiled at me. He had this catchy grin I felt I needed to reciprocate, even if I was still half asleep. I was nowhere near ready to join in with their conversation, though.

"You guys seemed to have had a good night last night," Mackenzie called out to me. "You guys were going hard on the dance floor. Could feel your energy, even from afar."

"It was a very fun night." I chuckled, peering back to Bruce. He gave me a tired smile as if to say, "come back to bed now, please."

Very enticing, but it was getting hot already.

"It's gonna be an even more fun day today," Mackenzie told me as I crawled out of the tent. "Absolutely killer line-up on the music front."

I was ready, but maybe after I'd eaten something full of carbs, brushed my teeth, and then had a coffee. Perhaps it would be then that I would be ready for a drink, or something similar.

"What's your name?" the man asked me.

"Thomas," I said, putting out my hand.

"I'm Travis. We're just camped next door," he told me. He pointed to the esky. "Would you like a beer, Thomas?"

Fuck it. The eating and teeth brushing would have to wait. "A breakfast beer…why not." He reached into the esky, pulled one out, and popped the cap with his lighter.

Travis cast his gaze to Bruce and pointed to the beer. Bruce laughed. "Sure. Why not."

Travis popped a second beer and I delivered it to Bruce, who was still consumed within the tent. He lay on his stomach with his head poking out. I sat in a camp chair, and we all sipped.

"Mackenzie and I were just speaking about how these events are such a vast comparison to early civilization," Travis put forth. "We all share. Reconnect with our roots. No technology. Dance at all hours of the day and night. But, like, I've been going to doofs since I was seventeen. I'm now thirty-six. I've seen it evolve into such a large, abundant community."

Travis had this soothing, weirdly familiar voice that I would have listened to all morning.

"What do you fellas do with yourselves?" Travis asked us.

"I'm a fine artist, and a bartender," I answered.

"Aspiring writer and restaurant waiter," Bruce added.

"I'm an ecologist," Mackenzie said. "Love me some plants."

"Isn't it fascinating knowing that what we do with our lives, or what we aspire to do with our lives, can be used to create so many different things?" Travis said, turning his gaze to the trees.

"What about you, Travis?" I asked.

"I'm a psychologist," he replied.

Bruce and I both locked eyes. Bruce then chugged a mouthful of beer and looked away, slightly rolling his eyes.

Travis observed us, taking a hoppy sip. "I'm sensing something here," he mentioned. "Whatever it is, no one needs to say. It's not any of my business, but if there is something, then just know I'm open ears. I'll be around all day if anyone needs to chat. I'm sure that by the looks of that line-up today, we're all gonna be quite *chatty.*"

Chatty didn't even scratch the surface. It should've been the most euphoric day of all our lives: the music, the colors, the forest. What could possibly go wrong? Nothing, I originally thought as Bruce and I trundled down to the swimming hole, the sun perched upon our necks and bare backs. I had a black bum bag draped across me. We had concocted a jungle drink in a plastic water bottle, inside it a heart-warming mix of whisky, honey and ginger ale, which went down as a treat.

"That Travis lad was a bit of a character, wasn't he?" I said, breaking a somewhat uncomfortable silence.

"Yeah. A bit spooky too," Bruce replied.

Why weren't our silences peaceful anymore, like they had been when we first met? Now, they were just concerning. Perhaps our spark was beginning to fade, blocked by both of our emotions—his lack of self-worth, and my fear of loss.

I then asked, "Were you thinking of chatting to him?"

Bruce sighed. "I dunno, Thomas. I'm not sure if a rave is the right time to just unload my problems like that, even if he is a professional."

"I mean, what do you have to lose, right?" I suggested. "You'll probably never see him again anyway."

Bruce was stubborn and he knew it. It was his way or no way at all. I didn't blame him, because at the end of the day, it was his adversity he had to overcome. Outside sources could only advise him so much. The rest he had to do on his own.

"Maybe," he considered. "I'll have a think about it and see how I feel later on."

Our bare feet gripped the dirt hill as we climbed down onto the rocks, the mud moist and cool on our toes.

"It was really interesting what Travis was saying, wasn't it?" I said as we laid out towels on a rock in the sun. The falls cascaded into the swimming hole beside us. Several other ravers bathed in the fresh-flowing water. I heard one of them call out how "bloody cold" it was.

"I just never knew raves like this had so much history behind them," Bruce added, laying on his stomach.

I also became horizontal, but on my back, the smooth rock soothing my spine into its grooves.

"That sun is so nice, but the more we sip on that drink, the more we're gonna forget to put on sunscreen," I mentioned with a chuckle.

"Mmm," was Bruce's reply. He already had his eyes closed, enjoying the sun too much already.

I reached into my bum bag and fished out the sunscreen. I lathered it on his back, massaging it into his muscles. He moaned in response. I then slapped some over my chest and stomach and looked around. The swimmers had left and an intoxicated couple had joined our party, interrupting the calming sound of the cascading falls. They laughed like hyenas as they crumbled the soil from the hill on their way down. He wore a pair of briefs, her just a bikini.

Once they reached the bottom of the hill, he immediately pinned her into a crevasse near the falls and began to kiss her. She laughed but was also hesitant. They couldn't see us tucked away further down toward the water, but we could see them. Bruce turned around to watch them. We were now the only people here: just us, and them. The lad began to rub her body and kiss her. She giggled but also sighed.

"Not here," she refused, trying to push him off her. "Someone could see."

He didn't give up. He kept kissing her, rubbing up her thighs. "It's fine. No one's down here. We're pretty hidden."

She laughed again. "C'mon. No."

He didn't stop. I looked at Bruce. His lip quivered. His eyes were knives. Before I could calm him, he sprung up and shot off toward the couple. Fuck. Fuck. Fuck.

"Hey, someone's coming," I heard her mutter.

It all happened so quickly before I could even scramble onto my feet. Bruce ripped the lad off her and began to punch him repeatedly in the face.

"What the fuck, man!" the lad bellowed. "Get the fuck away from me."

The woman screamed. I ran over. The lad fought him off, but Bruce kept grunting and throwing punches. I ripped Bruce off him.

Bruce was huffing and puffing. Even he couldn't process what he had just done. He just stormed off, climbing up the hill and out of sight.

"I'm so sorry," I apologized to the couple before chasing after him.

I followed him up the hill and across the grass.

"Bruce!" I called out to him.

He turned around, yelling at me through gritted teeth.

"Don't fucking follow me, Thomas. Just don't. For your own fucking sake, please!"

I stood rooted to the spot. He stormed away and I didn't follow. I just sat up against that same log Mackenzie and I had on that chilly winter morning. My first time in this now surly forest. We spoke about finally meeting the love of our lives one day.

I reached into my bum bag and rolled myself a cigarette. I then cried, because this love now seemed to hurt more than any stab wound ever could. It hurt so fucking much and I didn't know how to stop it. I could've chased after him, but I knew I needed to let him go.

However, I never thought that letting him go meant me returning to our campsite to an empty car space. He was gone. He left me here, kilometers from civilization. He also managed to leave a pile of Mackenzie and I's belongings in the tent.

"He left in a mad rush," Travis explained to me. "I asked him if he was okay, and he just said he had to leave."

I burst into tears, already feeling empty without him by my side, as if a piece of me had just disappeared in that yellow Ford Falcon, dust kicked up by its tyres. Travis sat with me. And it was only then that I realized; perhaps it wasn't Bruce that would seek advice from Travis. It was me that would be the one to talk to him. And his advice, alongside that given to me by Courtney, and by Mackenzie, all led to the same conclusion—that maybe it was time to let Bruce go.

Plunge and Disperse

If Bruce were a drug, his effects were finally wearing off, but the addiction still remained. A part of me wanted to reach out more, but a part of me also wanted to be set free.

"You can't do any more for him," Courtney admitted, drunk on a Friday night. We were at a bar in Coolangatta with Kat. "It's eating you up inside, and he won't talk to you. I mean, Bruce is a good guy, but he just seems so lost right now."

"It's true!" Kat agreed loudly.

"I can't just fuck him off. I love him," I pleaded. "I just want to know what this means for us, because I feel like he's running away from me. Everything seemed so good until the last bit of that fucking road trip."

"Yeah, but things can change within such a short period,"

Courtney advised. "You get to see him tomorrow anyway when we meet him in Brisbane."

As I got drunk that night, I wished he were right there by my side, just like he had been for what felt like eternity. I just wanted to help him through this, whatever he was going through. Little did I know that I was now part of his problem. He didn't even know it yet but looking back, he could feel it. I could feel it. We just didn't want to believe that it was happening. It felt like we'd worked so hard to create a life together, dreaming of a future that neither of us could fulfil right now.

The next morning, Courtney, Kat and I drove up to Brisbane. I'd been hanging out with Kat almost every night that week since Bruce had been quiet and Courtney was busy with Jake. Kat had also been the one to inspire us to take a spontaneous trip to the city. We were spending the weekend there for a concert we'd all bought tickets to. Bruce planned to meet us at our hotel in the city. He said, however, that he could only hang out for the day because he had to work that night. When he arrived, he didn't come and meet us in the hotel. Instead, he asked if I could meet him where his car was parked nearby. I spotted his yellow Ford Falcon in the street behind the hotel. Bruce was perched in it. He saw me approach. My heart was pounding. We'd spent a week apart, and I'd given him the space he needed. Deep down, I knew what was happening here, why he asked me to meet him in this sleepy side street, alone. But I didn't want to believe it.

He hopped out of his car, and we walked toward each other in the middle of the road. We locked eyes, and then he sank his head. We finally faced one another. Restlessness clouded his features, like he needed to get something off his chest. We hugged.

"How are you, babe?" I asked.

"Wrecked," he replied shortly.

I went to kiss him, but he pulled away and kissed me on the cheek. Another stab to the heart. Well, this was a mess, wasn't it? I wriggled my mouth and forced it upon his, holding on for dear life.

"What happened last night? I got a call from you at like 4am?" he asked me.

I ran my fingers through my hair, grabbing it anxiously. We moved to the sidewalk, into the shade beside his car.

"I was just in a…ah…bad place," I said sadly. "I was worried about you. You've been distant."

"Were you drunk?" he quizzed me. "Also, I'm really sorry about leaving you at the doof. I was messed up and I'm really sorry."

I nodded. "That's fine. We got a lift back with Courtney and Jake."

Where did we start? I knew we were both thinking it.

"Is everything okay?" I asked him.

Bruce shook his head. He sighed heavily. "I'm not feeling very good, Tom—about us."

I sighed. "Is there someone else?" It's the first conclusion I came to.

I could tell he was holding back tears. "I swear on my life that there's nobody else."

"Then what is it?" I questioned.

"I don't know. I just can't do this anymore. And it's obviously affecting you now too, which isn't what I want."

I could feel my heart break then and there.

"I don't understand," I said, shaking my head. "You're willing to throw away what we created together? I just want to help you."

"I've tried so hard to push past this feeling, Thomas. Hoping that it will just get better, but it's just not. I wish I wasn't feeling like this, and that I could just push past what happened to me. I'm getting help, but I need to do this alone. Fuck, I feel like such a dick. I'm so sorry."

Tears burned in his eyes. I didn't know how to feel. Angry. Sad. Anxious. Disappointed. Numb.

"I thought you were different," I said bluntly. "I thought *this* was different. You just…"

"We had a great time together, Thomas," he cried. "I tried."

I wanted to blame him. "So that's it?"

He continued to sob. "I think so. I'm so sorry."

I was lost for words. "Why did you ask me to be your boyfriend in the first place? Why did you chase me so hard? I just don't get it."

"I did want to be your boyfriend," he wept. "But I don't know. Everything has caught up with me. I shouldn't have a boyfriend right now."

I studied his teary eyes for a moment, holding back the pain of absorbing every word that left his mouth. I wanted to cry but it wasn't the time. We sat next to each other on the bonnet of his car, just staring off into the distance. Why was this happening to us?

I shifted my gaze toward the end of Lilley Street.

I nodded. "I'm gonna go," I then said.

"Okay," he uttered, wiping away his tears. "We can stay in touch if you want," he added between sobs.

I thought for a moment. "No. It's probably for the best that we don't do that," I admitted coldly, but I didn't mean it.

He nodded. "I understand."

We scanned each other again.

Was this the moment we were meant to hug?

We did. We hugged, and he cried harder, yet I was too numb to reciprocate.

"Thank you so much for the past few months. You've been so supportive of me," he said, holding onto me. I felt torn in two. "You're an amazing person, Thomas, and someone, one day, is gonna be able to love you like I can't. Don't shy away from love, okay?"

I broke away. "Goodbye, Bruce."

"Goodbye, Tom," he sniffed.

I walked away, for perhaps the last time. I wanted to look back, to take one last glance at him. I didn't right away, until I was in the alleyway. Then I turned around. His car drove away out of Lilley Street. And when it disappeared, that's when the tears pooled in my eyes.

Ricochet

It had been less than twenty-four hours since Bruce and I broke up. I woke up next to David in his bed, both of us naked.

It didn't take me long to find a rebound for Bruce in Brisbane that weekend. David and I had been casually talking online just before Bruce and I had met, and I turned to him after Bruce left.

"Serendipity," David called it. I had been on the phone to Dad in Lilley Street, telling him what had happened with Bruce. It was moments after Bruce had ended things with me. This was when David walked past me, and we caught each other's eye. I thought maybe one door closing could lead to another opening. Or perhaps it was the booze and coke I consumed that night with Courtney and Kat in the city which made me believe that. When I bounded into David's place still high at three in the morning, I had no barrier in letting him go down on me and suck my nipples to make me cum.

The novelty wore off, though.

He wasn't you, and this wasn't the happy little life we'd created for ourselves.

I felt hollow and stared up at the ceiling, seeing a sober me floating above, and I didn't like it. The reality of him not being here had hit me, and I knew it wouldn't be the last time I would feel this. I teared up as I gazed into space, hoping that my surroundings would change, and Bruce would roll over and grasp me tightly. Tears filled my eyes and spilled down my cheeks. I couldn't break down, not here in David's room.

And so, I scrambled to find my clothes and slip on my shoes. I then grabbed my phone and wallet and stumbled out onto the quiet street, the sound of nearby construction whirring. It only took me till halfway down the road to lose it, uncontrollably crying in the gutter. I rolled a cigarette to calm my nerves. I was a mess, but the cigarette helped, kind of. It was a band-aid for a bigger problem I hadn't even realized yet.

The hotel Courtney, Kat and I were staying in was only around the corner from David's house. I entered the dark room where the girls still slept, creeping into bed with Courtney, trying my best not to wake her. She breathed heavily as she opened her eyes.

"How did it go?" she asked me groggily.

"I'll tell you later," I said, feeling a tad better after sobbing my heart out on the street. "I need to sleep some more."

Even in the dream world, I still couldn't get away from Bruce. He continued to haunt me, and I did nothing to stop it. I dreamed of him lying next to me, us facing each other on our sides, transfixed in each other's gaze like twinkling stars. I stroked his face. It was silky soft, just like I remembered. Then I woke up, and reality dawned once more. Courtney and Kat had risen, and I guess so had I, with tears in my eyes. Courtney sat on the bed next to me while Kat showered.

"You okay, Tommy?" she asked me, putting her hand on my leg and patting it like a dog. "Ugh, that's a stupid question, I know."

I wasn't sure how to react when my friends were this sad, but Courtney always knew how to make me feel better.

"I just had a nightmare," I admitted, rubbing my eyes.

Courtney smiled at me. "We're gonna have a good day today, okay?"

I looked up at her sullenly. "Okay."

"I found this article this morning, and it says that you can experience the five stages of grief after the loss of a relationship," she informed me, her eyes downcast at her phone. "Number one is denial and isolation. Second is anger. Third: bargaining, fourth: depression, and fifth: acceptance."

I chuckled. "Feels like I'm feeling them all at once. Apart from the acceptance part."

Courtney gave me a half-smile. "You will, though. It won't happen overnight. In the meantime, let's focus on the here and now."

I tried hard to have a good day, but I was miserable, wrung-out, tired. The stroll to the art gallery felt heavy. I ambled through the concrete jungle of ants, all shapes and sizes, my sunglasses on in a crowd full of people, eyes full of tears. Anything could trigger me in this moment, whether it be seeing a gay couple holding hands, or a young woman in the markets singing a sweet song about love.

Not knowing if this would ever get any easier wasn't the hardest part. It was trying to digest the idea of never seeing you again.

Worthlessness consumed me but walking through the

abundance of art and creation in that gallery in Brisbane was a first step in my healing. I loved art, and it gave me inspiration and hope that one day, I could make a living from my creations. We tore our shoes off and stepped into a dark room with a 360-degree sound and graphic immersion. It showcased the perspective of a fish moving around in circles through gray trees and forests. Each time the fish reached a full circle of its environment, the forest grew in size. Art installations of Indigenous people began to appear through the trees, hiding behind the leaves. The fish kept swimming. The people then stopped hiding and joined in a dance. Lights and colors breathed from the trees, and the forest glowed green.

"You've been on your phone all goddamn day, Tommy," Courtney piped up over lunch in the gallery's café. She ripped the device from me. I had just been rereading messages from Bruce.

"Today we will *not* be on our phones," she declared. "Today we're gonna switch off and enjoy what we have around us."

As much as I was hurting, I smiled at her enthusiasm.

"What time is it? Must be time for a drink," Courtney conceded after her ever-so inspirational speech.

"Well, if I had my phone, I'd be able to tell you the time," Kat teased. She'd already had hers taken away by Courtney.

If it weren't for the M, the concert that night probably would've made me cry. I didn't cry that night, though. The love buzz didn't let me, nor did the wild Courtney or Kat. I sang along with the blonde goddess on stage.

I wanted to sing those exact lyrics to you, Bruce. I wanted to ask you if I was on your mind, and if you'd remember me if we became a thing of the past. I wondered if I screamed the words loud enough, you'd be able to hear me.

The love buzz eventually wore off and I was back to grieving my loss. I cried the whole drive home back to Coolangatta the next day, smoking a cigarette every half hour. Turns out Bruce wasn't my only problem at this point in time. *I* was my problem too.

I drew a sketch of Kings Canyon on a piece of canvas that afternoon, which, unsurprisingly had all the memories from our road trip flooding back. The dolphin painting, the hike through that red rock land of wonder, our first argument. It was like I was holding onto all of our memories and playing them back one by one. It was only then that I would hit that self-destructive replay button and the cogs in my brain would start going round and round again.

I soon decided the time had come to call home again.

"Hey, Dad," I said in a dark, emotionless tone. I was tired from crying. My eyes were red and sore.

"Tom, mate. How are you holding up?" were his first words. He sounded concerned.

I sighed. I didn't know what to say at first.

"Tom…talk to me," he pleaded softly.

"I'm not doing too good, Dad." It was the truth. I felt terrible. I felt worthless, disgusting, unmotivated. "I just miss him so much, and knowing that I might never see him again…"

"It was a surprise to me too, son. When I came to visit, I really did see something in him. I saw potential for you both. He's a silly boy for leaving you. But you know, everything happens for a reason. You know that. I know that."

"Why? Because I rushed into a relationship yet again? Just like I did with Peter…?"

"Sometimes we have to go through these lessons to really love ourselves," Dad explained.

I held back another wave of tears. "Well right now, I don't."

"And that's okay, Tom, but you will. You just need to start focusing on you and get yourself realigned. It's going to be hard at first, but eventually you'll get there. Are you sure it's not time for you to come home?"

I sighed and breathed heavily. "I don't know. Maybe I should."

"It's up to you, but you've always got a place here. Remember that."

I looked over at the painting I had drawn of Kings Canyon. "I'll come home soon, Dad. There're just a few things I have to do first."

Self-Reflection: Part I

When I returned to my life after that weekend in Brisbane, everything was different. I didn't feel contentment like I did before. I was much quieter too. In fact, I hardly talked to anyone.

I couldn't accept the fact that Bruce was gone. He was just a drive up the coast, but now, he felt much further away. A part of me just wanted to drive up and see him, to pull up at his beach shack and yell at him, tell him how much I loved him. But even I knew that was a terrible idea.

I couldn't believe it. I didn't want to believe it. I wasn't that happy, bubbly person at work anymore either. I mean, I was surprised the café rehired me in the first place. I thanked Courtney for that one.

It was like the planet had significantly shifted on its axis and I had been left behind to pick up the pieces, like an outsider in my own world. Something had to change, but I wasn't quite sure what yet.

"Everything all right, Tom?" my boss Julie asked me numerous times.

If she said those words one more time, I would most certainly lose my shit. I had already been fighting back tears all day, just waiting to finish my shift so I could let them all flow free.

The next Saturday had me hungover and lonely. I had called in sick to work, and just lay in my bed, staring up at the ceiling as my head spun, like that moment where you would stand up too quickly and everything pixelates into a fade.

I endlessly scrolled through social media, hoping that a message of hope would pop up. I craved connection, but the only message I received that morning was from David.

DAVID
Hey, how are you?

THOMAS
Hungover and in bed. How about you?

DAVID
I'm very much the same. Could do with cuddles

THOMAS
Me too

DAVID
Would you like to come over? I'll cook dinner for you

I thought I didn't have anything else better to do at this point. So, before driving up to David's, I caught up with Kat over breakfast. Kat and I had spent the night at my place getting drunk and high while Courtney was down in Byron with Jake for the weekend.

I chomped down on a plant-based beef burger with my coffee.

"What are you gonna do for the rest of the weekend?" Kat asked me, hiding the hangover behind her sunglasses. "The house will probably be super empty without Courtney."

"I think I'm going to go see that guy from last weekend," I admitted, sipping on my coffee and staring out to the festivities on Coolangatta Beach across the road.

A surfing competition was in full swing. It reminded me of nothing but him, out there riding those waves, dancing in the salty water.

"Maybe it's a good idea you get away for the weekend," she suggested. "If it makes you feel better, do it."

It was a gloomy day, yet the humidity crept in like it always did in the latter part of the year. The drive to Brisbane felt endless along the Gold Coast, even though it was only an hour away. I felt anxious on the drive up, and I wasn't sure if it was the aftermath of the hangover, or whether it was my gut telling me that going to see David was a bad idea. I didn't turn around like I should've, and I had to drive past Lilley Street to get to David's. I drove slowly, catching a glimpse of where my heart was broken.

I parked my car on the corner of the street David lived in and just sat there for a moment with the engine off. Something about this just didn't seem right. Why was I here, again? I hopped out of the car and could already see him at the end of the street waving to me, beaming with his toothy grin, wearing what looked like boxers and a T-shirt.

"Hey there, stranger," he greeted me, giving me a tight squeeze. "How was the drive?"

I reciprocated the embrace, but not as tight. The bomb inside me was ticking and it was only a matter of time before I blew, taking Lilley Street and David with me.

"It was good," I lied. "How's your week been?"

"Busy, but glad it's the weekend," David said, grinning at me and ushering me inside. "So, I was gonna cook a stir-fry for dinner. You're vegetarian, aren't you?"

"Yeah. You remembered." I was surprised.

"Definitely not something I could forget. Same with that sexy accent of yours. Are you hungry yet?" he asked.

"Not yet." Uncomfortable already, I dropped my bag on the ground and sat on the bed. I couldn't even look at him, not that he wasn't an attractive lad; I was just fractured right now. It was a terrible idea that I was here with him.

"Did anything interesting happen this week at work?" I asked, trying to make small-talk.

David was a marketing manager. "Nothing out of the ordinary," he shrugged. "It was just hectic busy as usual. How about you, how was yours?"

Should I have told him that I had been the lowest I'd been in a very long time, so lost and confused with life that I might just cry thinking about it?

"It was pretty average." I pulled my punch. "I just worked and exercised a bit."

I needed to work out more. These endorphins needed releasing, and they obviously weren't right now with how low I had been feeling. I had been drinking alcohol and puffing on smokes all week. Anything to plaster over the pain I felt.

David put his hand on my chest and moved closer to me, until he pretty much had his groin to my thigh. The longer he touched me, the harder his semi got. It wasn't even flattering like it was last Saturday night when I was high and horny, and not because I wasn't physically attracted to David, but because I had no self-esteem or love for myself right now. He kissed me on the cheek and then slowly moved on top of me. We locked lips. The time bomb ticked louder, ready to explode.

I gently pushed him off me. He didn't resist. He was a good lad, I could tell. He wasn't going to disrespect my wishes.

"I can't do this," I said at once, breathing out heavily. "I'm sorry."

"Is everything okay?" he asked, genuinely worried.

"I'm sorry. I shouldn't be here. This isn't fair on you," I told him truthfully. "I'm still very hung up on my ex, and the break-up is still quite fresh."

"That's okay, Tom. I understand." David stopped touching me altogether and just sat beside me, a comfortable distance away. "I know what it's like. But do you have to leave? You drove all the way up here. We don't even have to do anything physical if you don't want to. We can just have dinner and watch Netflix and fall asleep."

I took a brief moment to think about it, gazing listlessly at the Bob Marley banner over the window to his bedroom. "I need to go," I finally said. "You seem like a great lad, but I just need to be on my own right now."

It was the opposite of what I wanted, but it seemed like I had no other choice.

He nodded. "I get it. Do what you have to do."

I grabbed my backpack and walked toward the door. All I could say now was, "Thank you," before I was back on the street, the sun setting. A gust of wind blew all the trees' leaves about. I didn't even make it back to the car before the tap to the pipe of my tears burst open. I rolled myself a cigarette and drove myself out of there, passing Lilley Street for the last time. It was time to shed the layers and if that meant solitude, then I would just have to learn to become my own best friend.

Self-Reflection: Part II

With a dry mouth, I scrambled for water. Then I just lay there, watching my fan spin round and round. Waking up meant I had to accept that Bruce really was gone, again. He faded from my life more and more every day. Sometimes I didn't think about him, but it could be anything that would trigger a memory, triggering that longing for what we had. A lot of those memories were brought up by songs. Songs that we had listened to together. I tried to embrace my solitude by painting, but I just had no inspiration and I didn't know what was wrong with me.

I had woken up to an empty house for the third day in a row. After a miserable scroll through all my socials, I finally crawled out of bed, the blinding light of the morning rays fixed upon me. I just had to get to the kettle, and I'd be fine. The only sounds in this lonely little house today were creaks on the wooden floorboard as I paced in the kitchen. Waiting for the water to boil, I stared aimlessly out the kitchen window to the lime trees outside, the branches swaying with the wind. There didn't seem to be one cloud in the sky. Most folk would be jumping out of bed to get down to the beach, wade in the saltwater and bask in the sunshine. As for me, I just needed my morning caffeine hit.

It was my last day off before I had to go back to work at the café. The place that I had somewhat enjoyed before the break-up but now seemed like a place of restlessness and resentment.

After my coffee, I sauntered into the bathroom and studied myself in the mirror. I knew it was time. I didn't want to hide my pain with a bottle of liquor and a pouch of tobacco anymore. That's what I had done with my first boyfriend back in London three years ago. It took a long time to get over him because I just hid my feelings behind intoxication instead of facing the pain head-on.

I whacked my blue gym shorts and black singlet on, followed by my black corduroy cap. I took a last look at myself before I left the house, feeding myself a weak but determined smile.

"Hey, what can I do for you?" the blonde woman asked me as I entered the gym. She sat behind the front desk, wearing a bright blue collared shirt.

"Hey." I drew a sheepish grin, lost for words. "I'd like to join some sort of training program."

"Sure," she said less robotically. I think she knew that I needed her help and the only way she would be able to communicate with me would be to come down to my level. "We offer a few structured training programs based on your fitness levels and goals. I'm a personal trainer myself."

Her inspirational attitude made me smile. "Sign me up," I said.

In fact, I started a program that day. No alcohol. No cigarettes. No drugs. No junk food. My detox was underway.

I returned home from my first guided resistance workout feeling energized, and sore. It had been a long time since I had been to a gym.

The house wasn't as quiet as I left it, though. Courtney was home from Byron Bay, and welcomed me as soon as I stepped foot through the front door. House music erupted from the living room, and I could smell the alcohol on her breath the moment she hugged me.

"How are you, Tommy boy?" she greeted me, a thrilled grin on her face. Her eyes were puffy and black and her hair messy.

"I'm good. I just joined a gym," I said, clearly not impressed that our humble abode had been transformed into a club while I was gone.

"Nice, nice!" she exclaimed, squeezing my hips until I squirmed into the living room.

A shirtless Jake slouched back on the couch.

"Thought we'd finally come hang out in Coolangatta for a bit," Courtney said. "We needed a change of scenery."

Jake waved at me through glassy stoned eyes. "Hey, dude. How's it goin'?"

He reached out his hand. I shook it, trying to hide my lack of enthusiasm. "Good."

"You want a drink?" Courtney asked me. "We've got Bacardi. We went on a bit of a bender in Byron over the weekend."

"Nah, I've got work early tomorrow," I said bluntly, continuing to my room. "I want to work on my art tonight too."

"C'mon, Tommy. I did all of this for you." Now she seemed offended, but I didn't care. "I thought maybe you could use a good time with good company, y'know."

I kept the peace.

"I'm just tired after the gym, Court," I said, which was the truth. "Thank you, though."

I shut the door before I heard a sassy, "Suit yourself," from her.

They turned down the music. I whipped out a diary planner I had bought from the newsagent on my way home from the gym. I began to plan out my training schedule, and what I was going to eat for the week based on my nutrition plan. It felt good to have my life organized again, even if that included muscle aches and cripplingly anxious withdrawals. One moment I'd be pushing my body in the gym—lifting weights, releasing crucial endorphins I'd been starved of for some time—and the next I would be longing for him again, to have my head resting on his chest, hearing those deep heartbeats. There were times where it felt like someone had died. It was true to a certain extent. Our past selves had died. Somewhere between that road trip of freedom, and accepting the reality that we didn't really know what we were doing. We gave it all away for the spontaneity and adventure, something we couldn't have forever.

I just wanted to talk to you, have you close to me. But that's not what was meant to come from this part of my journey, was it? We had our own demons to kill.

I'd finished the second week of my training program with flying colours. And by that, I meant it was starting to feel like another drug. It was the kind of drug that was good for me, though, the kind that would help me physically and mentally. On my cardio days I would run, as far as I could, my feet sinking beneath the sand. I listened to Dermot Kennedy, my idolization for his serenades soothing and healing every inch, every sore muscle, every tear jerked.

One afternoon, on the walk back to my car from the beach,

I spotted a man sitting in his four-wheel-drive, staring out at the water. I tried not to alert him, but I could see his glassy eyes of sorrow. What was this man dealing with? What had he lost? Or, who? I wanted to knock on his window, to let him know that everything was going to be okay. But I decided not to. Even on the darkest of days, sometimes we have to be our own savior.

"Hey, Tommy," Courtney called out.

I was in bed, reading. I put the book down. Courtney asked if she could come in.

"Of course," I said. She was always welcome. She knew that.

Courtney sat on the bed at my feet. I knew there was something important she wanted to talk about. "What's up?"

"I just got off the phone to Mum," she replied. "Made me really miss home. Except for the fact that they'll be coming into winter soon."

I chuckled. "How's Nikki?"

"She's good. She misses me. Well, *us.*" Courtney paused a beat before continuing, "How's everything going with your training program? I can see that you're making progress so far. It's definitely showing. You seem a lot brighter."

I loved that she noticed. I'd been working hard to push myself out of that deep black hole of misery. I know it's not the only way one can heal from grief. But in this instance, it was mine. Turns out the world was still beautiful, yet I had my back turned to it for a little while.

"Thanks, Court," I said, blushing a little. "It's something I had to do if I was ever going to get some progress with everything. I've definitely learnt my lesson now."

"And what's that exactly? I'd love to hear it."

"Well, there's a saying that everyone has a garden," I

explained. "Some are neatly kept; some are a little rugged; some just need a little bit of color. The state of your garden says a lot about you. There will come times when someone will pop their head over your fence and gaze at your garden. And you have to say to that person, 'You can look, but you can't touch. I'm the only one that can maintain it'. But if you enjoy that person looking at your garden, and if they have a bright, well-watered garden of their own; only then can you appreciate both gardens side by side."

Courtney's mouth quirked into a smile. "I've been trying to tell you that for years, but obviously my words aren't quite as colourful as that. It's true, though, and it's great to see you working on that garden, lad. Wait until it's done. Boy, you'll be bloody unstoppable. Your plants will be up in all the best art galleries. In fact, tell you what the best thing is about all the rain in the UK?"

"What's that?" I asked.

"Everything's so green," she said. "A place for gardens to thrive. Let's go home, Tommy."

"But, what about Jake?"

Courtney laughed. "It was never a forever thing, him and me. The initial spark is disappearing already."

"So, we're gonna go back?"

"I think it's a good idea, before the humidity really sets in," Courtney suggested. "It's already getting a little too hot for my liking."

Courtney and I thought more alike than I realized sometimes. We were both profuse sweaters too. Living in England our whole lives really had made us uber-sensitive to hot weather.

"I do want to go back," I agreed. "How about when I get back from Central Australia in a few weeks, we go? There's just one more thing I need to do here in Australia. Just for my own state of mind and clarity."

Courtney rolled her eyes. "Do you *really* need to go all the way back to the desert?"

"If I don't, I'll feel incomplete on the journey I went on out there," I tried to explain.

Courtney smiled. "I don't understand that, pal. But, do what you need to do."

In The Wild

It felt like it had been a while since I had bought anything useful for myself. Every hiking backpack I browsed in the sports store seemed perfect, but I always struggled making decisions. That's why having a friend like Courtney proved essential.

"Are you sure you actually wanna do this?" she asked, and not for the first time. "You know there's plenty of hikes you can do back home."

I was sure. It might not have made sense to Courtney, or even my father, but this last adventure was my closure. My closure from Bruce, and from Australia. I had to do that hike. The Giles Track. The one that I wanted to do so badly when I was at Kings Canyon but didn't because Bruce didn't want to.

"This is the one you want," Courtney said confidently,

pointing at a green and gray hiking bag. "Not too big, not too small."

I gave her a grin of appreciation. "It's perfect."

"Please call me as soon as you finish the hike, okay?" Courtney reiterated as she dropped me at the airport two days later. Dad had said the exact same thing.

"And don't let those flies get the better of you," she added. "Gosh, you're gonna be a full-blown explorer when you're back, lad. We're not gonna know what to do with you."

I chuckled. "See you soon."

As I disappeared through the terminal, I felt it; my first solo adventure awaited me. I wondered what I would find when I stepped back into the dust. Two domestic flights. One overnight backpack. A twenty-two-kilometer walk. Then, it would be time to go home.

What I found first when I hopped off that bus from Alice Springs to Kings Canyon was flies, lots of them. But I wasn't surprised. They swarmed to the moist patches on my back, harassing me for a few kilometers before I arrived at Kathleen Springs.

Kathleen Springs was mostly empty that afternoon. I took a breather in the parking lot and signed my name down on the walker sign-on ledger before continuing onto the Giles Track. Into the valley, I watched on as some tourists were taking photos of an injured dingo. It had been infected with mange, causing its skin to rot, a bit like a zombie virus. I felt a sudden empathy for the creature and thought about how much like us they could be sometimes. Except for the most part, we would let our inner pain eat away at us instead.

The sound of the very few tourists diminished a hundred

meters along the narrow dirt track. As the spinifex scratched at my bare legs, I soon knew I'd made a terrible decision not wearing trousers. I walked at a fast pace through the scrublands, my earphones in and mindful melodies flowing. I cocked my head toward the ground, glad that I did. Purple surrounded me, with sunburnt flowers that had spiky stems. Perished lavenders I liked to think of them as. Accompanying them were twiggy bushes in the shape of flames. I now stood on a mountain ridge where the ground became so dry that it hardened and cracked in a perfect symmetry, imprinted like sacred geometry. Shifting my gaze further into the valley, I spotted a family of wallabies hopping on the side of the mountain ridge, into a safe cave. I couldn't help but smile.

The trail ahead of me was quite flat so I ran with high-beat music in my ears, dodging the trees as I picked up the pace faster and faster. I ran at least a kilometer before I was out of breath. And there I was, in the middle of the bush, nothing but trees and red dirt surrounding me. I pulled out my earphones and enriched myself in the serene silence, catching my breath back. I sat down on a nearby rock and ate a muesli bar from my bag.

I flicked back to a memory, of those muesli bars Bruce and I ate on the edge of Mount Greville, the calm winter wind soothing our sweaty skin. Time had been of insignificance up there as we caught the view of the lake and rolling hills at our brows.

The moment I stopped daydreaming and realized that there wasn't an oasis of any kind out here in the desert, I wondered why the hell I was in such a rush for. I had wanted to embark on this trail for a while now, so why didn't I just take my time? I began to think that perhaps my intentions for this journey stemmed from my yearning to truly do something for me; to show myself that I was capable of not just slapping paint on a blank page, or sketching without shaking. But here I was, in the exact place I wanted to be. I had painted it, manifested it, dreamt it.

Did I feel accomplished? Not in the exact way I had previously imagined. I thought this hike would be my way out of the worries. But it wasn't until I finally got here, in the flesh of the vast plains and endless scrub, that I realized there was in fact no way out. Life was always going to be these chapters of ups and downs. And once I realized this, it made much more sense. I used to seek happiness, and only happiness.

When I was younger, whenever I would feel sad, people would always tell me to try and be happy. The sad emotions were often rejected. And I don't think I ever fully felt them, because to me, they were seen as something I shouldn't be feeling. But when I grew older, I realized that there was no escaping the sadness. I would feel it numerous times throughout my life, sometimes on the most unexpected of days, in the same way I would feel happiness, and freedom.

As I chewed down to the last few bites of the muesli bar, I promised myself that I would do more things for me from then on. I promised myself that it was time to welcome my sadness just like my happiness. I had chosen to love a fractured soul who wasn't ready to let himself go in the same way I was ready to. And that was okay. It hurt, and that was okay. I had a right to feel that way. I guess the thing I couldn't shake from this was that, deep down, I knew Bruce loved me like I loved him, yet I still couldn't have him.

After eating and replenishing with water, I walked closer to the edge of the George Gill Range to catch a better view of my surroundings. It had me awestruck: the plains of browns, yellows, greens and oranges stretching as far as the eye could see.

I could spot the roadhouse we stayed at in Kings Canyon. I

really was in the middle of nowhere. And there, in the middle of nowhere, without warning, I would face my worst nightmare.

It started with a soft hiss, and a warm brush against my leg. I peered down to inspect what this entity was, feeling sheer panic, like when you dig into your pocket and your phone or wallet is no longer there.

I glanced at a large brown snake weaving across the ground next to my feet. The adrenaline made me run. I ran as fast as I could, but I kind of wish I hadn't, because it was only soon that I lost balance in terror, tumbling off the side of the cliff face.

The first feeling I had was collision, slamming into several rocks on my tumble down the rabbit hole. Pain punched each body part as I rolled to the bottom of the range, taking a surfeit of rubble with me.

I reached the ground, bruised and battered after multiple tumbles and failed attempts at gripping to the cliff face. I think I lost consciousness for a few moments just from the shock. I was focused on nothing but my leg, which was in agony. I stared down to my knee. Multiple deep scratches caused rivulets of blood to trickle. I tried to rise, but my left leg wouldn't let me put any weight on it. I screamed at the attempt.

"Help!" I bellowed, dispersing a deep echo through the valley. No response.

The sun started to set. The evening alpenglow settled, leaving a brisk dusk breeze. I surely was in trouble here. The temperature dropped with the sun, and I managed to crawl under a tree nearby. I was covered in cuts, bruises, and dust, low-key panicking but also trying to stay calm. I couldn't help but yelp and groan at the sight and feel of my leg, so tender and brittle. I knew as soon as I regained consciousness at the bottom of the mountain range that I'd done something to it. I'd never experienced this sort of pain before and it was the only thing I could focus on. I was terrified, and I'd seen *Into the Wild* enough times to know how situations like this ended.

Night approached quicker than I thought it would. I gave up on the intention of crawling back up the mountain, it was far too steep. I was in no state to be climbing, nor to walk anywhere for that matter. Thankfully, I brought my pop-up tent, which I somehow managed to set up in spite of the pain. I would've made an emergency call, but my phone had gone flat. Next time I'll bring a portable charger, I thought. If there even was a next time.

As I lay in my tent, listening to the dingos howl, I tried as hard as I could to not think about the ache. I reached into my bag and popped two ibuprofens, hoping that would numb me a little. I panicked as I took a generous gulp, down to my last bottle of water. I hoped that the rangers would send a search party the following day when they realized I never finished the trail. I had high hopes when I closed my eyes, too exhausted at this moment in time to dwell on where I was, and what had happened to me, or how seriously lost I was in this desert. But it didn't take long to come to terms with how much trouble I'd really gotten myself into.

Surprisingly, I slept through the night. The blinding light of the morning sun struck me, and I woke up covered in sweat, zipping open the tent to gather fresh air. The first thing I did was gulp down some water to hydrate myself. I had to be sparing as I was now down to half a bottle. I really didn't prepare myself for this "overnight hike". I was out of food too. I just sat there, outside the tent, under the tree, thinking of what my next move would be. Maybe I was dead, and this is what hell looked like.

I spent the morning yelling "help" as loud as I could, over and over, hoping that someone would be hiking the track and hear me. Alas, no luck. I'd lost my voice by the time the sun reached the center of the blue dome. This made me terribly thirsty, and I was now close to a few mouthfuls of water left. Perhaps a helicopter would come for me soon. I could feel myself becoming weaker the longer I was deprived of food. I hadn't eaten anything since that muesli bar. I tried not to focus on things like hunger, and the still-throbbing pain from my leg. I tried to focus on the scenery and napping during the day under the tree on my sleeping bag.

It felt like forever before the sun set again, though I managed to crawl to gather some nearby wood and dry leaves to make a little fire for myself for the night. But, it wasn't big enough to send a smoke signal.

I caught myself gazing deeply into the flames. Reaching into my bag, I fished out that folded up piece of paper, the same one with those poetic words of love written on them. I unfolded it and stared at the words. It was like I wanted to make myself cry. I closed my eyes, letting the flames almost kiss my face with warmth. I could almost taste marshmallows, their sweet toasted gooey centers. I could feel Bruce's warm hand rub my left shoulder as we sat by that magnificent fire at Lake Moogerah. It was enough to see me through the night, and hope for a better day.

29

Redemption

For being so scared and alone, I didn't find it hard to sleep out there in the wilderness. Especially if I laid on a comfortable angle on my back, which stopped my leg throbbing.

I woke up on the second morning to the ear-deafening sound of a helicopter. And springing up in my sweaty state, I clambered out of the tent as fast as I could. Was this the start of the search party? I mean, I had been out here for two whole days now. Today was the hottest of them all and I'd officially run out of water.

My mouth dry and coarse like leather, I squinted at the sky. It wasn't a helicopter, just a figment of my imagination. And of hope. It was the driest of days, or maybe it was just the fact that I was weak, injured and feverish. I sheltered under the same immense tree next to my tent, examining my injured leg. The cuts were now purple and angry. I turned my gaze heavenward, at an eagle soaring high in the sky.

As I perched myself up against the trunk that had been my sanctuary, I noticed the dry rock holes in the ground that I presumed filled with water when it rained. I began to dig into the red dirt and mud beside the tree. I used dead tree wood as a shovel, digging deeper and deeper into the earth. I found very little liquid, clambering on all-fours to lick at it. I didn't know whether to vomit or feel grateful. A little bit of both at this stage. Then, glancing down at the scratched-up watch on my wrist, I could've sworn it was eleven twenty-two.

Ouch! What the fuck was that? I looked up at what had poked me. No! It couldn't be.

"How is this possible?" I gaped at her. Her being my mother, standing before me, wearing the same turquoise dress she was wearing at The Blue Bar in Alice Springs those months ago. She just smiled at me, not feeling the need to answer my question.

I shook my head, pressed my back up against the tree, fragments of mud around my lips. I screamed at the top of my lungs, then cried. Was I going completely crazy? Was this the end? Was I going to die out here? I didn't want my family back in England to hear about me on the news: *British Backpacker Dies in Australian Outback*. No. I couldn't let that happen. But I was also at the point of giving up all hope of survival.

"Don't worry," she whispered to me.

"Y-you're not real," I groaned weakly, shaking my head more rigorously.

"I've always been real, Thomas," she said, smiling at me. "I'm always with you no matter what."

"Why are you here?"

She didn't answer. She gave me a last smile, then disappeared.

I extracted a memory of when I was a baby. My mother would bathe me in the kitchen sink and hold me tight in her sweet, nurturing arms, until I was cleaned of all impurities.

It felt like I was going bonkers, like all this sun and dehydration was sizzling me to cinders. I closed my eyes and was taken somewhere else. Somewhere colder, fresher. Somewhere dramatic, somewhere scenic. The fresh smell of pine-trees lingered within my blocked sinuses. The interspersed tingle of snowflakes dropped from the sky upon my neck, towering rocky mountains just visible within the thick mist. Everything: the smells, the feelings, the sights, it all made me think of her—my guardian angel on the days where I was at arm's length of giving up. My boots crunched through the icy powder beneath my feet, and I stamped in it several times, before I began to slowly sink. My ankles numbed and tightened.

I opened my eyes back up. A plethora of clouds now blocked the sun, and a cooling sensation tingled my skin.

Was that thunder? Or was I just imagining another glimmer of hope like the helicopter?

Nope, there it was again. The clouds darkened and floated toward me, the former red dust desert switching to a shade of dim beige. From what I'd just seen, I had no expectation that any of this was real. I could've been in a warped-out simulation at this point and I wouldn't have questioned it one bit.

I closed my eyes again, the sky growling. And there it was: my hope, arriving safe and sound. It started with one drop, then another. I tilted my head to the sky, breathing deeply, in and out. In and out. In and... Yep, this was definitely real. It was the realest thing in my entire life. The droplets accelerated to patters on the dirt, the smell fresh and earthy, just like I had remembered. I opened my mouth and let the water fill me up like a glass. I thought back to that day in Buderim, walking around without a rain jacket, holding his hand and smiling while we sipped a morning brew at that shipping container overlooking the misty coastline.

But I wasn't there anymore. I was here, given one last chance. The mud washed off my face in the torrential downpour. What were the odds of rain on this day in the driest of all land? I couldn't help but laugh, as loud as I possibly could. It wasn't like anyone could hear me anyway. But then again, no one needed to.

I wiped my face clean so I could see clearly. And there it was: the object to the end of my demise. I just had to write for help. I picked up a large piece of sandstone from the ground and crawled over to a big boulder about five meters away. It was there that I began to carve "HELP" in the biggest letters I could draw. The letters began to drip down the rock in the rain as I wrote them, but they were still noticeable.

How did it take days to come up with this idea? Maybe it was my will to live finally coming to the fore. Maybe before this moment, I didn't want to be found or saved.

I smiled to myself weakly as the sound of a helicopter approached, even harder when I could feel the wind of the blades mess up my hair even more than it already was. I laughed with a beaming grin by the time I felt those hands of comfort and heard the words, "Everything is going to be okay."

My eyes closed and I thought of *me*.

Dominoes

A light sprayed across my eyes, although this didn't convince me that I was still alive.

"Hey, Thomas…can you hear me?" a woman's voice called.

I regained sight, which was a tad blurry at first. White walls, plastic tubes, and crinkled white sheets. A repetitive beeping from beside me. I wasn't dead, it seemed.

"Where am I?" I knew I was in a hospital, but where exactly was I? The plump woman to my side wore navy blue scrubs and a smile that I was far too weak to catch. If only I weren't so groggy.

"You're at Alice Springs hospital," the nurse informed me. "Thomas, how is the pain in your leg?"

My left leg was elevated on a pillow. An IV drip had been inserted into the crease of my arm.

I coughed. "Not too bad."

"Good stuff. You got brought in just at the right time. Any longer out there, and it could've been a different story."

She proceeded to take my blood pressure. A white and black analogue clock ticked on the wall. Unfortunately, it wasn't twenty-two past eleven. Perhaps that time had passed.

"Do you remember much?" she asked.

I nodded. Everything. I explained to her what I remembered as best I could, except for seeing Mum out there in the desert. I would keep that to myself, for now at least.

"It's lucky you're still alive, honestly," she told me. "There must be someone watching over you."

I daydreamed out the window. The clouds had dispersed, unveiling a thick blanket of sunshine. "There is," I said. She came in many forms, my mother. I now knew that she was with me at the best of times, and the not-so-best.

"Where's your accent from?" I asked the nurse.

She chuckled. "New Zealand. Although, I'm not as far away from home as you are."

Where was home? Was it a destination, or was it the people in my life that had stuck by me through every wave, every hurdle, every still lake—in this thing we call life?

Out there in the parched wilderness, it seemed like a test of the loyalty I truly had for myself. Until this year, I thought London was the only place I could feel at home.

And just like that, there was another one of my angels, and it was then that I felt completely safe. All it took was that familiar face. That luscious blonde hair. That smile as if to say, "you fucking idiot." We were in the middle of Australia, but I could undoubtedly call this place home now that she was here.

"You are one stupid sod," Courtney piped up, shaking her head.

Fair. That was the greeting I deserved. I couldn't help but smile when she rushed over and hugged me tight.

"A stupid news-headlining sod," she corrected herself.

"What are you talking about?" I asked her.

"Oh yeah, I didn't get to the part about you being all over the news," the nurse said. She turned to Courtney. "I'll leave you to do the filling in. I'll be back later on."

She left, and Courtney shook her head some more. Her smile faded. "You could've died out there. Great headline, though: *British backpacker lost in the NT for three days, survives.*"

I couldn't help but chuckle. "Thought it was going to be my art that brought me that kind of attention."

"Thomas!" she yelled. "C'mon, this is serious. I lost it when I saw you on the TV getting wheeled out of that helicopter. And in that moment, everything became so real. We've been friends for so long, Tommy. You're pretty much my brother. I can't lose you."

Courtney hardly ever cried. And if she did, she did it when no one was watching. For the first time in years, I reaffirmed that she actually had tears stored away in those ducts. I sighed as she pulled over the cream plastic chair in the corner of the room.

"I know. I'm sorry. I never wanted it to end up like that," I apologized. "At first, I just wanted to complete the journey that Bruce and I started. But then it began to feel like I was trying to prove a point. I'm not sure who to, though."

"Probably to him at first, until you realized that...you were proving a point to yourself." She paused. "A point that maybe needed to happen. I don't know, I wasn't out there with you, so I can't know for sure. But you do."

I sniffed, looking out the window again, watching clouds form. Perhaps the Territory would see some rain on this day, like it did when I was lost in it.

"Life's such a weird, fucked up rollercoaster, isn't it?" I mentioned.

"It is, but you're not alone, Tommy," Courtney smiled. "We're all right there with you, rolling along."

"She's right, you know," said a deep voice.

I then realized I could've spent the rest of my life there in that small hospital room if I had to. Because standing right in the door, brighter than the flowers in his hand, was Bruce.

On this day, I had recognized two things: one, that my choices made an impact on not only my life, but the ones around me, especially the ones that would do anything for me. And two, that people come, and people go, and then they may come again. And that is okay.

Courtney shot a glare over at him as he stood in the door waiting for an invitation. I didn't think he cared anymore. I thought that day in Lilley Street was going to be the last time I saw those almond eyes.

"You *can* come in, you know," Courtney said rudely.

She eyed me protectively. "He flew over with me today," she told me. "Insisted that he did."

He entered and placed the flowers on my bedside table. I could smell them, even though they weren't under my nose. Courtney sighed at the waft of awkward silence that now filled the room.

She cocked her head to Bruce. "Don't think for a *second* that I completely trust you again," she told him sternly. She then peered over to me. "I'll give you guys some time. I'm going to see what food I can get around here."

She left, leaving him by my bedside. He sat in the chair by my bedside. We didn't speak for a few moments, both lost for words. Where would we even start?

After asking how I was, to which I replied with a thumbs up, he blurted out, "I'm sorry."

"For what?"

He shrugged. "I don't know. I feel somewhat...responsible for what just happened."

I half-smiled. "Don't. It's just dominoes."

"What do you mean?"

"Life. Dominoes. They fall the way they're meant to, regardless of the outcome. There's no stopping them."

"That's a great analogy. Are you sure you're not the writer?" he said.

I chuckled. "Most of it never goes onto a page like you, though."

It wasn't that painful talking to him again. Not as much as I imagined anyway. Then again, I never thought the day would come where we would even be in the same room together again.

"I've been writing a lot lately," he mentioned. "Hell, I've written more the past few weeks than I have, like...ever. I think a novel is on its way."

I managed to produce another smile. "I bet it's all amazing too. How is everything going with you?"

He knew I would ask whether he could walk freely with his thoughts yet.

"Things are better now," he told me, which was a warm relief. "I did get diagnosed with PTSD, though. But I've been talking about it all. The psychologist in Noosa has helped a lot."

"That's really good to hear, Bruce. I guess sometimes it really does take the perspective from someone outside of your comfort zone to come to terms with all of it."

He sighed. "Yeah. I just wish I would've done it sooner, before it came between us."

I paused, unsure of what I would say next. "I think it had

to," I finally said. "We both had things we had to overcome. And we couldn't do that together." I felt so wise saying these words to him, especially with how detrimental my desperation had become those weeks ago.

"Did you overcome what you needed to?" he then asked.

Looking back on it, in the most fucked up of ways, I certainly had. In the face of death, I had overcome more than I could have ever imagined.

"If I hadn't, we wouldn't be having this conversation," I finally replied.

He nodded, putting his hand on mine. "So, what next?"

I took my hand back almost immediately, sifting it through my hair. "I think Courtney and I will be going back to London when I can get out of here," I revealed.

His smile faded, but he soon turned it around. "That will be good for you both. To see what's happening back on that side of the world."

"What about you?" I asked. "What's your plan?"

"Might be time for me to go back to my Irish roots soon, too, actually. It's been a while."

I arched my brows at him. "Surely there's a few more waves to catch in Australia now that summer is on its way, though?"

He laughed. "Funny you say that actually, because that first surf after my initial consultation with the psychologist was the best I've ever had. I've also been starting each day with listing five things I'm grateful for. Surfing is always on that list. Lately, you've been making an appearance too. I miss you, Thomas. I really do."

I wanted nothing more than to jump up out of this bed in my pale blue gown and hug him harder than I ever had before. However, I did not have the energy and my leg wouldn't allow it.

"I miss you too, Bruce. You know that."

"A part of me wishes we could just go back to the way things were between us," he said, mildly frustrated.

Things could never go back to the way they were, not exactly. And that was the true beauty of it. We'd grown, and our shorter selves simply couldn't reach us now, even on their tippy toes. Our edges would stay buffed on their own accord. Perhaps one day we'd meet again on a lone orbit around the sun, prior to another collision. But I didn't bank on it. My mother had always told me that everyone we meet has a purpose in our lives. It could be for something as small as learning how to spell the word "hippopotamus", or understanding how to fill up the oil in a car properly. Or, it could be for something like remembering to smile. I'll never forget the smiles we shared that day: smiles of acceptance, smiles of the present.

The phone plugged into the socket on the wall next to me vibrated. Bruce pointed to it. "Want me to grab it for you?"

I nodded.

"You've got an email I think," he said. He handed my phone to me. I unlocked it, my eyes enlarging as I read it. The anticipation grew on Bruce too. "What is it?" he asked.

"It's that art competition I applied for a few months ago," I blurted out, shaking my head in disbelief. "I won!"

Big Ben

Two months had passed since I left Australia. I strolled out of the gym, beginning the day with a face full of sweat. The sun hadn't shone for an entire week in the great city of London, nor had Big Ben chimed once to let the concrete playground know that it was still alive. They had been conducting maintenance on it the whole time since I had been back. I, however, wasn't here to worry whether Big Ben was working or not.

Actually, I had met a real Ben at a sticky party in a crowded warehouse that night. Flashing neon lights sprayed onto my pupils, ground-grumbling bass music in my ears. His eyes caught mine within the crowd. Courtney was off pashing a lad she had met on the dance floor, leaving me to socialize. Turns out I knew nobody here, but now I did. He had those eyes—almond, with a slight flicker of green. He scoped me out across a group of dancers and pushed his way through.

"Having a good time?" he asked.

"Better now that you're here, lad." I certainly hadn't lost my smoothness.

He had the accent too: Irish. So bloody Irish.

I shook his hand and introduced myself. We ambled to the bar together. It reminded me of when Bruce and I had our moist night out in Noosa. However, Ben and I would not be rolling in any dewy grass, that was for sure. London…in the middle of winter…fuck that right off. Although, the warehouse was sweaty enough to take my shirt off. Well, Ben took it off for me, and I peeled off his. I kept glancing at that complex tattoo on his chest, a slithering snake across his smooth muscular pecs.

We rubbed our perspiring bodies together in the crowd, kissing each other in whatever spots our mouths could reach.

Surprisingly, the sex was good, though. Took us a few hours to cum but we finally milked each other in the end. His room was clean and boasted a well-planned color palette, of whites, baby pink, and beige. I woke before he did, horny and ready for round three. I tried waking him discreetly with soft kisses on his shoulder and bare butt caresses, but no response.

Okay, maybe I would watch some porn and go from there. I was strangely in the mood for "outdoor amateur" on that morning in his blacked-out bedroom. I couldn't even tell if it was sunny or not today, but it didn't matter. What mattered was that I was rock-hard after watching the first thirty seconds of a video. I then stumbled upon another, of a mystery man jerking off in the forest. His head had been cut off by the camera, but what drew me in was the tattoo stretched across his chest: the snake. I studied Ben in his slumber, at his tattoo, then back at the phone. It *was* him.

And I was right next to him, kind of spooked, kind of turned on. He rustled in the baby pink sheets.

"Morning," he grumbled. I turned off the screen to my phone quickly before he cocked his head in my direction. "Want to go again?"

I wouldn't waste data on my phone compared to the real thing. Ben's head popped underneath the sheet as he crawled closer. I lay back and closed my eyes, smiling. It didn't take long to be laying back together, sweaty again, his head on my chest, feeling somewhat wholesome. Or was I just filling a hole that belonged to someone else?

"Got much planned today, Ben?"

"I'm actually meant to be going for a nude photoshoot today with some of the lads."

Another porno perhaps. Each to their own, I wasn't going to judge. I considered messaging Bruce when I left Ben's place. But each time I went to type a message, I deleted it.

I returned to my apartment, to my half-completed art canvases in both the living room and spare room. Home.

My first art show was the following day. To say I was nervous would have been an understatement. I felt strange on this crowded train. It was somewhere between being able to feel the energies of those around me and smelling them too. I wore a scarf, a black blazer and chinos I had known and loved over the past year.

I missed Australia. The sprawling windswept beaches and hot, humid weather, where one could just wear shorts all day long and bask in the sun. It was also good to be back home, snug and content. I missed him more than I could say, though. We hadn't spoken in a few months, since we left the hospital in Alice

Springs actually. I had been busy painting. The announcement of my competition win came an influx of commissions. I was now doing what I loved, just like I had wanted from the start. I just had to ride the wave of getting there and enjoy the little things in between.

Like ants, workers trundled into Charing Cross Station, ready to scurry home at the end of a long day, spilling in every direction. It was overwhelming, but only in contrast to the relative quietness of my apartment.

As I sauntered toward *Café 22*, formerly known as *Paula's*, I looked at myself in the window front, at the person I was now. I wanted so badly to enter but didn't. It wasn't the right time. Her café's new design was superb, though. Neon green, eclectic, and modern. It glowed and caught the wandering eye.

I kept walking, eyeballing my reflection as I strolled past. An older man swept across the pavement in front of me, wearing a red and black wizard's hat. His clothes ratted and worn, he walked aimlessly. He didn't look so good, but his hat showed character. I wondered if he wore it so someone would notice him. I sure noticed him, but I knew others would mock him, see him as nothing more than a crazy old man and go right on their way. As weird as it sounds, this man led me to where I needed to be, and I stayed behind him the entire time. I didn't overtake, appreciating him for walking the streets without shame.

I walked and walked, turning down a quiet street just off the main road. As I ambled down it, the contrast between here and central London was marked: no cars, no voices, but a whole lot of light. Light beamed from every terrace house. It was dinner time, and I smelt savory scents wafting from several doors as I passed them. I pulled up to number thirty-seven, the old blue and red terrace house with the teal gate. It creaked as I opened it. I knocked on the smooth wood, waiting patiently as footsteps along the hollow floorboards grew louder. I took a deep breath. The door swung open.

"Hey, Abigail."

She was surprised when she saw me, even though I was expected. "It's so good to see you, Thomas!" She hugged me. "How have you been?"

"Really busy, but I can't complain."

I stepped inside with her. The house wasn't how I'd left it. The walls in the front hallway had been painted over. From old mahogany to a soft white, it certainly looked different. Paint tins sat on the floor, with a ladder adjacent to the staircase.

"Excuse the mess, darling," Abigail told me. "I've been helping your father do some work on the house. You know how us oldies get. This is the kind of change we get excited about now." She chuckled, and so did I.

"Yeah, he was saying. It looks nice," I said, following her through to the kitchen.

"It's just fresh. It's a beautiful house. It just needed a little... sprucing up."

The kitchen was exactly as I had left it, the same kitchen Dad and I would play Yahtzee in almost every night when I was younger, at the table his father had given him. Dad loved second-hand furniture, especially when it was handed down from the generations above himself. I loved that about him; he could find sentimental value in almost anything. It also made him a wee bit of a hoarder, but I wouldn't have it any other way.

"So, are you nervous about tonight?" asked Abigail.

"Beyond words," I confessed.

She placed her hand on my shoulder. "Don't worry. You'll do great. It was a well-deserved outcome. Those pieces going up in that gallery will be loved and appreciated by many."

I drew a smile, feeling myself go red. I seldom knew how to

reply to compliments about my art. In this instance, Dad saved the day.

"Dad, you didn't need to wear a suit!" I called out.

He winked. "I've got to look the part, son. Tonight, I'm playing proud father."

"Well, I think you look dapper," Abigail said, admiring his black and white attire.

"Thank you, honey." He pecked her on the lips. "You ready, Thomas?"

I smiled sarcastically. "Nope. Not ready."

"Don't worry," Dad assured me. "Everyone who is meant to be there is going to be there, looking at *your* art."

I chuckled playfully. "Yep. That's the problem."

Once Abigail stood under the kitchen light, I saw that she wore old track pants and a sweater.

"I can't come, if that's what you're implying." She noticed me looking at her clothes. "It's my sister's birthday tonight, and we've got a dinner to go to. But I'll be ready for a wine or three when you folk decide to come back."

Abigail glanced up at the clock. "You guys should get going by the way. You're going to be late."

The more I got to know Abigail, the more she reminded me of Mum, even her mannerisms and sass. Perhaps she would soon become some sort of a mother figure for me. It was too soon to say, because I'd had my fair share of people in my life who I thought were going to be around a long time and weren't, like Bruce. But based on our last interaction, I was beginning to wonder if this might have been partly my fault.

I wondered where you were then. Were you still in Australia, gliding through waves and browning like a perfectly cooked vegetarian burger patty, maybe shacked up with a tanned Aussie beauty and living life in the sand? Or, were you back in Ireland, reconnecting with your family like you said?

Dad and I tackled the chilly air and strolled down the soundless street, the smell of dewy leaves perfuming the night. Misty exhales floated above us.

"Do you think Bruce will be there tonight?" Dad asked, breathing into his gloves for warmth.

I shrugged. "I don't know. I invited him to the Facebook event, but he might've missed it."

He laughed. "I highly doubt that. By what you told me about your last encounter, it seemed like he had genuinely gotten the help that he needed, and that he was asking for forgiveness."

"And I've forgiven him, Dad. I just...I don't know. I wasn't ready for things to go back to the way they were. I needed some distance from him after everything that went down, from what happened out in the desert. Everything."

"And now that you have distanced yourself?"

I sighed. "I think it's over between me and him now. He's probably found someone else anyway. And I've been loving just focusing on my art. The past few months have been amazing. Busy, but amazing."

"It makes a difference when you love what you do. Gosh, Thomas, I'm so proud of you." He gave me a firm tap on the back. "You've really gone leaps and bounds to get where you are now. I'm a really lucky father."

I shivered. "If it wasn't so cold right now, I'd stop and give you the biggest hug I've given you ever, but I don't want to stop until we get inside the gallery."

We power-walked over a broad bridge, the crisp river below, city lights at our brows. We approached an old building. Several people gathered outside, talking amongst themselves, some smoking cigarettes. Through the open wooden doors, my nerves heightened, the gallery full of people. Chatter and laughter filled the rooms. Art pieces and installations were draped across the pristine white walls. I had never seen the gallery with this many people in it. I had never heard it this loud either, with red wine being poured in each room. Dad and I maneuvered our way through the crowd. I caught his eyes, as if to signal that I really needed a drink. He was already pointing toward the closest wine table. We poured ourselves a glass each.

"Good turnout, hey?" Dad observed, hitting my glass softly with his.

"A lot more people than I expected, to be quite frank. The red wine tastes expensive too."

"Get used to it, son. This won't be the last of these that you attend."

"Tommy! Harry!" a voice called out.

I was just about to scope her out, but she found me instead. Courtney fast approached, a glass of red in her hand. She wore a gorgeous black jumpsuit that made her look like a completely new woman.

"Jesus, Court! You look amazing!" I exclaimed.

"Tommy, my brother. You see…" She softened to a whisper. "I never go to events like this. This is a first for me."

"It's definitely a first for all of us," I confirmed. "I'm so happy you came."

"Wouldn't miss it for the world, lad. So, where's your artwork? I haven't seen it yet, but I also haven't been game to go into all these crowded rooms by myself."

"Let's go find it," Dad suggested.

We walked through three rooms before finding them. My pieces had their own section in the least crowded room. We liked it there, it was much quieter. There was a small group of people admiring my collection of framed originals. They scurried off after a long gaze, leaving one young man in front of them, his hair combed back neatly, but a tad shorter than I remembered it. He wore a neat black overcoat with one of his hands tucked into a pocket, the other wrapped around a glass of red. He turned around.

"Thomas," he said.

I was lost for words. "Bruce?"

Dad took over from my awkwardness. He stood forward and shook Bruce's hand. "Long time no see, lad. Glad you could make it."

"Good to see you, Harry," he replied with a grin. "Hey, Courtney. How's it going?"

"Hey, Bruce," she greeted sarcastically. "You just keep popping up everywhere, don't you?"

Bruce chuckled. "Apparently so."

"Why didn't you tell me you were coming?" I asked, astounded.

"I wanted to surprise you," he admitted.

"Well, you succeeded. I'm very fucking surprised."

He nodded awkwardly. "Uh…good."

Why did all of this have to be so cumbersome to begin with, and in front of my art pieces?

Courtney turned to Dad. "Harry…did you see those scones on that table in the last room?"

Dad stuttered. "Yes…yes, I did."

"I'm a little peckish after the dinner I had. Want to maybe join me for a scone with jam and cream?"

"Absolutely," Dad agreed confidently.

"We'll be back in a bit to check out your art, Tommy. We're just a little hungry," Courtney fibbed. She couldn't have been more suspicious if she tried.

Dad and Courtney marched off, leaving me face to face with Bruce.

We stood still, locking eyes for a moment, before I said, "You've really got to stop just showing up without letting me know."

He giggled. "I thought you liked surprises."

We stood side by side in front of the frames. I couldn't even remotely stay angry at him. And there the original presented itself, hung high and loud in the room: my winged rainbow companion. Surrounding it were several other paintings. From one to another, it presented a story blooming with detailed color, of two men falling in love, buying a house together, and a dog, soon leading to a wedding amongst the alpacas. Looking at my signature written on the bottom left-hand corner of each piece, I felt a sense of silent achievement.

"You never showed me these drawings," he said. "Except for the rainbow angel one."

"You're seeing them now," I told him with a slight subtle cheek. "Maybe it'll inspire that happy ending if you ever write a romance novel."

He laughed. "Maybe I am writing a romance novel."

Before I could respond, Dad and Courtney were back, ushering us.

"They're doing the speeches. Tommy, c'mon," Courtney called out.

The party had gathered in the foyer of the gallery, all bunched together while a lady at the front spoke over a microphone. She wore a glittery black dress and had a distinct posh tone in her voice. From what I could gather, she wanted all the new gallery artists to move to the front. Eleven of us bunched up behind the lady in a line across the room. Multiple cameras snapped, glistening eyes upon us. Usually, this kind of attention would zap my nerves and freeze me whole. However, there were two things that calmed my breath: my full glass of red wine, and those almond eyes at the back of the room. The lady gave her speech to congratulate all of us, and a round of applause followed. I couldn't resist locking eyes with him. Because I knew that when I would this time; he'd smile, and I'd smile.

Just On Time

The art show was a success, even though I seemed to avoid networking the same way I would if I saw an ex in a shopping mall. One of my original pieces sold for one thousand pounds, though, which had me chuffed.

The sun thawed the frosty night into the following day. Courtney and I took a morning stroll in the park near Dad's place. We'd spent the night there playing Yahtzee and drinking more wine after the art show. Bruce didn't join us. He'd already agreed to meet some of his friends for drinks but asked me to have brunch with him the next morning.

"How long has it been since you've been in that café?" Courtney asked me. "Must be years now."

I nodded. "Yeah, since Mum passed away. Bruce said he has something important to tell me."

"And of all places, you told him to meet you there?"

Courtney questioned many of my motives, only later to understand that there was a method to my madness sometimes.

"It just seemed like the right place. The right time."

We sat on a bench in the middle of the park, watching people walk past while we basked in the warm sun. Rays sprayed onto our faces, paired with a winter chill.

"What do you think he has to tell you that he hasn't already?"

I shrugged. I honestly didn't know. That man had been full of surprises ever since I'd met him, so anything was possible at this point.

"You know I just want to see you happy, right, Tommy?"

I nodded. "I am happy. With, or without him."

Courtney chuckled. "The indoor plants in your new apartments are pretty impressive too, I must admit."

I winked. "My idea of the perfect garden."

I soon strolled over to *Café 22*. Mum's old stomping ground. The timing felt more aligned than ever. He hadn't arrived yet, so I sat at a table next to the window upon entering, taking off my jacket. It was warm inside, homely. The café had evolved, just like the world had. I could intrinsically picture her standing at the counter, welcoming patrons in with that friendly grin of hers. She had that kind of smile I would never forget. And I didn't have to. I could daydream for the rest of my life if I wanted to. She had saved my life a few times now, and who knew, maybe it would happen again.

Scrolling through my Instagram feed whilst waiting, I stopped by a photo uploaded by an old friend. Mackenzie from back in Australia. The shirtless selfie on Coolangatta Beach had me squinting. A familiar face stood next to him in the photo, the aqua waters and white sand at their rear. It was the lad I met on my first night in Australia. Turns out I was right, his name was Sam. **Three months with this scallywag**, the caption read. I shook my head in disbelief, wondering how in the world those two ended up together. I thought about my Cupid-like companion and envisioned him shooting both Mackenzie and Sam with sharp arrows, piercing them right in the heart.

The sound of coffee brewing made everything seem right.

It seemed even more right when you walked through that door.

He sat down across from me at the table. I put my phone down.

He took his black puffer jacket off and draped it over the chair. "Hey, sorry I'm late."

"It's fine. I only just got here."

A waitress approached us. We ordered coffees. The usual.

"This place is so nice," Bruce admired, glancing around. "It's exactly how I pictured it to be. I know it might not be exactly what it used to be, but it does have a warm vibe about it."

"It still feels the same to me, it's just been modernized," I said.

It didn't take long for our coffees to arrive. We sipped and gazed out the window.

"Damn, I've missed this, Thomas."

"What's that?"

"Just being in a café with you."

"I'm warming up to it." I smiled. "So, you said you had something important to tell me?"

He turned his head from me to his coffee mug.

"I've got a few things to tell you actually."

"Right?"

"So, the first thing I want to tell you is a bit grimmer than the rest," he began. "But ah, Joe…my abusive ex, turns out he did it to someone else. Someone pressed charges, and then Joe breached the restraining order, and now he's in jail for a year."

"Wow, I mean, that is good news that he's gotten his justice."

"Yeah. I spoke up about it and testified against him last week."

I imagined Bruce in a courtroom, having to stand up and face the same person that hurt him, that had broken him into the same million pieces that took quite some time to mend back together.

"Wow," I said, truly proud. "How did that make you feel?"

"At first I thought it would break me," he admitted, "but it actually made me feel really good. It felt like it was finally getting put to rest, and that I could continue the rest of my life knowing that justice has been served. And knowing that he no longer has power over me."

"One hundred percent," I agreed. "Good on you, Bruce. I really am proud of you."

"Thanks, Thomas. I really appreciate it. I have to thank you as well. You did help me through a lot of what I was going through. I think without you by my side for most of it, I'm not sure what I would've done. Or if I would even be here for that matter. When we were in Uluru, I found out that Joe had abused a friend of a friend, and I was just so broken and angry and embarrassed that I couldn't bring myself to tell you. At the time when I found out, it felt like my shitty experience with him was like a disease that had spread to other people that I knew, and that somehow it was my fault. But I soon realized that none of it was my fault. And it was a shitty thing that happened to me, but it didn't make me."

"You've come so far, Bruce. It really is admirable."

"Yeah, I mean I know I'll never forget it, but I've learned

that I'm not alone, and that it's much better to talk about our struggles than to keep it all bottled up inside."

I told him how happy I was to see him happy again. He smiled. I smiled. The atmosphere around us was preheating like an oven.

Were our edges really ready for another flame-lit collision?

"Okay so, next thing I wanna tell you," he continued, this time in a much more gleeful tone. "So, uh…last night…when you were talking about romance novels…"

"Go on."

He was hesitant, but I knew he needed to spill some beans. "So, the novel I've been writing, it's ah…based on our relationship."

"I see. Like, an exact replica?"

He shrugged. "More or less."

"So, I could get my own character if it gets adapted for film one day?"

He slapped my arm playfully. "Don't mock me, mister. I lost sleep over having this conversation."

I shrugged and smiled. "That's a real bummer, Bruce."

"So, you're okay with it?"

I smirked gamesomely. "About as much as you're okay with me painting pictures of you and hanging them in art galleries."

He smiled. "Well…cool."

"Cool."

"One more thing."

"Yes?"

I took a generous gulp of my coffee. I loved him; it was undeniable. I loved him so fucking much, and I didn't care who heard it. There was only so much work I could busy myself with to try and tell anyone otherwise, including myself.

"There's something I just wanted to read to you," he told

me. "I know you're probably getting sick of me reading to you, but…"

"This better be good."

"It is. I promise."

He reached into his pocket and fished out a cream-colored piece of paper—from the same book I knew all too well.

I was in this sarcastic mood and no one could stop me. "Hey, I've got a piece of paper almost exactly the same, except mine's covered in red dirt."

He shook his head, trying not to laugh. He unfolded the piece of paper. "So, I had this really surreal dream the night I left you at Brisbane airport once we got back from Alice Springs," he explained. "It was the night I'd decided I wanted to write this novel, like properly. It was also the night that I realized what I really wanted. This is it."

My smile faded as he began to read.

"Thomas. I hope you're out there somewhere safe, and I hope you approve of the road I'm traveling on. I know you're there with me always. I can feel you. You're in my words, and you're in my dreams. I love closing my eyes and getting taken back to our happy place, where I see you from afar, outside Paula's. It's back to how it was, before this new shift in time took it all away. I watch you leave, and the contrast of your chinos and sweater stands you out against the overgrown plants consuming your mother's old café. I call out to you, but you can't hear me. You walk down the street, and I follow. You're wearing this rainbow cap which is like a beacon in the crowd. I call out to you again, but there's no chance of you hearing me over the noise of the streets. I just follow the rainbow cap and watch you run into this wide-open field which dips down into an amphitheater. Where are you now?

I scan the thousands of vibrant people inhabiting this field. *One Love* by Bob Marley is playing on a huge stage. I glance down at what I'm wearing. I'm now just as colorful as everyone else dancing and smiling around me.

"Bruce!" calls out a familiar voice.

I scan around and see two people waving at me in the distance. It's Harry and Abigail, waving enthusiastically at me from afar to get my attention. They're standing around a barbecue, wearing rainbow aprons. I'm eager to approach them, but I'm also nervous of this place, and do so with caution.

"Bruce!" Abigail greets me with a big grin on her face. She's flipping burger patties and onions on the barbecue.

"Nice to see you, Bruce," Harry says, shaking my hand. "I've got some burgers on for us. Tom told us you were coming. We'll set some aside for you?"

"Uh…sure. That'd be lovely," I say, still reserved but also grateful.

"Go on. He's waiting for you in there," Harry says, pointing over to the dancefloor of hundreds of people.

"See you soon, Bruce," Abigail smiles.

I walk across the right side of the amphitheater to see if I can spot you, but it's difficult because everyone is dressed in rainbow. I look out for your hat, but I see a few people who have the same one.

Where are you?

I feel two arms reach around my neck, two legs wrap around me and a body on my back. You catch me off guard, and I stumble into the ground. I lay beside you, my leg over your waist. We both laugh.

"Nice to see you finally showed up," you say, gazing into my eyes with those alluring azure spheres of yours.

I feel so content with you here, and it's like we're back on the dewy esplanade, rolling in the grass and with sparkling hearts in our eyes. But this time, we aren't dizzy from spinning around in circles.

"It's so good to see you, Thomas!" I exclaim.

I stroke your arms, just to convince myself that this is real.

"It's always good to see you, my love," you tell me. "How fun is this place!"

"It's amazing. I wanna stay here forever."

I kiss you, and it feels just as good as it did the first time we met. In the back of your car under the stars of that brisk June night.

"This is our world, mister," you say, pointing at your heart, and then mine. "This is the world that you and I created—the world that we can always come to, whenever life feels like it's filling up with water and we can't swim. I'll always be here. I'm not going anywhere. It's always sunny here, just like it was when we were in Australia."

You're right. I shake my head, grinning in disbelief. "I could marry you, Thomas."

You chuckle. "Is this a proposal, Bruce? Because I expect more alpacas, and the best vegetarian burger patty known to man."

I chuckle, looking up at the sky. I hadn't even noticed that there wasn't a cloud in sight. I followed you from the overcast streets to the sun-soaked open field, and here we lay in the shade of the tree's branches, creating memories fit for the immortals.

It is here that we'd continue to laugh at night together. Chasing away the days. Rolling in dewy grass. Blanketed by the stars. Dizzy but unafraid. We'd dance in the crowd of colors, just an arm's length from touch.

It is here that we'd continue to do life things, You and I. We'd buff our comet edges until they were smooth and soft.

Hell, maybe we could both be explorers, Thomas. I don't know. There's one thing I do know for sure, though. It's always eleven twenty-two here.

Always."

Bruce folded the piece of paper back up into fours, awaiting my response.

"That," I began.

"That?" Bruce mirrored, arching a brow.

"*That* could quite possibly be the most incredible thing anyone's ever told me," I finally spat out.

Bruce clasped my hand and there was no way in hell that I was going to pull away this time. I didn't take my eyes off him for quite a while, too. And when I did, it was to study the green analogue clock perched circular above the coffee station.

Timing was everything. It was a glance into alluring almond eyes. It was neatly trimmed gardens. A comet connection. Seeing to believe.

What did I see now? A clock, its hands bold and sharp, with that goddamned time on it again.

And then, I saw *her*, standing outside, on the other side of the window. Only a sheet of glass between us now. My mother, Paula. The one who brought only the humblest of hospitality to this part of the suburb once upon a time. She smiled at me ever-so clearly, beaming with a nod of acceptance. Bruce looked over too, and it was in that moment that I thought maybe, just maybe…

"Can you…see her?" I asked him.

Bruce frowned slightly. "Her?"

"Yeah," I grinned. "My mother."

Bruce shook his head. "No, Thomas, I can't see her. Only you can." He paused. "I can see him, though. He's standing right there, on the other side of the window."

"Who?"

Bruce's eyes glazed over. "My brother," he said.

I didn't see Bruce's brother. I never had, only in photos. I only saw her.

"We're connected in that way, Thomas, don't you see?" mused Bruce. "When the numbers appear, it means they're here. But we can only see them, and communicate with them, when they want us to."

I turned my gaze from my mother—glowing grin still stretched on her cheeks—back to Bruce.

I'd caught him talking to his brother once, in a place surrounded by sandstone. But the timing wasn't right to talk about it then. We'd have to wait until he wrote that book about us. When we could finally go over all the little details.

Acknowledgments

Firstly, I pay my respects to the traditional owners of the Country on which this story was written and mentioned in its pages.

I wrote most of this book in late 2019 and early 2020, while I was in the process of moving solo to a new city. I was excited, nervous, and everything in between. Writing this story allowed me to revisit some of my favorite places in Australia. It also helped me realize that I was going to be okay, even when things seemed uncertain at times, or dark.

When I first started writing WTHT, I had no idea what it would turn out to be. And although the first draft was written in solitude, the path that followed was by no means walked on my own. I have some incredibly supportive and inspiring people to thank for that.

To my stellar team at Deep Desires Press for believing in this book. Craig Gibb, you've made me feel comfortable throughout the entire publishing journey. Many thanks to my brilliant editor Margaret Larson for your close eye to detail, as well as my proofreader Francisco Feliciano for that much-needed final sweep.

A massive thank you to Jack Niko T for the stunning cover illustration. You read the manuscript, and from that, you've truly brought this story to life. It's exactly how I imagined. Even better, in fact! You are one talented artist, and a great friend.

To my very first beta reader and editor, Dominic. You really helped put the early drafts on the right road. And while the finished project has changed majorly since then, your invaluable feedback definitely inspired me to share this story.

A big shout out to the Bookstagrammers, bloggers, reviewers, and everyone in the world who messaged, liked, shared, commented, boosted, and supported me in any way.

To the dear readers who picked up this book and found a

sense of belonging somewhere along the journey, know that this story was written for you as much as it was for me.

Thanks to my friends and family for the ongoing support and memories over the years. My dad. You are the best man I know. Thank you for always being there for me, for accepting and supporting me, for encouraging me every step of the way to achieve my dreams, but for also teaching me the importance of patience.

And finally, To Mum. You won't get to read this book, but there is a piece of you within these pages. You loved words and your poetry still inspires me. I think it's safe to say where I got my love of writing from too. I love you.

About the Author

Jordan was born and raised in Australia and loves queer stories of all sorts. When he's not writing or reading, he's out in nature or parenting his overactive dog Misty.

Jordan's been published in print with Currency Press and online in numerous publications such as SBS Voices, We Are Explorers, Buzzfeed, Time Out, YMCA Australia, and elsewhere. He's also performed his work at the Australian storytelling event Queerstories, as well as the National Young Writers' Festival.

Being a passionate member of the LGBTQ+ community, he believes it's important to have raw, relatable, and positive queer representation in the stories we read.

More Great Books
from Deep Desires Press

All the Lovers
Harry F. Rey

Still hung up on ex-boyfriend Shawn, Nick tries, tries, and repeatedly fails to find a meaningful connection in a parochial gay society still defined by closets and cruising. With fabulous best friend Mylo and straight-laced flatmate Jenna by his side, Nick's journey to self-discovery forces him to confront not only his own demons, but those of all his lovers as well.

All The Lovers is a sexy, hilarious, and eye-opening chronicle of Nick—a working class teenager from the North of England exploring love and sex in a pre-Grindr world.

Symphony for Connor
Shane Ulrrein

David Schoenberg is shy, nerdy, and has big dreams of becoming the next great composer, dreams that seem to come real when he's admitted to a prestigious music school.

It's here that David meets and falls in love with Connor. Connor is handsome, a gifted composer, and the biggest flake in school. He's everything the studious, hard-working David isn't, and no matter how David feels about him, it seems Connor would never return that affection.

This all changes when the truth comes out after a wild party and David and Connor form a deeper bond than either of them has ever known. But with this deeper bond comes a darker side to Connor, putting David to the ultimate test as he must decide if he can stand with the greatest love of his life.

CPSIA information can be obtained
at www.ICGtesting.com
Printed in the USA
LVHW042007200922
728862LV00005B/220

9 781777 666842